O9-ABF-131

THE UNFORGETTABLE LOGAN FOSTER AND THE SHADOW OF DOUBT

Also by Shawn Peters

The Unforgettable Logan Foster

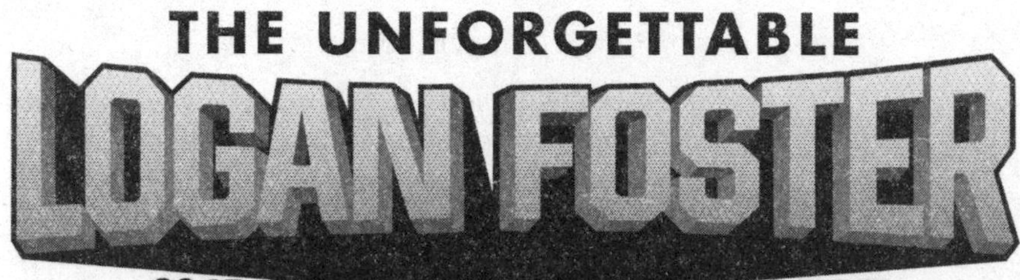

by **SHAWN PETERS**

HARPER
An Imprint of HarperCollins*Publishers*

The Unforgettable Logan Foster and the Shadow of Doubt

 For information address HarperCollins Children's Books, a division of HarperCollins Publishers, 195 Broadway, New York, NY 10007.
www.harpercollinschildrens.com

Library of Congress Cataloging-in-Publication Data
Names: Peters, Shawn, 1971- author.
Title: The unforgettable Logan Foster and the shadow of doubt / by Shawn Peters.
Description: First edition. | New York : Harper, [2023] | Audience: Ages 8–12. | Audience: Grades 4–6. | Summary: Twelve-year-old orphan Logan and his superhero friends embark on an adventure to stop the evil supervillain Necros and find the true identity of Logan's birth mom.
Identifiers: LCCN 2022029564 | ISBN 978-0-06-304772-3 (hardcover)
Subjects: CYAC: Superheroes—Fiction. | Orphans—Fiction. | Birthmothers—Fiction. | Friendship—Fiction. | LCGFT: Superhero fiction. | Novels.
Classification: LCC PZ7.1.P4487 Uo 2023 | DDC [Fic]—dc23
LC record available at https://lccn.loc.gov/2022029564

Typography by Corina Lupp
22 23 24 25 26 LBC 5 4 3 2 1

First Edition

To Sara, who never had even a shadow of doubt.

Hello. My name is Logan Foster. I am a twelve-year-old orphan living on the Westside of Los Angeles. Even though I am extremely small for my age and should be in seventh grade, I'm almost halfway through my freshman year in high school. That's because I have an eidetic memory. I've retained every word, sound, and image that I've seen or heard since I was three (which is when I was abandoned in Los Angeles International Airport and became an orphan).

Also, I am your big brother. That is a fact.

If you already know these facts because you read the last letter I sent you after I pretty much saved the world about three weeks ago, you should feel free to skip the next two hundred words.

If you do *not* know any of this, it means you did not read what I wrote previously, possibly for one of the following reasons:

1. I sent a printed version of my first letter, but it got lost in the mail. In 2014 alone, more than 85 million pieces of mail were deemed undeliverable.
2. I sent an email to you, but it ended up in your spam folder. According to Statistica.com, there are over 107 billion spam emails sent every day.
3. My first letter got to you either via snail mail or email, but it was written in English, and you are one of the nearly 6.5 billion people on Earth who do not speak that language. Of course, that also means you cannot read this either.
4. You are not my sibling and have no idea what I'm talking about.

If option four is the case, a mistake has been made. I have noticed this happens frequently.

It seems everyone makes mistakes.

But assuming you are who I think you are and have read what I wrote to you last time, I hope you will continue reading this now.

I'll give you a moment to decide.

★ ★ ★

Okay, if you're still reading this, I am going to assume you read my last letter . . . at least the important parts.

I had thought that after being fostered by Gil and Margie and discovering that they were actual superheroes called Ultra-Quantum and Quicksilver Siren, and then outsmarting an immortal villainess named Necros, life *might* get kinda "normal." I assumed I'd get to slow down, hang out with my best-friend-slash-neighbor Elena (who also has superpowers), and just deal with everyday kid stuff instead of being hunted by supervillains and secret organizations.

Instead, life has gotten even stranger, because right when I should've been getting closer to my new foster family, I discovered something that just might lead to finding our parents, and maybe you too.

So now I'm writing this all down to tell you exactly what happened, because I don't want to keep any secrets from you.

Secrets may make you feel like you have control, but they're almost always the reasons things get *out* of control.

5:50 P.M.
SUNDAY, OCTOBER 31

"We aren't going to make it in time. That is a fact!"

That was me, sitting in the middle rear seat of Gil and Margie's minivan as we raced westward down the Marina Freeway, weaving through traffic like an Olympic slalom skier.

"I'm aware of the situation, Logan." Margie exhaled, her knuckles glimmering silver as she gripped the wheel, passing cars on both sides. "We need a bit less critique and more ideas of what we can do about it! There's no telling how bad the damage will be. Gil, what if you go ahead?"

From the passenger seat, Gil swallowed hard, which is odd because he doesn't have actual saliva. As you probably remember, Gil was a MASC scientist when an experiment went wrong and transformed him into a mass of dark-matter-infused atoms held together by his leftover human consciousness.

"Alone? I can't! I mean . . . you know . . . if it's just me it won't . . ."

Margie shook her head, and I'm pretty sure I heard the steering wheel bending in her hands.

Ahead, the freeway ended, gently narrowing and descending to surface streets on the eastern edge of Marina del Rey. According to Google Maps on my new iPhone, we were still twelve minutes from our destination with traffic.

"We're still twelve minutes from our destination with traffic."

Margie's shoulders rose up next to her ears, but then she forced them back down. "There has to be a way to shave off time. Even one minute could make a difference. A shortcut or something!"

That's when I got an idea.

"I have an idea. According to a *New York Times* article I read when I was researching the safest bike routes to school, there are forty-five hundred intersections with traffic lights in Los Angeles. Six of them are between us and where we're going. That is a fact. The traffic lights are synchronized—"

"Could you skip to the idea part, Logan?" Margie asked like she was trying to be patient. She didn't sound at all patient.

"If we get all green lights, we can reduce our travel time by fifteen percent. Possibly more. But if we hit even one red, we will encounter several more."

Margie glanced over to Gil. "Can you get us all greens?"

Gil nodded. "You *red* my mind."

No one said anything. It was the only sensible response.

"Okay. I'm gonna go . . . do the thing."

Gil disappeared from the front seat in a flash, streaking ahead of us to the next traffic light a hundred yards away. It was just turning yellow as the cars around us began to slow, but Margie accelerated instead. My hands squeezed the armrest and I involuntarily started listing all the ingredients in a Twinkie.

"Enriched bleached wheat flour, water, sugar, corn syrup, high fructose corn syrup . . ."

Before I could even get to polysorbate 60, Gil appeared next to the intersection's controller box and his hand vanished inside it. There was a small spark and suddenly, the light changed to green.

Several cars on the cross street had to slam on their brakes, but before they could identify what happened, Gil had flashed off to the next intersection.

Margie just kept her foot on the gas, and Gil's timing got better as he went. There was a lot less sudden braking, and the air wasn't quite as full of the sound of skidding tires—other than ours as we took turns at high speed.

On the sidewalks, I noticed kids dressed up for Halloween, dragging their feet like zombies or prancing around like cartoon unicorns. But there were plenty of comic book costumes too. And every one of those kids was totally unaware that real-life superheroes were blasting down the street in a month-old minivan that they leased after their last vehicle was crushed by an earthquake-making supervillain named Seismyxer.

Margie made a careening left onto Via Marina, leaving a twenty-foot arc of rubber in the intersection, drawing head turns from the trick-or-treaters. Meanwhile, I was starting to feel a bit nauseated, but I wasn't sure if it was motion sickness or just me worrying about the fact that we were probably already too late.

With all the traffic lights behind us, Gil reappeared in the passenger seat, panting.

"Will it be enough?"

"I don't know. I just don't know."

Margie's face hardened as she took one last turn, cutting the wheel hard and power sliding back to the right into a parking spot across from a dock that stretched out into the marina.

And then we were out of the car, running down the ramp toward an unassuming houseboat that loomed over the small sailboats and pleasure crafts around it. We paused for a moment at the gangplank.

"Listen," Margie warned. "We don't know what's waiting in there, but we have to assume the worst. There's no one else to clean this up. It's just us. Understood?"

I did understand, so I nodded. Gil did too, though I think he looked a lot less confident.

After one deep breath, we boarded the houseboat, threw open the door to the main cabin, and saw it.

"Oh no," Gil whispered. "We're too late."

He was right.

In the middle of the floor sat a three-month-old, black-and-white-spotted Great Dane puppy, sitting at attention, surrounded by several torn-up couch cushions and a still-growing puddle of pee that was slowly spreading with the gentle rocking of the boat.

No matter how fast or powerful they may be, superheroes can't be everywhere at once. That is a fact.

6:41 P.M.
SUNDAY, OCTOBER 31

Do you have a favorite Halloween costume genre, like old-school horror monsters, superheroes, or sports stars? Growing up at the El Segundo Transitional Orphanage—aka ESTO—we didn't exactly have a lot of options, but some of the boys got pretty inventive. They'd take a few rolls of toilet paper and turn themselves into mummies or cut up old sheets to be ghosts. One boy named Oded stuck Cheerios all over his face, covered his hands with red paint, and called himself "Cereal Killer." I thought it was a pretty good joke, but I'm pretty sure he scared off more than a few PPs—prospective parents—when they asked what he'd been for Halloween.

This year, after helping Gil and Margie mop up an impressive amount of puppy pee, I got dressed in my first-ever commercially produced costume. It was a replica of the suit and mask worn by TideStrider.

I think I got it for free because, technically, I saved TideStrider's life when I came up with the plan that freed him, my foster parents, and some other heroes from Necros. Free costumes were an unexpected perk from MASC, the Multinational Authority for Superhuman Control. They are the ones who boss around all the heroes and also make all the superhero merchandise and movies in the world. They gave me the eighteen-dollar costume as a thank-you.

MASC gave me something else for free that I liked a lot less. It was a watch with a GPS tracker and panic button that I was required to wear at all times, since I'd accidentally memorized their entire supersecret database and Colonel Gdula thought my brain was now pretty much a threat to all civilization. If I pressed the panic button three times, it would summon a commando rescue team. The watch was Gdula's way of making sure I wouldn't get abducted and tortured for the information I had in my brain, but mostly, I just used it to tell time.

Anyway, when I came out of my bedroom on the houseboat dressed in an aquamarine bodysuit and sleek mask, Margie was putting a leash on our dog, Bohr, while the puppy stared at Gil intently, barking every few seconds.

We named the dog after Niels Bohr, the Danish physicist who won the Nobel Prize in 1922 for his model of atomic structure. Gil came up with the name, which was both nerdy and a pun, because he said he was sure the puppy would be a "Great Dane" just like the scientist. Margie liked the name more than the joke so we agreed to it, but the dog was not as accepting. He had barked at Gil ever since we brought him home.

"This dog has a *bone* to pick with me."

The dog growled at Gil while Margie groaned at the pun.

"He can tell you're nervous," Margie offered as she stood up, leash in hand. "Dogs can smell fear."

"They can smell a lot more than fear," I added. "According to a *Science* magazine article from February 2020, not only are dogs' noses a hundred million times more sensitive than humans', they can even sense low levels of radioactive energy. You have no scent at all, but you're radiating more energy than almost any creature on this planet. So, that combination may be very confusing to Bohr."

These facts did not appear to make Gil feel any better, which was surprising. Like me, Gil usually appreciates facts.

"Who's ready for some dockside trick-or-treating?"

That was Margie as she led Bohr out across the gangplank, with Gil and me following behind. Gil and Margie

were both dressed as regular humans, even though neither are. It was the one night a year when they could have worn their superhero costumes without being noticed. But they made it clear Halloween is for kids, and though I'm a little old for trick-or-treating, it was my first Halloween with Gil and Margie and they really wanted to take me. I wasn't going to turn down free candy, especially since Margie's ability to cook food that tastes good to human tongues instead of her alien taste buds had not improved in the past month.

However, their plan had some holes in it. It turns out that people who live on boats don't expect a lot of trick-or-treaters. For over an hour, we strolled up and down the docks of the marina, searching for other boats that were decorated with pumpkins or spooky lights. In all, we only found about a dozen. I ended up with seven candy bars, two bags of Smartfood, a clementine, and several fishing lures as my "treats." I almost certainly would have gotten a bigger haul if we still lived on Kittyhawk Circle, but I was not allowed to go back there.

Even if you don't have an eidetic memory like mine, you probably remember there were good reasons to think Necros might come looking for me at my last known address. So, as soon as MASC set up a temporary West Coast HQ in one of their hidden storage facilities under Venice Beach, they activated the "Page One Protocol" for

Gil, Margie, and me. That's what MASC calls it when they give a superhero a completely new secret identity. Colonel Gdula wanted to reassign Gil and Margie north of San Francisco and send me to a different country altogether. He mentioned Uzbekistan. But Gil and Margie refused to leave the area or let me get deported, which I appreciated. I did some research and Uzbekistan is the only country that borders five other nations with names than end in "stan," which is interesting. But I didn't want to leave Gil and Margie, who I actually like living with. I also refused to move too far from Elena Arguello, who is my best friend.

So, our Page One Protocol meant that Marjorie Morrow and Gilbert Grant became Margaret Matthews and Guillermo Grover. That allows them to still go by "Margie" and "Gil," which is good, because it's very suspicious if someone calls you by your new first name and you don't respond.

I'm now Logan Lewis according to my new school registration. MASC has a thing about alliteration and names: Peter Parker, Lois Lane, Reed Richards. I asked Colonel Gdula why and was told it was "classified."

So instead of going to San Francisco and Tashkent—the capital city of Uzbekistan—we moved from our old house in Westchester to a houseboat in Marina del Rey. It's only five miles from Kittyhawk Circle, but it's a different zip code, has different schools, and the boat can actually move to different places, which may help us stay "off the grid." Gil had to leave his day job working for a cable company, and Margie couldn't be a substitute teacher anymore. So now, Gil is the overnight IT specialist at a reality TV production company in Culver City, and Margie is a part-time personal trainer at a gym in Venice. And me? Well, I'm just the newest, youngest, weirdest freshman at a different school, Marina High, so my identity hasn't really changed all that much. Just my location.

After trick-or-treating, Margie went back outside with Bohr to play fetch in the parking lot, while Gil waited inside for me to get out of my costume.

"Do you have a lot of homework this weekend, Logan?"

"I did it on the bus ride home."

Gil got excited as he asked, "Did you wear those new noise-canceling headphones I got you? They're *bass*-ically the best on the market."

I ignored the pun and answered truthfully. "They are excellent at blocking out the sounds, but they also feel strange on my ears."

"Oh, well, you don't . . . I mean if they don't . . . we can look for others that feel better." Gil's smile disappeared as he struggled to complete the thought. I appreciated that he had tried to help me with my ASD-related auditory sensitivity, which can make me feel overwhelmed and unable to focus when there's lots of noises nearby. But before I could say so, Gil changed the subject back to homework. "And did you . . . like we talked about . . . make some mistakes on purpose?"

I assured Gil that I had intentionally misspelled one word on each of the worksheets and substituted the sine of 32 degrees (.52992) for the cosine of 32 degrees (.84805) on one of my math problems, guaranteeing I would not get a perfect score.

"That's smart . . . I mean . . . making one mistake on a math problem isn't a *sine* of a bad student. But still, I'm glad you did it. Just in case."

The "just in case" he was talking about was the possibility of Necros and Dr. Chrysler searching for reports of a new student with my kind of memory. Gil and Margie agreed not to make me redo grades I'd already passed just to blend in better with kids my own age, but they wanted me to stay off Necros's radar. That was their term for it. The thing is, the way to stay off the radar is to fly low . . . much lower than you usually would. That didn't feel a hundred percent right to me.

"It doesn't feel a hundred percent right to me," I explained, "It's like I'm hiding who I really am. I'm not a superhero like you. I'm just Logan, and Logan gets facts right. That is a fact, Dad."

I'd promised Gil that I'd try using that term for him

to see how it felt, but I couldn't help noticing that he did a funny little dark-matter scramble whenever I called him "Dad." His body literally glitched as if being a father was something his consciousness hadn't quite adjusted to. So, I watched his molecules rearrange themselves for a millisecond, but when he recovered, he knelt down so we could look eye to eye.

"We don't want you to be anyone except you. But we want you to be safe too. And for the record, I think you're every bit as much a superhero as I am."

This did not feel like a fact, and I was about to argue the point when Margie walked in the door with Bohr, who immediately let out a piercing bark that startled Gil. He involuntarily vanished in a flash of light and reappeared across the room behind the sofa.

I guess even heroes aren't heroes all the time.

2:18 P.M.
THURSDAY, NOVEMBER 4

Apparently, I am now a wizard.

I don't mean it like, "Harry—yer a wizard," which is what Hagrid said in chapter four of *Harry Potter and the Sorcerer's Stone.* I am only a wizard on Thursdays 2–4:30 p.m., when I'm part of the Marina High Dungeons & Dragons Club.

Since this was my first time having a new identity, I decided to find a hobby where I could get extra practice pretending to be someone else. Also, Gil and Margie told me I needed to join an extracurricular club to start making friends. I originally looked to see if there was a cat-video appreciation club, since they are my absolute favorite types of videos, but there wasn't. After researching the options that did exist, I realized D&D might put me in touch with other people who enjoy reading super-long books, calculating probabilities, and memorizing charts. So, I gave it a try.

After school on Thursday, I made my way to a history classroom and saw that a large table in the center of the class had been transformed into a miniature castle that was made of something very familiar.

"It's hand-painted Lego. I had mono last year and went kinda nuts with the crafting. Welcome. I'm Chris Gifford, but you can call me Giff. I'm president of Marina High's D&D Club. I'm also the Dungeon Master."

Very tall and super pale, Giff was a senior who spoke in a reedy voice, except when he was pretending to be a monster or a giant. But since he was talking as himself when we met, he squeaked a little as he introduced me to the other two members: Zach Wong, who was built like a teenage powerlifter, and Nicky Dinh, a sophomore who was almost as short as me.

I assured the group that I already knew how to play, even though I'd never done it before. That's because I'd read the entire *Player's Handbook*, *Dungeon Master's Guide*, *Monster Manual*, and several other sourcebooks before I showed up.

"Okay, good. Since you're up to speed on the rules," Giff proceeded, "you'll need to roll a character. Any ideas?"

Before I could respond, the door to the classroom opened with a thump and someone walked in.

They had a super-light-brown complexion; short, fringy jet-black hair; a nose ring; and black jeans with seventy-nine different rips in the legs. To be clear, I didn't immediately know how many rips there were, but I counted them afterward in my memory.

"Is this where a gal can go to get her *nerd* on?"

Giff looked at Zach and Nicky, but neither spoke. It was like this newcomer had cast Silence on them. It's a second level spell for bards, clerics, and rangers in case you were wondering.

"Let me put it another way," she continued when it became clear no one was replying. "Is this the D&D Club, or have I just interrupted the least interesting cult in the world?"

Giff finally spoke up, introducing the rest of us. "And you are . . . ?"

"Connie DeWitt. New kid. From New Orleans. I'm a thousand miles away from my home game but I saw your flyers in the caf. So, we gonna roll some dice or is this gonna be like that season of *Stranger Things* where they never get around to playing? Because if that's where we're headed, I'm gonna skip the Upside Down if it's cool with y'all."

Apparently, that one pop culture reference was all it

took to get us back to creating our characters.

I know I said I joined the club to try new things, but after careful consideration, I ended up choosing to be a Halfling Wizard named Nagol. Super-high intelligence. Really short. Very low dexterity. Basically, I ended up being me, just with my name reversed.

On the other hand, Connie decided she would be a gender-fluid goliath barbarian.

"You know," Giff pointed out, "you could be a female goliath. Or a male. There's no advantage to being one or the other in D&D."

Connie's eyebrows scrunched together and the edge of her lip curled in a half smirk, half sneer. "We're playing a game with gnomes, orcs, and devil spawn with purple skin, and you're gonna get caught up on whether my barbarian has a wiener?"

"According to chapter two of *Mordenkainen's Tome of Foes*," I pointed out, remembering one of the several books I'd read, "certain drow elves have the ability to decide which gender they will be for the day. They're called the Blessed of Corellon."

Connie grinned at me. "Guess I'm 'hashtag blessed.' So, here's how it goes; the pronouns you should use for my barbarian are *they/them*. If you accidentally misgender my character, the first time I'll gently correct you. The second time, I'll go into a frenzied rage. Deal?"

Everyone including me nodded. No one said anything about anyone else's choices for the rest of the time.

"Okay, great session! Welcome to the club, Logan and Connie." Giff exhaled as we wrapped things up, a little sweat beading on his forehead. "We'll start the campaign next week, same time and place."

Everyone started packing up. Giff, Zach, and Nicky each had dozens of dice that they bagged up like it was a ritual, sorting them by color or design. I was transfixed and found myself craving my own dice horde. By the time I looked back around, Connie was out the door.

I knew almost nothing about her, but whatever motivation she had for joining the club, it wasn't about making friends or staying under the radar. She didn't seem interested in either.

5:37 P.M.
THURSDAY, NOVEMBER 4

I don't know if you grew up with our parents or with foster parents, but did they ever bring you to their workplace? I understand it's relatively common. There's even a national Take Our Daughters and Sons to Work Day in late April.

I was not that interested in going with Gil to his IT job since it would've meant staying up all night. I had even less desire to see the gym where Margie was teaching people how to lift weights. But going to visit them at MASC—that was *definitely* interesting. So, after D&D Club was over, I took the bus to the new HQ that MASC had built under the Venice Beach Boardwalk and got them to show me around.

"It's not quite Hollywood Boulevard," Margie explained as we strolled up the boardwalk past costumed street performers, hulking weight lifters at Muscle Beach, and dozens of people in skintight swimsuits. "But overall, it's a place where no one is going to notice anything out of the ordinary."

Once they led me in through a secret elevator at the back of a thrift shop, it was clear the new location wasn't as impressive as the old MASC headquarters under Monolith Studios. But it seemed to have most of the same amenities. There were high-tech labs, control rooms, a cafeteria, and of course the kind of training rooms only superhumans can use.

We were just passing one of those gyms when the doors slid open and my best friend, Elena Arguello, emerged, covered in sweat. Behind her was the hero Quarry Lord, who was still walking with a bit of a limp after barely surviving the fight with Seismyxer and Necros nearly a month before.

"Logan! I saw you out here so I asked Luther if we could take a quick break."

Elena had officially joined MASC as a hero trainee after she showed off her long-hidden superstrength during the escape from Necros's lair. That meant, for the past few weeks, she'd spent a lot of time training with her new mentor.

"How's it going, my dude?" Elena asked as she put her

hand up for a high five. It was also very sweaty, but I agreed to slap it anyway because it was the first time I'd seen her since moving away.

"Have you been practicing those bike skills?"

I had, so I said so.

"I have. I am now officially adequate at bike riding. But I don't think I'm allowed to ride back to the old neighborhood yet."

"You're one hundred percent right about that, Foster! You go near Kittyhawk Circle without my clearance, and I'll wipe your mind cleaner than a dry-erase board on the first day of school." Colonel Gdula's voice boomed down the hall as he turned the corner and saw us together. I don't think he needed to be that loud, but in my experience, he'd rather yell at me than talk to me.

In case you forgot, Colonel Gdula is in charge of MASC's operations west of the Mississippi River. He's used to people doing what he says without much discussion. I almost never do what he says and I always want to discuss why, so I am not his favorite person. Then again, I am not certain he has favorite people. The only things I'm sure he likes are wearing burgundy camouflage and chewing on cigars, as he does both at all times.

"Arguello!" Gdula's voice took on a new level of military authority as he put his hands behind his back. "You're supposed to be practicing hand-to-hand combat techniques with Stonefist."

"Who's Stonefist?" I asked.

"That's me, Logan," the massive hero with stone arms informed me with a slight grin. "Luther—aka Stonefist—because someone told the media team that Quarry Lord was a dumb name."

"Stonefist is Arguello's training officer," Colonel Gdula said, I assume, for my benefit, though he was staring at Elena. "It's his job to make sure she learns how and *when* to use her powers. Isn't that right?"

"Yes sir, Colonel," Stonefist agreed, shooting a look to Elena. "I'm confident Elena understands the importance of following *all* trainee guidelines."

Gdula squinted back at him. It was hard to tell if it was a sign he was skeptical or if some smoke from his cigar had drifted into his eyes. "You're confident, eh? Well then, I guess we're all set!"

Even I could tell he was being sarcastic.

The colonel turned to my foster parents and continued. "I've been getting reports on dozens of superhumans disappearing all over the globe in the past two weeks. And I'm not just talking about unaffiliated Class D supers lying low. We've had several MASC heroes drop off the radar. Cryoborg was last seen weeks ago in Alaska, and the London HQ just released a bulletin saying Shadow Paladin hasn't reported since before Halloween."

"Shadow Paladin?" Gil asked, his eyebrows lowered. "Why do I know that name if he's based in Europe?"

"From the movie posters," Colonel Gdula replied with a snort. "The media operations team was going to go worldwide and release his first movie this Christmas, but now there may be no point. I'm telling you, this threat is far more global than what we dealt with a month ago."

Margie made the face she makes when she's concerned. It's one of the ones I've learned to recognize since I've been living with her.

"Is there any pattern to the disappearances?"

"The only thing they all have in common," Gdula responded, turning his attention to me in a way that I didn't appreciate, "is they were all names that your foster son gave to Necros when he was blabbing our database to her and that traitor, Dr. Chrysler."

"I don't think . . . that's . . . totally fair," Gil stammered in my defense.

"Logan was forced to give Necros that information to save our lives, and he is the only reason any of us escaped. That includes you, Colonel!" Margie asserted with no hesitation.

Stonefist stepped in between my foster parents and Colonel Gdula. "Regardless, what are we doing about it now? Have we initiated Page One Protocols on the rest of the compromised superhumans?"

Colonel Gdula exhaled a cloud of smoke that encompassed his reddening face. "We're trying, but we have a serious manpower shortage. Right now, I've got covert recovery teams combing through rubble under Hollywood Boulevard. They're trying to recover equipment and technology we can't afford to lose; and meanwhile, the entire MASC creative team keeps complaining they have nowhere to shoot the new season of the TideStrider show, like that's somehow my concern. On top of all that, I have no doubt that Necros is still after the database intel this boy has stuck in his hard-drive head, so I've got to keep a team on standby at all times in case she shows up near Foster."

Elena's face paled. "You really think Necros would come to get him herself?"

"She's too smart for that. But I do know two things: she wants the information he's got in his brain and she knows how to hold a grudge."

"She certainly does!"

A loud, brassy voice tinged with a light Georgia accent piped up from behind me. I turned to see a middle-aged woman trucking down the hall toward us. She had a wild smile on her face and frizzy hair that fell in curls around her heart-shaped face. Her broad shoulders and chest strained against the seams of her lab coat as she continued interrupting Colonel Gdula.

"Necros had it out for the Borgias for most of the fifteenth century due to a broken promise regarding a certain Michelangelo statue. Won't say which one, but it rhymes with *Shmavid.* Anyway, she waited all the way to 1503 to take out Pope Alexander the Sixth and his son Cesare as revenge. Do *not* mess with Necros! Am I right?"

"I don't know about the historical facts," I replied, thinking her question was a real one. "But you're correct about the last part."

Colonel Gdula's head dropped, and he shook it side to side slowly before introducing us all to the woman.

"This is Dr. Katie Augustine. She has been heading up the lab in MASC's East Coast HQ for the past decade and is our leading authority on Necros. Since Dr. Chrysler betrayed us and bugged out with the bad guys, we need a fresh set of eyes. She's here to help us sift through what we know and help us uncover what the old son of a gun was cooking up while he was secretly working for the other side."

She quickly nodded and said an effusive hello to each of us until she reached Gil, at which point her face lit up even brighter and her arms went wide.

"Oh . . . my . . . stars! Gil, is that you? I haven't seen you since you moved out West! I heard about the accident with the dark matter and your powers and, ugh, let me hug you. Can I hug you? Are you huggable?"

Without waiting for Gil to answer, Dr. Augustine threw her arms around him and hugged him hard enough that it likely would've hurt his bones if he had any.

"Katie . . . I mean . . . Dr. Augustine . . . so good to . . . that's tight . . . this is my . . . Margie?"

Margie stepped forward with a smile on her face.

"I think what Gil is saying is I'm his wife, Margie."

Katie released Gil from her viselike hug and brought her hands up to her mouth. Either she was excited or worried about her breath.

"Of course, I know who you are, Quicksilver Siren. The hottest new heroine MASC has seen in a decade. Though I'd say you're a *villain* for taking Gil away from the rest of the women on this planet. Am I right?"

Katie looked around at the group as no one answered.

"If we are done with the trip down memory lane," Colonel Gdula announced, clenching the cigar between his teeth even harder, "I need to brief Ultra-Quantum, Quicksilver Siren, and Stonefist on the recent disappearances. And, Dr. Augustine, I'm sure you have quite a bit to do as well."

Colonel Gdula stalked off toward the nearest briefing room and Stonefist, Gil, and Margie gave each other a glance before following him. However, Margie turned back as she went through the door, and I heard her telepathically whisper in my head: *We'll be done in a bit. Please, stay out of trouble.*

And then Gdula and the heroes were gone, leaving me, Elena, and Dr. Augustine in the hall, standing in silence.

Some people might call it an awkward silence, but as I have said before, I don't find things awkward. They just are what they are.

"I understand you two actually met Necros."

That was Dr. Augustine. Elena nodded as her hand drifted up to her own neck.

"If you'd call being captured, threatened, and almost killed by her as 'meeting Necros,' then, yeah, I guess we did."

Dr. Augustine's face lit up. "I want to hear everything! Come on."

5:47 P.M.
THURSDAY, NOVEMBER 4

I gave Dr. Augustine a detailed summary of our encounter with Necros as we all walked to her lab, which was beyond messy. In fact, it made her hair seem tame and well maintained by comparison. I wondered how she found anything but also couldn't help being curious if she might be hiding something under her piles of papers and devices.

I am not a prejudiced person. You should know that about me. Because I believe that facts are vital in almost all scenarios, I understand that prejudging anyone or anything means making an evaluation before facts have been observed. Also, as someone who is prejudged frequently, I find prejudging to be mean a lot of times, and I see very little value in being mean. All that said, I was a bit suspicious of Dr. Augustine strictly because the last MASC scientist who had been nice to me almost got me killed.

"Have you ever had a brain PET scan, Logan?"

That was Dr. Augustine. Apparently, my retelling of the Necros encounter had gotten her interested in talking about my memory. Her interest did not make me less suspicious of her.

"I'm asking because I've read research suggesting people on the spectrum often have special isolated skills in memory, but yours seems . . . different."

"You're referring to the 2014 study by Andrée-Anne S. Meileur, Patricia Jelenic, and Laurent Mottron, I assume."

She nodded and smiled, "That's the exact one, not that I should be surprised. My understanding is that *true* eidetic memory is far rarer, especially having it across multiple senses like you do."

"So, you're saying I'm unusual, even for someone like me?"

"No, I'm saying you're special . . . for anyone. And studying superpowers is kind of my full-time gig. That's why I asked about the brain scan. I mean, it isn't exactly a day at the spa, but it doesn't hurt and it could tell us a lot about which parts of your cerebrum are functioning in overdrive. I bet that gray matter of yours would light up like a Christmas tree if we gave it a little bit of radioactive tracer. Am I right?"

Once again, I felt the compulsive urge to answer her possibly rhetorical question until Elena stopped me.

"I'm curious about something else, Dr. Augustine. How does someone become an expert on Necros without having ever met her?"

Elena might have been suspicious too, but if Dr. Augustine noticed, she didn't show it.

"Oh please, call me Katie or Dr. A. or anything that doesn't sound so formal. I don't know if you've noticed, but they are super uptight in the buttocks region around here." She laughed and then caught herself. "Oh, I am *not* supposed to say things like that, especially around young people. I need an industrial-strength filter implanted between my brain and my mouth. What was your question again, Elena?"

"Elena asked how you became an expert on Necros," I reminded her.

"She sure did! I guess you can say I'm part scientist, part historian, and part detective—a sci-stor-ective! I know, it's not a word. But it should be. Anyhow, after getting my third PhD, I was recruited by MASC and started analyzing data from actual encounters with Necros. That led me to look back at historic events related to her activity. Then I pieced it all together until I had more than a millennium of her escapades assembled into a timeline. Did you know the Spanish Inquisition was actually the Catholic Church trying to locate her because they thought she was the devil? And the Bermuda Triangle's legend started when she was headquartered off the East Coast and didn't want visitors. She has always had something going on: being worshipped as a god on an island, being feared as a vampire in the mountains, creating her own cryptocurrency for paying her henchpeople around the world. I've reviewed over a century of MASC's records, and there aren't many gaps other than that one short break Necros took about thirteen years ago."

"What happened thirteen years ago?" I asked, suddenly curious.

Dr. Augustine hesitated for the first time. "I am probably not supposed to say. Neither of you have security clearance."

The way Dr. Augustine stuffed her hands into the pockets of her lab coat as she held her breath suggested she was physically holding herself back. I wasn't the only one who noticed, apparently.

"You knowwwww," Elena said, drawing out her words and making a little frown. I had never seen her do either of these things before. "We didn't ask you for any security clearance before talking all about our firsthand run-in with Necros. We told you everything, didn't we, Logan?"

I thought I understood what Elena was doing and I wanted to help. But technically, we didn't tell her *everything* because that would have taken hours or possibly days.

"Technically we didn't tell you everything because that would have taken hours or possibly days. But we did not hold back any important details. That is a fact."

I tried to mirror Elena's pouty frown. I think I might have instead looked like I was trying to suck something out from between my bottom front teeth.

"Fine!" Dr. Augustine exhaled at once. "Officially, the story is that Necros was injured or incapacitated for a period of about three years because during that time, there were zero reports of her using her powers in any form. But the *unofficial* story is she spent those years . . . becoming a mom."

"That's impossible!" Elena blurted out, looking back and forth between me and Dr. Augustine.

"It should be," Dr. Augustine continued, "but the evidence is there. We know she was working with a brilliant former MIT professor named Dr. Wendell Clarke during that period and that he died about a year before she officially reemerged. But during that downtime, we only have a limited number of security videos and photos of her."

"Videos and photos from MASC?" I clarified.

"No, from TARGET."

I assumed "TARGET" had to be an acronym for some global security program no one knows about. I generated a list of possibilities:

1. Tactical Aerospace Readiness: Ground Emergency Team

2. Terrestrial Authority Regarding Global Environmental Threats
3. The Allied Response Group for Existential Terrorism

None of them made any real sense. Apparently, I must have looked confused.

"Logan, I'm talking about Target. The store. She was shopping. Here, look at this."

Dr. Augustine hustled over to her desk and sat, quickly entering a series of keystrokes to unlock the terminal. She then opened a folder called "Necros_Sightings" on her desktop, which contained a list of hundreds of chronologically sorted subfolders named after dates and locations. Dr. Augustine scrolled past dozens before arriving at a highlighted folder that read "Mama Necros."

With a click of her mouse, the screen filled with photos. Some were grainy and looked like they came from cameras whose lenses were almost as old as Necros herself. Others were clear, digital images. But they all were of a woman who looked exactly like Necros, except for two things. Firstly, she wasn't wearing a gown or a supervillain costume. She was wearing normal-people clothing, except for her ever-present gloves. And second . . .

"Holy flipping crud! She's pregnant!"

That was Elena, and she did not say "flipping" or "crud."

5:55 P.M.
THURSDAY, NOVEMBER 4

I am not an expert on pregnant women. That is a fact. However, I was paying attention in my seventh grade health class, when they explained what happens to a woman's body when she is with child. So I can say that in the pictures Dr. Augustine showed us, Necros looked like she was either pregnant or hiding a kickball-sized supersecret weapon under her sundress.

"How is that even possible?" Elena asked, looking slack-jawed at the images. "She drains the life out of anyone she touches, so if she . . . and someone else . . . it takes two people, right?"

Dr. Augustine just kept flipping through the pictures on her computer screen, showing Necros in various stores, in various stages of pregnancy, and some with a taller man with light-brown skin, glasses, and high, wispy curls on his head. "In general, yes. It takes two people to make a baby. But maybe I'm out of touch. I haven't had a date in months."

Elena raised her eyebrows at me and stifled a giggle.

"How Necros got pregnant is one of dozens of questions we just can't answer. These pictures were also taken from all over the place: London, Tokyo, Boston, Cape Town, even here in LA. Was she moving around to avoid capture, or did she just have pregnancy cravings and travel the world to get her favorite foods? Who knows? The man in the pictures is Dr. Clarke. Could he be the father? Or was he just the one who devised the process that allowed her to carry a child? Did the baby survive? Did Necros pass down her powers?"

As Dr. Augustine rattled off questions, I added the one that she didn't mention.

"How many babies did she have? She definitely was pregnant more than once."

Elena looked even more confused, if such a thing was possible.

"How can you possibly know that?"

"Security cameras have time and date stamps. Look at the photos. Some of them are more than two years apart, but Necros is pregnant in all of them."

Dr. Augustine nodded. "He's right."

Elena sat down on the nearest seat and hung her head, not even bothering to push aside the stack of papers on the chair. "You mean Necros might have multiple preteen Mini-Mes?"

Dr. Augustine continued listing off theories and Elena seemed to listen, but I was distracted. This is not normal for me. I'm usually very focused on the thing I'm very focused on. Like when I'm watching videos of kittens sleeping and making little kitty biscuits in the air with their paws, I can watch them for an hour straight, categorizing them by the color of their fur or how many biscuits they make per minute. But as Dr. A. talked to my best friend, I knew I had missed something important.

So, I replayed the security pictures in my mind: Necros dressed like a regular person with a big belly, Dr. Clarke by her side, bags and bags of maternity merchandise. But there was no new information that I'd missed. So, I went back a little further, to when Dr. Augustine was scrolling past all the other folders of Necros sightings. Dates. Places. And there it was, a folder that read "Los Angeles International Airport" labeled with the date I was found abandoned in a Jetway.

On the day I became an orphan, in the exact place it happened . . . Necros was there. That is a fact.

As the reality of that fact washed over me, all my assumptions of what happened that day shifted; if Necros was there and so was MASC, then it was likely memories might have been erased. That could easily be the reason the police never found any clues how I got left behind! And if that was true, there might be images of me and my parents . . . *our* parents somewhere in MASC's files.

I felt something rising up in my brain—not memories, but feelings.

Alexithymia is the medical term for when a person cannot name the emotions they're feeling. I saw the word for the first time in my medical records at ESTO, and it's pretty much a perfect description of what I experience daily.

All I can say is that what I was feeling was a lot.

Even though I knew it would only get me in trouble—and Margie had clearly asked me to stay *out* of trouble—I had an impulse to reach for the keyboard. But before I could, Dr. Augustine started typing again.

"Anyway, the whole 'Mama Necros' thing is old news around here. Right now, I gotta focus on breaking into Dr. Chrysler's encrypted files to see if we can find out why supers are disappearing all over the planet. It turns out the old guy had an entire secret server built into our system where he kept all the stuff MASC wasn't supposed to know about. It's my job to find out what's in there." Dr. Augustine sighed as she logged out of her workstation and tried to log back in as Dr. Chrysler, only to get rejected.

"Don't suppose he dropped any juicy clues about his password when he was holding you two captive, did he? That would be helpful. Am I right?"

I believe I nodded and said, "Yes, you are right." But I wasn't really thinking about her question. My mind was elsewhere. It was in the Los Angeles International Airport, almost ten years ago . . . the last place and time that I couldn't remember. I'd always thought that was the day my eidetic memory began, but now, I had a new theory.

That was the day my most important memories were taken away.

8:03 P.M.
THURSDAY, NOVEMBER 4

Back at the houseboat, I was still feeling overwhelmed, trying to sort out whether I was feeling confused, intrigued, or anxious most of all. But then I noticed I was also feeling hungry. Margie insisted she needed to take a shower, so Gil offered to make me mac and cheese for dinner before he had to head out to his late shift, working IT. This was advantageous on two fronts:

1. Gil makes it with extra cheese which makes it super gooey.
2. It meant Margie wasn't involved in the process.

While I waited for the pasta to cool, I found myself

feeling impatient about more than dinner. "Do you think I could come to MASC HQ again soon?"

"Probably. I mean, we'll have to get permission."

"Speaking of getting permission . . ." Margie said, exiting the bathroom with her hair wet and in a towel. She had a strange, singsong tone to her voice and was clasping her hands together, her fingers intertwined. "Gil, why don't you tell him."

I looked to Gil and watched as he tried to start a sentence about a half-dozen times.

"Yes . . . Right. Well . . . I . . . or we . . ." Margie gestured for Gil to take a deep breath, ignoring the fact that he no longer has lungs. "We have officially started the process of getting permission . . . to adopt you."

I don't think I reacted to this, but Margie leaned on the counter next to me.

"That doesn't mean we're adopting you anytime soon, Logan. Things take forever with MASC. Take Bohr, for instance."

I looked down and saw the puppy chewing on the leg of a kitchen stool.

"We applied to get a dog a year ago."

"Right . . . I mean . . . you know what they say about filling out forms. It's like sitting on the toilet. You're not finished until all the *paperwork* is done."

That was Gil making a toilet pun. Usually, I like them.

But in my mind, this wasn't the time for jokes.

"If MASC knows something about my birth family, they'd have to tell us about it before they approved an adoption request, right? Like if they had information about whether I had a sibling—they couldn't just keep it from me or cover it up, right?"

Margie and Gil looked at each other and both pursed their lips. I think it was a look of foster-parental concern.

"Of course . . . Logan . . . I mean, MASC exists to protect people . . . and families. That's why we joined. If anything like that had come up in the background check they did back when we first brought you in, we would never keep that from you."

"You have plenty of reasons to mistrust Colonel Gdula," Margie acknowledged with a small frown. "But is it possible that you're feeling this way because talking about adoption is making you uncomfortable, like you're giving up on finding your birth family?"

"Because we wouldn't . . ." Gil sat next to me at the table. "I mean . . . you know that, right?"

"Logan, we love you," Margie said, taking my hands as gently as a superstrong person can, and I did not pull them away since that's something I'm working on. "And we will support you in any way. In *every* way. That includes being your forever family. But it's not a decision you need to make today or next week or anytime until it's right for you. The paperwork just gives us options down the road, and we didn't want to keep anything from you ever again. Okay?"

I nodded and I knew they meant it when they said they wouldn't keep any secrets from me. But I could also see they were both still convinced that MASC's mission meant they were always the good guys, consistently doing the right thing. I wasn't so sure. If they were willing to make up movies and comic books and news stories every day to fool billions of people, it seemed likely that hiding the truth from me wouldn't be such a big deal. So, if I wanted to learn why Necros was at LAX on the same day I became an orphan, I was going to have to figure that one out myself.

9:12 A.M.
FRIDAY, NOVEMBER 5

Have you ever gone on a field trip? Assuming the answer is yes, have you ever noticed there are very few field trips to an actual field? That's because schools do most of their teaching in classrooms, but for centuries educators have reserved special lessons for "out in the field," which was another way of saying "out in the real world." Of course, if the class went to a hay farm, that would truly be a "field trip."

All that said, I definitely learned something I would not have been taught in school when my Earth Sciences class went on a field trip to the Santa Monica Mountains. We were going to study erosion, which is the process by which rocks and soil are worn away by the natural friction created by water, wind, or ice.

There were fifty-six of us, all Marina High freshmen except for Mr. Almonte, the driver, and Ms. Gupta, our teacher, crammed into a yellow 2005 Blue Bird Vision school bus. I knew this because it was the same bus I had ridden to school several times, and Mr. Almonte was the same driver every time. His shoulders always rose above his ears when he drove. And just like on most of my rides to and from Marina High, I had a two-person seat all to myself.

It was fine with me. I never mind having my own seat as I tend to get carsick or bus sick. (I don't think there's a real difference.)

I could hear the other kids talking about how amazing the view was each time we cruised around a banked curve, the hillside falling away on one side or the other. But I couldn't look out the windows without feeling like I was going to barf. So, I closed my eyes, put on the not-so-comfortable noise-canceling headphones that Gil had bought me, and tried to distract myself by mentally rewatching the latest video from Princess Purrnella, my new favorite social-media superstar cat. As I have already shared with you, I think that cat videos are pretty much the very best kinds of videos. In her most recent post, Princess Purrnella got into a staring contest with her own reflection. It went on for more than two minutes and every second was hilarious.

Then, still trying to keep my mind off the curving canyon road, I counted every flake of Raisin Bran Crunch I'd eaten at breakfast. But that was only interesting for so long and my mind started to wander to the images of pregnant Necros next to Dr. Clarke. Dr. Augustine had said he could've been the baby's father. So, I started mixing and matching their features to imagine how their child might look now. I envisioned a girl who was tall like Dr. Clarke but pale and super intense like Necros. I created a composite that was short like Necros but with wild, curly hair like Dr. Clarke, and a complexion that was halfway between their two skin tones. What I got was someone that looked a lot like me.

Just then, we went over a bump in the road and my headphones jostled off my ears as a pair of angry voices toward the front of the bus caught my attention.

"Stay on your side of the seat, freak."

The voice was low for a freshman, and openly aggressive.

"I didn't ask you to sit here, steroid boy. So why don't you dial it back, huh?"

The reply came from a higher voice, dripping with attitude.

Three rows ahead, an oversized jock guy was sitting

next to Connie from D&D Club. Even though I could only barely see the boy's profile from my angle, it was impossible to mistake the way he was sneering at his seatmate.

"If you were a dude, I'd wreck you."

"The only thing you're wrecking is my sense of smell with your breath. It's called a toothbrush, dude. So why don't you put your EarPods back in, turn up whatever butt-rock band you've got on Spotify, and try shutting up for the next fifteen minutes, okay?"

Before the big guy could respond, there was a sudden, concussive POP! and the entire bus lurched to the side. My eyes went wide as the bus ground up hard against the rock face on the right of Mulholland Drive. On contact, the front door shattered and pulled away as sandwich-sized chunks of orange-brown stone crashed through the windows and slammed into everyone ahead of me. I barely ducked down under my seat to avoid the biggest rocks, but then the bus heaved the other way and started to spin.

We made two full, 360-degree rotations. It felt like a carnival ride where you spin for three minutes straight.

When the bus finally came to a rest, the air inside was thick with rock dust, tire smoke, and the groans of my classmates. My head spun, but I knew immediately I had been lucky. Even through the haze and confusion, I could see several people on my side of the bus hadn't taken cover in time and were bruised and bleeding. I just had a few scratches.

As I tried to get my equilibrium back, I noticed a

few people stand unsteadily, including Connie and her unfriendly seatmate. But while the jock headed toward the rear of the bus, Connie stumbled toward the front and looked like she was about to head out the wide-open exit.

The thing was, I couldn't see any ground outside the door. No dirt, no pavement—nothing. Just open air and a canyon stretching out for miles.

"Connie!" I shouted as I leapt to my feet, rushing forward and catching hold of her spiked leather bracelet as her foot hovered over the step down into nothingness.

"What the hell are . . . whoa!"

I think Connie might have been mad at me at first. Maybe she doesn't like being touched very much either. But when she realized why I did it, she backed away from the door and gripped my wrist to steady herself.

"Siéntese! Back to your seats and sit down!"

That was Mr. Almonte in the driver's seat, waving at the students as we all suddenly experienced something strange and genuinely disquieting. The bus felt like it was tipping forward slowly.

Connie and I both got back to our seats, and as we did, the nose of the bus seemed to stop moving. It maybe even rose back up a few inches. That's when it became clear that the whole bus had to be precariously balanced on something, which was why it was rocking back and forth like a seesaw. However, we were not on a playground and a bus should not behave like a seesaw. That is a fact.

The front of the bus was hanging over the edge of the cliff, and the rest of the vehicle hadn't decided yet if it was going over too.

"Everybody, stay in your seats. I'm going to back up!"

I'd heard Mr. Almonte tell students to sit down before, but for once, everyone listened, staying where they were as he gripped the gearshift, put the bus in reverse, and leaned his foot on the gas.

From outside I could hear tires spinning on gravel, trying to grip the ground; trying and failing.

"We need to evacuate this bus!" announced Ms. Gupta, who was in the front seat, directly behind Mr. Almonte. "Exit through the back. Rashida, you go first and call nine-one-one! Anthony, when you get down, I want you to help everyone off. Come on, people, quickly and calmly."

Everyone swarmed toward the back, pushing to be first out of the emergency door.

"I said *calmly*!" Ms. Gupta shouted and apparently her teacher voice worked because the pushing stopped. As everyone moved to the rear, I could feel the tail of the bus settle down a few more inches and the tipping sensation decreased.

"Mr. Almonte, I need help with this student. She's hurt."

That was Ms. Gupta, moving over to the front seat on

my side of the bus. Mr. Almonte slid out of the driver's seat and joined her as they both leaned over a girl I didn't know. I could only see half of her face. The other half was streaked with blood. She wasn't moving, but I noticed her lips mumbling as she drifted in and out of consciousness.

Then I looked to the back, where the other students were crowding toward the emergency exit, even though they could only get out one at a time.

"Can you hear me, Stephanie? Stay awake!" Ms. Gupta's voice pulled my attention back to the front of the bus where the teacher was trying to keep the girl conscious.

"Jump down!" a boy's voice called from the back of the bus as more people hopped to the ground.

Like watching a tennis match, my head toggled back and forth from the front of the bus, where Ms. Gupta was trying to revive Stephanie, to the exodus from the back. I noticed a pattern. Each time I looked forward, I could see a little bit more of the canyon out the windshield, and every time I looked toward the exit, it looked a little higher. More canyon up front. Less students in the back.

This was a problem.

Which is why I yelled out, "This is a problem! Stop getting off the bus! Everyone get back on the bus, now!"

9:15 A.M.
FRIDAY, NOVEMBER 5

You know that your big brother is someone who often says things people don't understand. I try to be clear, but when I tell people facts, I get all sorts of reactions. And yet, I'm not sure I have ever said anything that confused people more than when I told my classmates to get back on that teetering bus.

"Are you crazy? If we stay here, we're all gonna die."

That was Connie's not-so-sensitive seatmate, who was sneering at me. Almost everyone else grumbled and nodded in agreement with him.

"I am not crazy. I am telling you a fact. If we stay on this bus, we all *might* die, or we all might live. But if people keep getting off, approximately half of us will definitely die. Do you want to be the one who decides which half that is?"

The grumbling stopped all at once. Ms. Gupta broke the silence.

"What are you talking about, Logan?"

"Physics. I know this is an Earth Sciences class, but this is really simple. The engine and the fuel tanks at the front of this bus weigh over one ton. The people who are still left on this bus weigh about one-and-a-half tons. That is an approximation. I don't know what everyone weighs, and I've been told it's considered rude to ask. Right now, the bus is balanced. But if we keep getting off, at some point the front will weigh more than the back and the entire bus will go over the cliff, taking anyone who's still on it with it."

"Well, we can get out and . . . hold on kinda." The jock's sneer evaporated as he tried to work through a solution, but I already had.

"The only chance we have to save *all* of us is for everyone to get back on and crowd the back of the bus. We need everyone!"

As if to prove my point, a gust of wind from the canyon swept up the cliff face, rocking the bus like a ship at sea. There was a chorus of screams and *Whoaaaaaa*s until the bus stopped swaying so much. Finally, Ms. Gupta spoke up.

"He's right. Help the students that got off get back on now! The rest of you, pack the last three rows. Stand on the seats if you have to. Let's move. Anyone that doesn't do it will need to write an extra report by Monday!"

Her threat didn't make a lot of sense, since there was a chance we wouldn't be alive Monday. But apparently, teenagers will do anything to avoid extra homework.

A lot of people were sneaking looks at me like they were trying to decide if I knew what I was talking about. Or maybe they were just getting a look at the new kid. That happens too.

Luckily, once the first five or six people got back on the bus, everyone noticed the rear of the vehicle easing its way closer to the ground. Seeing the results, a few spoke up.

"It's working!"

"The tires are back on the ground!"

"Get on! Everyone, get on!"

I turned to Ms. Gupta and the hurt girl, Stephanie. "We need *everyone* to get as far to the back as possible, except for you, Mr. Almonte."

The bus driver's eyes went wide.

"What am I supposed to do?"

"You're the bus driver. You're going to drive the bus." I felt that what I was saying was obvious. "This is a 2005 Blue Bird Vision bus with a wheelbase of two hundred and thirty-eight inches, a Caterpillar C7 engine up front, and rear-wheel drive, isn't it?"

Mr. Almonte's head cocked to the side. "Do you work for the bus company?"

"I do not. That is a fact. Another fact is that if we can

move this bus back, even a few feet, we won't be in danger of going over the edge. It's the fulcrum equation that says in a class one lever—"

"Logan!" That was Ms. Gupta. "This isn't a time for more physics."

Mr. Almonte agreed vigorously. "Besides, I already tried backing up. The wheels just spun."

"Yes, but last time the students' weight was evenly distributed throughout the bus and the tires were only barely touching. By putting all the weight away from the fulcrum, the tires are now in *full* contact with the ground. That raises the coefficient of friction, and while I know you didn't want more physics, Ms. Gupta, it might actually work this time."

Mr. Almonte and Ms. Gupta exchanged a look. Don't ask me what the look was meant to convey because at this point, I wasn't trying to understand the complexities of adult nonverbal communication.

After a pause, Mr. Almonte muttered a prayer and eased himself back behind the wheel, at which point I did my best to help Ms. Gupta carry Stephanie to join the rest of the students at the rear. We laid her down in the last unoccupied seat just as I heard the diesel engine revving.

"Everybody hold on to something!" Mr. Almonte called back over his shoulder. "When I put it in gear, if we move at all, it's gonna be sudden."

People grabbed the nearest seat back, window frame, or even each other as the motor rumbled and whined with increasing volume. That's when Mr. Almonte wrapped his right hand around the gear shift and slammed it upward into reverse.

The bus bucked, and the sound of the gears gnashing sent a shudder through the floorboards. Everyone's heads snapped forward as the rear tires grabbed on to the ground and dragged the bus back five feet in one giant lurch.

"Come on, cariño!" Mr. Almonte was leaning on the accelerator as he tried to coax the bus to do his bidding, which is impossible, of course. But I didn't tell him that.

The front axle grinding against the edge of the cliff sounded like the world's biggest can opener as the bus retreated another five feet, then ten, until only the front wheels were still over the edge. Finally, the engine noise died down.

"It worked!"

I don't know exactly who yelled it, but then everyone was yelling and cheering and several people were crying. One of them was Mr. Almonte.

Ms. Gupta was all business.

"One at a time, everyone exit the bus and find a place on the side of the road to sit. I said one at a time!" Ms. Gupta clearly felt she needed to be more involved in the process, so she turned to me and gestured to the injured girl. "Logan, can you keep an eye on Stephanie?"

I felt the urge to tell her I am not fond of blood or other sticky things, but she didn't give me the chance.

Ms. Gupta cleared a path to the emergency door, using her teacher voice to line people up in the aisle. But she wasn't the only one talking loudly.

"Yo! Sloth people! Move your butts before something else messed up happens!"

That was the jock guy. He seemed unaware that everyone else had just survived a near-death experience too, and they were all showing a lot more patience than he was. He definitely was unaware that his former seatmate, Connie, was standing behind him in line, rolling her eyes every time he mouthed off.

I turned away when I heard a soft groaning from Stephanie, lying in the seat, as she shook her head weakly and tried to wipe the blood from her eyes. Looking closely for the first time, I could see that she had a jagged, angry gash stretching several inches from her eyebrow to the edge of her left temple. It looked awful, and as I stared I felt a different kind of nausea than the motion sickness sweep over me.

I sometimes throw up when I see blood—but you know this about me by now.

Once again, trying to keep down my breakfast, I closed my eyes, fighting the burning sensation of the Raisin Bran Crunch creeping back up my esophagus.

"Move! Let's go! It's like a three-foot jump, nerds. Just go! It's not an *American Ninja Warrior* course. Just grow a pair of . . . pair . . . uhhhhhhhhh . . ."

The bro-tastic voice caught in the middle of the phrase

and then started to slur. I opened my eyes just in time to see the big jock guy's eyes roll back in his head as he slumped to the ground, out cold. It was like every muscle in his body had turned to jelly. I definitely did not feel bad for him, but I was curious why it happened.

Several students shouted as he fell while a few others pulled out their phones and started recording. At least one of them decided to tell the teacher what had happened.

"Ms. Gupta! Chad just passed out!"

All eyes were now on the unconscious jock sprawled on the floor. All eyes except, I noticed, the one person who was touching him. Off to the side was Connie, who was holding his hand. At first, I assumed she was trying to help him, but then I noticed Connie's eyes were closed and her other hand was outstretched, just barely touching Stephanie's leg, lying on the bus seat.

Ms. Gupta wove back through the crowd to tend to Chad, but I couldn't look away from Connie. Like most of the people on the bus, Connie was covered in abrasions from the crash, but as I watched, several of the small cuts on her cheek glistened for a moment like they were dusted in glitter and then started to heal up as if the skin was regrowing in a time-lapse video.

Then I heard Stephanie gasp and when I looked to her face, I saw what should have been impossible. The massive cut on her forehead had all but disappeared, the glittering edges of the wound knitting together until the gash looked like nothing more than a scrape. Stephanie's eyes opened wide, focused on me.

"What happened? Where am I? Who are you?"

I answered as simply as I could.

"The bus crashed, and you got hurt. You're lying on a seat. I'm Logan . . . I'm new."

When I turned back, Connie had already stood up and was slipping through the crowd to the exit, taking advantage of everyone watching Ms. Gupta as she tried to revive Chad. No one had seen what happened with Connie, except me.

Ms. Gupta coordinated the orderly exit from the bus while simultaneously coaxing Mr. Almonte to carry Chad to safety. Conversely, Stephanie was able to get off the bus under her own power just as a parade of fire trucks, ambulances, and police cars roared up the canyon road, sirens blaring. They blocked off Mulholland and began their rescue efforts, even though there was very little rescuing to be done.

I was one of the last people off the bus. There was no reason to wade through all my new classmates, who were covered in a mixture of rock dust, sweat, and, in many cases, blood. It was not a sanitary situation.

But once I got off, I spotted Connie to the side of the road, alone and away from the rest of our class. Across the way, a paramedic was shining a light into Stephanie's eyes and applying two Band-Aids to the wound which, until minutes before, looked like it would require serious stitches. Chad, on the other hand, was lying on a stretcher, his head lolling side to side while the EMTs monitored his blood pressure. The rest of the kids were just standing around, holding their phones, posting pictures to their stories or texting friends who weren't on the field trip. Not one even looked up at me as I walked through the crowd and over toward Connie.

"Hey, hero boy. Did any of them even thank you?" Connie asked, hands firmly planted in the back pockets of her ripped jeans.

"No," I admitted. "But I didn't do it to be thanked. I did it so I wouldn't die."

Connie nodded. "I'm a big fan of not being dead too, and if you hadn't kept me from taking that step out . . . I'm pretty sure you saved my butt back there. So let me be the first one to actually say thanks."

I nodded and tried to smile. I have no idea if it looked right because I never do. But what I was really thinking about was wanting to know more about what Connie had done on the bus. I just had no idea if there was a subtle way to bring it up. Subtlety is not my strong suit. That is a fact.

Still, I tried.

"I hope everyone will be okay. That girl, Stephanie, was in rough shape."

"Is that her name?" Connie betrayed nothing. "I bet she'll be fine. She was able to get off the bus on her own."

"What about that big guy? Chad?" I asked, still trying

not to let on. "He didn't seem hurt at all and then he was out cold. Do you think he'll be all right?"

Connie leaned back against the guardrail, crossing her arms as her expression darkened. "I doubt it."

There was a pause, and for the first time, I considered the possibility that whatever had happened to Chad on the bus might be permanent. But then Connie smiled and interrupted my thought process with a twinkle in her eye.

"He'll still be a grade-A tool bag whenever he wakes up. There's nothing those EMTs can do about that. It's incurable."

I was pretty sure that was both a joke and a fact, but before I could confirm it, I heard Ms. Gupta's teacher voice once again.

"Students, I need everyone to gather. We're going to contact your parents *before* this ends up on the news."

Connie shrugged and slowly meandered back to the group. "Thanks again, hero boy. Guess I'll see you at D&D Club on Thursday, assuming we live that long."

"It's Logan. My name is Logan."

Connie kept walking and replied without looking back. "I know."

5:21 P.M.
SUNDAY, NOVEMBER 7

When Margie picked me up from the crash site on Friday, I told her almost everything that had happened, including how I used my understanding of physics and the bus specifications to save myself and my new classmates. When I retold the story to Gil that night, I shared all the same information, plus a little bit of the math I did in the moment. But I didn't tell either of them about what I'd seen Connie do, because I ran through the possible results and found many of them less than ideal:

1. They could insist that I report Connie to MASC even though Connie clearly was trying to keep her powers secret.

2. They might be required to tell MASC themselves.
3. They could pull me out of Marina High out of concern that being in a school with a superhuman might draw attention.
4. They could potentially not believe me and think I injured my head in the accident.

So, I kept that one piece of information to myself and instead asked Margie and Gil to make a formal request to MASC for me to visit Elena's house as soon as possible. Then I texted Elena that I had several facts I had to tell her. She said she had stuff to share with me too, so I asked Gil and Margie to expedite the request.

We had to sign seven different forms, submit to a digital lie-detector test, and there was still a twenty-four-hour waiting period to get the approvals, but they finally came through midday Sunday. A few hours later, I was picked up by a MASC team, placed in a large cardboard box, and delivered by an Amazon van to Elena's father's house. This was all designed to throw off any of Necros's operatives in case they were watching Gil and Margie's previous home.

Squatting in the box and sweating through my T-shirt, I texted Elena that I'd arrived after I felt the MASC delivery guy wheel me on a dolly to the front door and put me down on the porch. I assume he rang the bell before walking away, but I couldn't see for sure. This wasn't a high-tech delivery device with hidden cameras and a built-in video monitor. It was literally just a box. They hadn't even given me bubble wrap.

The doorbell chimed and I heard a distant, muffled female voice call out. "I'll get it, Dad!"

But then I heard a lower, gruffer, and much closer voice reply as I heard a door opening. "It's no problem, baby. I'm right here."

Suddenly, I was in the air. Or to be more precise, the entire box was in the air, lifted up like a carnival ride. I weigh eighty-five pounds, and whatever or whoever picked me up snatched me up like I was lighter than a roll of toilet paper.

"Mira, baby! It's a big box. Did you order a new punching bag?"

Instinctively I must have yelped a little as I tumbled around inside the box. Or maybe I grunted. I'm certain I made an involuntary noise because, suddenly, I wasn't being tossed around anymore.

"What was that?" The voice got even lower and rougher as I felt the box placed on the ground.

"Dad, it's okay! It's just—" I think there was a worried tone to Elena's voice, but before she could complete her thought, five outrageously thick and calloused fingers ripped the cardboard away in one sweeping pull.

The box fell apart around me, and there was Elena's

dad, Arturo, holding a big meaty fist by his ear, poised to punch whoever had snuck into his house.

"Logan? Why are you in a box?"

Elena laid a hand on his shoulder softly. Even though she's already about six inches taller than her dad, she slumped her shoulders in a way that looked either uncomfortable or apologetic.

"Dad, I told you some people were assigned to deliver Logan here."

"When you said *deliver* him, I didn't realize he was going to be in a box." Arturo shook his head and extended his oversized hand to me, pulling me up with zero effort. "I'm sorry, Logan. They should've at least marked the package as fragile."

"It's okay," I assured him. "It was an honest mistake."

"Yeah," agreed Elena. "Lots of people think Logan is fragile, but they don't know how gangster he really is."

I think Elena meant that as a compliment, but her statement wasn't a fact. Still, I decided not to correct her.

It had been a month since I'd been in Elena's dad's house, but it all looked the same: lots of pictures of Elena when she was younger, including several from when Arturo and Elena's mom, Vivica, were still married. There were also tons of posters of classic German cars, which were the kind of cars Arturo repaired. And the thing that was the most the same was the way the house smelled like the best Mexican food ever, which made sense, because Arturo might be better at cooking than he is at repairing cars, which is saying something. He must have noticed me inhaling deeply through my nose because he grinned.

"I'm making carnitas on the grill. I assume you're staying for dinner?"

Arturo turned and headed through the kitchen and out the back door into the yard, snatching a pair of tongs and an apron off the counter as he went. I made sure to hang back to get Elena alone for a moment.

"You told your dad I was being 'delivered'? Who does he think was delivering me?"

Elena reached out with a smile and tousled my frizzy hair, which had been made even messier than usual after a half hour stuck in a cardboard box.

Instinctively, I started muttering the rules of the Geneva Convention.

"He knows about MASC, and what happened last month, Logan. That's part of what I wanted to tell you."

That was important information. My mind needed a moment to process what I was hearing. But then I realized what Elena had just implied.

"That's only part of what you want to tell me? What's the rest?"

"You know the big mystery about how I got my powers? Not a mystery. It's a family secret."

6:38 P.M.
SUNDAY, NOVEMBER 7

The dinner with Elena and Arturo was one of my favorite meals ever: Arturo's slow-cooked carnitas tacos with homemade corn tortillas were out of this world—and not in Margie's "alien-cuisine" sorta way. But what made it even better was that while we munched, Arturo shared an origin story straight out of a comic book.

"Twenty years ago, I had my first garage out in Barstow. It wasn't much of a shop, but it had a studio apartment above where I lived, and it was the perfect location to be the first place to get gas or radiator fluid for anyone driving across the Mojave Desert from Nevada. That's pretty much how I built the business: towing hungover dudes coming home from Vegas whose cars were in even worse shape than their luck.

"One night, I get a call for a tow waaaaaaaaay out in the desert. Like in an area that doesn't even really have roads. The guy says he'll pay triple, but he needs me to bring my flatbed. I hop in the wrecker, rumble up north a bit, get lost once or twice, and I finally find this guy standing next to a Land Rover that's running just fine. And the dude wasn't any gambler that took a wrong turn. He was some kind of professor type: tall, skinny, a wild 'fro, and an accent that sounded kinda English but not quite. I point to his Land Rover and say, 'Your ride doesn't look like it needs a tow.' The dude just laughs at me, which I wasn't a big fan of.

"Then the guy pulls a shovel out of the back of his Rover. I'm on high alert, thinking that he's some psycho trying to bury me in the desert. But he goes over to this sand dune and starts digging something out."

"What was it?"

That was me. It seemed like the most obvious question.

"It looked kinda like a meteor or a satellite, but also kinda like a giant burnt chicken nugget mashed up with refried black beans. Just this mass of rock and metal and stuff I don't even know what to call it. And it was glowing in the dark a little. Not a steady glow either . . . like throbbing. I wasn't looking to mess with nothing like that, but this dude pulls out a wad of cash thicker than my wrist, and I've got a pretty thick wrist. He hands me a grand and tells me that if I put the thing on the truck, bring it back to the garage overnight, and keep my mouth shut, he'll give me ten thousand dollars, cash. You gotta understand, I was getting fifty bucks for a tow job back then. I put on my thickest gloves, wrapped this glowing junk pile in a chain, and cranked it onto the flatbed.

"The professor dude said he'd come by first thing in the morning to get it. So, I drove back, locked it up in my shop, and headed upstairs to sleep, if you can call it that. All night, it was like I was dreaming, but also kinda floating, and I swear wherever I was in the dream, everything was pulsing and getting hotter and hotter every few seconds.

"When I woke up, my bed was soaked with sweat. I drank about eight glasses of cold water and an entire carton of orange juice. Then I went down to my shop and it was wide open. The garage door was up, the glowing thing was gone, and sitting on the driver's seat of my tow truck was an envelope with ten thousand bucks in it and a note that said, 'Thank you for your assistance and your silence.' I was definitely not about to mess with that dude, so I hid the cash in my freezer and went back to work. I was still feeling weird and hot all day, but just before I closed up for the night, a man and a woman, both wearing suits and well-shined shoes, show up in a black SUV and start asking questions. Have I seen anything strange in the past twenty-four hours? Did I get any weird work calls? They show me a picture of the dude who hired me and asked if I'd seen him. I figure they must be government, but they never showed me any ID or a badge. Meanwhile, I've got a chunk of actual, cold cash in my freezer telling me 'Cállate, bobo! Just keep your mouth shut!' So, I hit them with a bunch of 'no, sir' and 'no, ma'am' and the whole time my heart is going like the pistons in a BMW M3. Eventually, they get tired of asking me questions and leave, and as soon as they go, I slammed down the garage door . . . and it was closed forever."

I was confused by that last part.

"I'm confused by that last part. Why was it closed forever?"

Arturo smiled as he took a drink of his lemonade. "Two reasons, Logan. First, I slammed it so hard that the metal at the bottom crumpled and dug into the pavement. I was so strong all of a sudden, I could do stuff with one hand that would take a jackhammer a half day. I figured those people asking all the questions probably would be back if word got out that I was suddenly Chicano Superman. So that brought me to the second reason. I knew I couldn't stay in Barstow. I took the ten grand out of the freezer, drove my flatbed over to my buddy Andre's shop, and sold him the truck in exchange for another twenty large in cash and an eighteen-year-old Mercedes convertible that needed a new wheel bearing and brakes. I threw my suitcase in the back and drove west until I hit the ocean. As soon as I got here, I used the money I had to open my new shop in the Marina and that's been my life ever since."

I was amazed. It was such a good story, and clearly one that had never gotten out.

"But you aren't in the MASC database! I have the whole thing in my head, and your name isn't anywhere in it."

"My dad never told anyone, Logan," Elena explained as she reached her hand across the table and laid it gently on her dad's. "He didn't even tell my mom about his powers . . . or mine when they finally started to appear."

Arturo nodded along. "I didn't even say anything when Elena hit puberty—"

"Dad!" Elena protested and blushed. I don't know why though. Everyone hits puberty eventually. At least I hope so for my own sake.

"I mean, you went from being slightly ahead of everyone else to suddenly getting much stronger and faster than the other kids, and I did my best to help you keep it low-key. But with your mom, I just played it off like it was no big deal and she was overreacting. I should've told you both then, but I was afraid. And keeping it from Vivica . . ." Arturo leaned his elbows on the table and turned back to me. "I made a lot of mistakes. I thought if people found out, Elena would be treated like there was something wrong with her. I didn't know it could help her be a hero!"

"I'm not a hero yet, Dad." Elena smiled.

"Sure you are, baby. In fact, why don't you rescue all these plates and silverware into the dishwasher?"

Elena rolled her eyes, but in a funny way. It looked like both Elena and her dad were getting along even better than they had when I was their neighbor. So, I asked her about it while we did the dishes.

"Yeah, things have definitely gotten easier since he told me about his powers. It's like we can both let down our guard since no one's hiding anything," Elena agreed as she rinsed glasses, like everything she was saying was normal. I guess for her, it was. "Last week, MASC asked my dad if he'd be willing to come on board and be trained, but he turned them down. He said we only needed one hero in the family.

"I'm just glad I don't have to lie to him about what's going on anymore. My mom, on the other hand . . ." Elena trailed off and the smile on her face faded. "I want to tell her too, Logan. I mean, she's my mom and hiding anything from her feels awful. But Colonel Gdula is totally against it and my dad agreed. They both said that it might make things harder."

"When Margie and Gil kept the truth from me, it caused problems. But then again, I can't say life has gotten easier since I've known the truth either."

"Makes you wonder about Necros," Elena mused. "I mean, if her kids survived, do they know she's a monster, or is she just Mom to them?"

"The concept of monster mothers is nothing new. I got

into epic poetry for a while in fifth grade; and in the Old English poem *Beowulf*, two of the three main creatures coming after the hero were monsters, Grendel and Grendel's mother, and that story is over a thousand years old."

Elena put the last plate in the dishwasher, closed it, and turned to me. "Is that why you risked being stuffed in a box to see me, Logan? To tutor me in ancient epic poetry? Or is something else up?"

"There is definitely something else up. Multiple things, actually."

I started out with the realization that Necros and MASC were both at LAX the day I was abandoned.

"No one at the airport that day reported remembering anything about how I got there or who I was with, and we both know that MASC loves to erase memories. I'd have to get back into those files to confirm it, but I don't think Gil and Margie will help. They're pretty convinced that MASC wouldn't keep the truth from them, even though it's exactly what MASC does."

Elena exhaled. "Eesh, that's tricky. I mean, it's not like Colonel Gdula is your biggest fan. You'd need to have a pretty good reason to show up at HQ."

"I might have it already," I explained, and then told her about the bus accident, this time including Connie's apparent superpowers. I may have spent some extra time on explaining exactly how I'd saved everyone on the bus because I know Elena appreciates those details.

"Dang, Logan! Why am I wasting all my time training to be a hero when I could just hang out with you and be saving lives on the regular?"

I told her that I thought that was a very good idea before realizing it was more of a joke than a question.

"Does Connie know you saw what she did?" Elena asked.

"I don't think so. And I have no idea if she knows about MASC or would even believe me if I told her about it. But someone with her powers could help a lot of people, and if I brought Connie in, Colonel Gdula might not even notice that I was there."

Elena listened and nodded along before responding. "I don't know Connie, but having powers and keeping it to yourself can be lonely. Maybe you should just talk to her?"

It was a good idea, but I had an even better one.

"What if *we* talked to her together instead?" I asked. "That way she'd know I wasn't making it all up. You could come to my new school. There's no rule against you coming to the Marina."

Elena considered it for a second. "Sure, I'll be your wingwoman. If nothing else, it's a chance to hang out without you having to be shipped over in a cardboard box."

4:45 P.M.
THURSDAY, NOVEMBER 11

All week, I avoided talking too much with Connie. She asked me if I wanted to grab lunch off campus on Tuesday, but I told her I'd brought a lunch. That was a fact. I had a bologna and grape jelly sandwich made by Margie. Clearly, I would have enjoyed a different lunch experience, but I declined because I was saving the big conversation for Thursday, after D&D Club.

The game session went well. My halfling wizard successfully cast several spells and Connie's goliath barbarian collected a half-dozen goblin heads as trophies. The others were more than a little disgusted, but I reminded everyone that ancient Celtic warriors did the same thing.

(Technically, I'm not sure I *reminded* anyone of that fact, since they never knew it in the first place.)

Anyway, afterward, I caught up with Connie in the hall outside the classroom.

"You were very efficient in terms of goblin elimination today."

Connie smirked at me. "You're one heck of a sweet-talker, you know that, Logan?"

I did not know that about myself, so I shared that information.

"I did *not* know that about myself."

As we headed down the hall, we continued to talk about our D&D game.

"My barbarian took a lot of damage today. Good thing Nicky's cleric cast that healing spell."

I am not very good at segueing from one subject to another because my brain usually stays on just one thing. But even I saw my opening.

"Speaking of healing, there's something I wanted to discuss with you . . . something about the crash last week."

Connie's smirk vanished as she faced forward and kept walking toward the end of the hall. "What's there to talk about? The bus tried to do an Olympic cliff dive, and you were the only one who didn't freak out."

"That is one semifactual account of what happened," I agreed.

I trailed along as she pushed through the exit doors, knowing that Elena was waiting outside. She was sitting on the stairs and stood as we approached. Connie slowed.

"Hey, Logan," Elena offered with a wave. "And you must be Connie, right? I'm Elena. Logan has told me a lot about you."

"He has?" Connie asked. "That's funny. I don't think he knows me well enough to tell anyone *a lot* about me."

Connie took a small step back, then looked to me and shook her head as she turned and headed quickly off campus.

"Dude, I don't know what your deal is or why you think I am looking to be set up, but I'm all good, okay, Cupid? No offense to you, Elena. You're definitely easy on the eyes, but this isn't how I roll."

I noticed Elena's dark bronze cheeks flush a little as she kept pace with Connie. Then, just as we got to the street, Elena reached out for Connie's wrist and held her back.

"It's not a setup, Connie. Just listen to Logan for a second, okay?"

Connie didn't pull back her arm, but she didn't back down either. "What are you, his muscle?"

Elena looked over to me and shrugged a little bit.

"Actually, yeah. But that's not why I'm here either."

"So why are you here?" Connie asked impatiently and then looked to me. "Why am *I* here? Why are you ambushing me after D&D Club?"

I looked to Elena, who gave me a nod. I assumed that it meant to go ahead.

"After the bus accident, I saw you do something that healed Stephanie's injuries. That is a fact. It also looked like you healed yourself a little, but I am less sure if that is a fact. Either way, what you did should be impossible unless you have some sort of superpower. I also happen to know that superpowers are real and that you are definitely not the only person on the planet who has them. So, if you would like an opportunity to help people with your powers and still live a semi-normal life, Elena and I know people who can help you do that."

Connie looked me right in the eye, then tilted her head up to stare intensely at Elena, who was almost a head taller.

"I'm gonna take my wrist back. Cool?"

Elena released her grip and Connie walked off down the street away from the school, taking long strides like she was eager to put some distance between us. But after a few moments, Elena went after her, catching up in the parking lot of a rundown mini-mart a block away.

"Hey, just wait! I know what you're thinking . . ."

"You do?" Connie turned and asked, but her raised eyebrows made me think it wasn't a sincere question. "You know what it feels like to be accosted by a classmate and a stranger who think comic books are real? Or do you know how exhausting it is to be the new kid and have everyone trolling you like it's a sport? Or maybe you know how it feels to be so done with a conversation that you wish you *did* have superpowers so you could teleport out of it? 'Cuz I'm kinda feeling all of that right now."

I've seen a few people stand up to Elena and it hasn't gone well for them. But this time, Elena didn't start punching or glowing or anything. In fact, she looked down at her own feet.

"What I know is how it feels to have a secret that you're afraid will get out. I know what it's like to be able to do stuff, except you can't do it without being called a freak. And I know it feels like you're the only one who feels that way, and that's the worst. But you're not alone. You're different . . . but not alone."

As she finished speaking, Elena looked up and met Connie's eyes for a beat. I thought Connie was about to say something to Elena, but instead she turned and walked away again.

"This is not happening. You can miss me with all this drama. I'm getting outta here! Hey, you!" Connie called out to a guy who was just getting into a Mazda Miata at the far end of the lot. The driver looked startled as Connie approached his open door.

"I need a ride."

"What?" he responded. The driver appeared to be just a few years older than Connie, but he already had a full tattoo sleeve on his left arm. He used that arm to shoo Connie away. "Get outta here."

"Connie," I called out to her, "it's not a good idea to get into the car of a complete stranger unless you are using a ride-sharing app. And I don't see an Uber sticker in that car's window."

"You don't know me. Maybe this is my new boyfriend, Tony." Connie walked to the passenger-side door, opened it like it was her own car, and sat down. "Isn't that right, Tony?"

"I'm not Tony. You ain't my anything. So, get lost. There's a bus stop right over there!"

It was when not-Tony gestured across the street with his non-tattooed arm that we all saw he had a long thin metal strip in his hand, like an oversized ruler with a notch in the end.

"What the heck is that?" Connie asked.

"It's a slim jim," I replied, having read several historical texts on car theft, including *Stealing Cars* by John A. Heitmann and Rebecca H. Morales. "It's a thin ribbon of metal designed to manipulate a car door's locking mechanism."

Elena was incredulous. "Dude! You're stealing a car in the middle of the afternoon, a block from a school?"

That's when not-Tony got a wild look in his eye and reached across Connie, slamming the passenger-side door behind her. Then he pulled a screwdriver out of a pocket and held it up menacingly close to Connie's face while yelling at us. "Back off! I'm taking the car and your annoying friend to make sure you two don't do anything stupid."

With that, the car thief jammed the tool into the ignition and the engine roared to life. Through the windows, I could just make out Connie struggling to get out as not-Tony used his other arm to pin her to the seat.

I considered hitting the panic button on my watch, but before I could press it, Elena took three athletic running steps and was in front of the Miata, refusing to move as she laid both of her hands on the hood.

"You aren't going anywhere."

The thief revved the engine. I supposed he was trying to scare Elena, but she stood her ground. That's when he put the car in gear and started to roll forward . . . except, after a few inches, the car stopped.

"I said . . . you aren't . . . going anywhere!" Elena hissed through gritted teeth as the muscles across her shoulders and neck went taut and began emitting a faint glow.

At the same time, I heard a strange, soft beeping coming from her and noticed a tiny, flashing LED light on one of her earrings.

"Elena, you're beeping."

She didn't react. Maybe she didn't hear me because the engine was getting louder, or maybe because the force of the car was starting to push her backward. The soles of her sneakers were squealing as she slid slowly across the blacktop, the 181 horsepower under the hood driving her back.

I ran around to the side and saw not-Tony's incredulous expression. His eyes were wide, and he was shouting things that I assume were curse words. But Connie's expression was completely different: it was more like the face people sometimes make when a video game has amazing graphics.

Still, impressive as Elena's strength was, it was clear that her footwear and leverage were overmatched by the Miata's engine. And just when I thought she was about to give up, Elena's right arm flared bright yellow and she dropped her elbow onto the hood *hard*, like a pro wrestler. In an instant, the front end of the car buckled, and then the engine died as a geyser of steam exploded out from around Elena's elbow.

There was a brief silence before the car thief threw open the door and sprinted wildly around the corner, sneaking terrified looks back over his shoulder as he ran.

Elena wrenched her right arm from the twisted metal that had been the Miata's hood. She didn't seem interested in running after not-Tony. Instead, she went to the passenger-side door and pulled it open.

"Are you okay?"

Connie stepped out, slightly shaken but trying to look like she wasn't. "I'm fine. But your arm . . ."

Elena seemed to notice for the first time that her entire elbow was bloody and burned. "It's not that bad. I dunno how I'm gonna keep this from my mom, but—"

Before Elena could finish the thought, Connie reached

out and touched the injured arm, and just like on the bus the week before, I watched as the lacerations and burns mended themselves. But this time, it was Connie who got light-headed and almost fell if not for Elena catching her.

"You didn't have to do that," Elena said, easing Connie back up.

Connie smiled in a crooked way.

"You didn't have to atomic elbow a car for me. I guess we're even."

Elena brushed a few hairs out of her own eyes and smiled in a funny way that I hadn't ever seen before, holding Connie's gaze for a beat. I wondered if that was what flirting looked like, but then I realized there were other concerns.

"Not-Tony is getting away."

Elena pointed to her earring, which was still beeping. "No, he's not. This is a MASC trainee tracker. Anytime I use my powers outside of HQ . . . well, you'll see."

An instant later, the car thief appeared again from around the corner, stumbling backward as a van full of MASC commandos skidded to a stop, blocking his way. With them was Stonefist, looking more than a little exasperated.

"Who the fuzz are they?" Connie asked, although she didn't say "fuzz."

"These are the people Elena and I were telling you about."

While the commandos surrounded the car thief, Stonefist took a direct path to Elena.

"Are you trying to get me fired?!"

Elena shook her head, raising her hands like she was either trying to apologize or surrender. "I know, I'm not supposed to use my powers, but—"

"You're not *allowed* to use your powers without supervision, Elena! You are so lucky I was only a few blocks away as part of Logan's surveillance detail. If anyone else got here first, Gdula would be coming down on you like a ten-ton hammer. You wanna blow your cover before you even have a superhero name?"

Elena's head drooped as she looked up at Stonefist.

"I'm sorry. I messed up."

"Yeah, you did!" Stonefist agreed, but then his expression changed to something less stern. "That said . . . daaaaaaaaaaang, Elena! Did you really do all this to the car?"

"I did," she replied, a small grin on her face as she raised her eyes. "I was able to focus the energy into one arm, just like you've been teaching me."

"Wheeeeeewwww! You're a natural." Elena smiled at the praise until Stonefist put his hands on his hips and his eyebrows lowered. "But you can't be testing that stuff out on small-time crooks. It's like using a sledgehammer to swat a mosquito."

"Hey! Who you calling a mosquito?" not-Tony protested as the commandos surrounded him.

Stonefist looked back at the car thief and approached

him, while one of the commandos pulled out a small, plastic case from their pack.

"I'm sure this is quite confusing. But you, young man, are actually on a new reality TV show called *The Prank Bank*, and you've won a pair of wireless earbuds. Go ahead and open the box. Try them on. Then you'll hear about the rest of your prizes."

I wasn't exactly sure what Stonefist was up to, except that I knew he was lying. Tricking people by telling them they've won a prize is actually very common. The Federal Trade Commission reported that con artists scammed people out of 121 million dollars in 2019 by making them think they'd won a sweepstakes or lottery. I'd read up on it when my sixth foster family had fallen for one of those schemes, right before they returned me to ESTO.

Apparently not-Tony wasn't aware of these statistics because he stopped being suspicious and, instead, ripped open the case and pulled out a pair of gleaming white earbuds.

"These look sick," the car thief admitted as he put the buds in his ears to see how they felt.

"Just wait until you hear how they sound."

That was Stonefist, who held up a smartphone and touched the screen with his thumb. Suddenly, not-Tony's eyes fluttered and he went stiff like he was in a trance, a light hum filling the air.

"That sounds like the Houdini chair," I pointed out. Stonefist nodded.

"Newest portable edition. There's even an app for the phone to activate them." Then he turned to a stocky, powerfully built woman who appeared to be the commandos' team leader. "Sergeant Bricker, finish up wiping the creep's memory and disable the convenience store's cameras. Then roll the car up against a light pole with him in the driver's seat and send the police an anonymous tip."

"Yes, sir," Sergeant Bricker replied crisply. "We'll arrange it to look like the subject peeled out, hit the pole, and knocked himself out cold."

As the team began their cover-up, Stonefist turned his attention to Connie, who had her arms crossed defiantly. "And how about this one? Do I need another pair of Houdini buds?"

For a moment, Connie looked like she was tensed and ready to fight back if anyone tried to mess with her. But before it came to that, I stepped in.

"Actually, she's with us."

6:13 P.M.
THURSDAY, NOVEMBER 11

Once we got to the MASC temporary HQ, there was a lot of explaining to be done. Like, well over an hour of explaining by several people.

Elena explained why she'd used her powers in public. Stonefist explained why she shouldn't be suspended. Colonel Gdula explained why it was actually *my* fault and how I should have my memory wiped. Margie and Gil explained why that was unacceptable. And eventually, once there was less shouting, I explained that Connie has superhuman healing powers, followed by Connie explaining a lot of stuff that none of us knew.

"My powers aren't exactly 'healing' if you gotta know,

and considering how many of you are standing around me right now, it seems like y'all *gotta* know."

Connie settled into a chair in the MASC ready room while Dr. Augustine scribbled notes. I just listened.

"I'm a conduit for life force. That's the best way I can explain it. Like, I'm sure there's a more nerdy, scientific term for it, but I've just always called it life force. When someone is hurt or sick, their life force goes down."

"Like hit points in D&D?" I asked because I thought I understood.

"Right. If I touch someone whose life force is tanking, I can give them some of mine, which can heal up cuts or even broken bones, but it makes me feel like trash for a while. That's what I did for Elena in the parking lot."

Elena smiled in that funny way again as she rubbed her arm where Connie had healed her.

"But that's only when things are desperate. Most of the time, I'll try to touch a fully healthy person and transfer some of their juice to the person that's hurt. It's like a blood transfusion, with the donor being down a pint for a while until their body naturally builds back up. That's what I did to that Chad dude on the bus."

"Can you absorb life force too?" Dr. Augustine asked, chewing on the end of her pencil.

"You mean as an offensive power?" Colonel Gdula piped up, showing interest.

Connie chuckled. "That would be so badass. But unless I'm hurt, I can only transfer the energy, not store it. So, nah, I can't just suck somebody dry unless it has somewhere to go."

I still had questions, and from the notes Dr. Augustine was taking, I think she did too. But Colonel Gdula didn't need to hear anything more. He was smiling for once.

"This is like stepping in a cow flop and coming out with a Snickers bar stuck to your boot!"

The colonel seemed very pleased with his own simile, while most of the other people in the room crinkled their noses. I definitely found it disgusting. That is a fact.

"We can always use a superhero with healing powers, or whatever you wanna call it. All I care is that the rest of the supers can go pedal to the metal and get patched up in a flash. That's like having a few extra heroes in the field. Ultra-Quantum and Quicksilver Siren, we're going to need to get this little missy trained up right quick. You're *both* going to mentor her."

"*Little missy?* What century do you think you're in, Colonel Camo? My name is Connie DeWitt. Learn it!"

Colonel Gdula started to get red in the face, but then his eyebrows lowered. "DeWitt? DeWitt . . . Why is that name so darn familiar?"

At that point, Dr. Augustine's face lit up for a moment and then she started flipping through her notebook.

"Anya DeWitt is part of our database," she announced loudly before making eye contact with me. "I mean, she's one of the names that Necros stole last month."

Without even thinking about it, I found myself repeating the information aloud. "Anya DeWitt, thirty-one seventy-seven Dauphine Street, apartment two B, New Orleans, Louisiana. Powers: touch-based empath. Possibly mind control—"

"Hold up." Connie stood, suddenly agitated and looking at me. "How do you know where we live? And why do you know so much about her? She told, like, three people about her powers her entire life."

I found myself speechless for once, so she turned to Colonel Gdula next.

"Do you know where she went? You better not be the ones who took her!"

"Took her?" Colonel Gdula interrupted. "She's missing? Since when?"

Connie's anger seemed to break into something smaller and sadder.

"Two weeks ago, she just disappeared. I didn't call the police at first because my mom's been in some trouble before. Nothing serious. But when the cops showed up, they were more interested in telling me I couldn't be alone in our apartment than actually going out and finding her. So that's when I called Uncle Jimmy, and he flew me out here to stay with him until . . . I dunno."

"Dr. Augustine, update the database and add Connie's mom to the list of missing superhumans," Colonel Gdula announced. "Connie, I need to know everything about your mother's disappearance. Siren, Ultra-Quantum, and Stonefist, I want you to hear this too."

Dr. Augustine nodded and headed back to her lab while Colonel Gdula led Connie, my foster parents, and Stonefist to a secure room. When I tried to follow, he stopped me short.

"Let the people with real powers handle this. Arguello," the colonel called out to Elena, "you're on babysitting duty. Foster gets out of line, it goes on your record."

Elena gripped the back of a nearby chair and bent the metal.

"I swear, even if I live to be a hundred, the day I got to knock that gasbag out will still be the best day of my life."

I could see Elena was angry, but I was feeling something different, and for once, had no issue naming the emotion. It was guilt. Elena must have noticed.

"Logan?" she asked, much quieter. "You okay?"

"Connie's mom is missing because of me. I'm the one who gave Necros her information. That is a fact."

"You're also the one who saved me, your folks, and probably thousands of other people by keeping like ninety-seven percent of the database safe from her. Those are facts, too."

I couldn't argue. Everything she had said was accurate, plus it also made me feel a little better.

"You're not the bad guy here. Necros is," Elena insisted, with the smallest hint of a smile at the corners of her mouth. "Speaking of which, you have questions about her, and right now, Colonel Gdula is too busy to notice us snooping. Come on. Let's find Dr. A."

MASC's top scientist was in her lab once again, bouncing from one cluttered workstation to another. Her mess had somehow grown since the previous week. I don't think most people would have noticed, but I could see there were dozens of new, half-built gadgets and piles of notes strewn about.

"Logan! Elena! You two really are joined at the hip. Am I right?"

I knew this was a figure of speech, but I still shook my head vigorously to make it clear we were not joined by any body parts.

"We sure are," Elena offered while holding her hand up to stop me from correcting her. "So, whatcha working on now, Dr. A.?"

"Oh, still trying to crack Dr. Chrysler's password and analyzing data from a few new heroes. Speaking of which, bravo on bringing in Connie. Her powers sound fascinating!"

Elena shrugged a little. "Logan is the one who found her."

Dr. Augustine approached me, rubbing the top of my

head in a way that seemed friendly but was a bit rougher than I would assume she meant it to be.

"You're a superpower magnet."

"It's more likely a coincidence, but I suppose it's possible. May I change the subject?"

As I mentioned before, I'm not very good at segues.

"What's on your mind, Logan?"

"We've been thinking a lot about Necros being a mother and we have questions."

Dr. Augustine's smile vanished as she dropped her rear end down on the nearest stool. The seat cushion expelled an airy sigh due to the force of her landing on it.

"Ugh, why didn't you just keep your mouth shut, Katie? Listen, you two, I wasn't supposed to tell you any of that—"

Elena interrupted, but not in a rude way.

"We know, but we can't unsee it now. And Logan is really smart. He might be able to help you figure out something you hadn't noticed before."

Dr. Augustine looked up at me and sighed, but then nodded. "Yeah, well, I guess once you drop a Mentos into a Coke bottle, you can't put the cap back on. But honestly, I think it's a dead end. After we collected the last images of her pregnant, we didn't even get a whisper of her whereabouts for more than a year."

"When exactly did she come back?"

That was me, even though I suspected I knew. Dr. Augustine moved to the nearest computer terminal and logged in, once again navigating folders until she reached the one I expected her to open. It was the one from the day I was found at LAX.

"This was the first evidence we had that she was still alive. When she turned up at the airport ten years ago, we got a facial recognition alert."

I looked through the photos in the folder. There was Necros, looking more like a well-dressed traveler than a supervillain. She was holding a wide-brimmed hat in one hand, looking up at a screen full of arrivals and departures.

"We didn't get a hit on her until she took that hat off."

I listened. I might have even nodded. But my attention was really on the very corner of the photo. Peeking out from between a trash can and a large, rolling suitcase, was a blurry image of a very small child wearing an even blurrier T-shirt. But I knew what it said, even if the letters were illegible. It was my "World's Best Big Brother" shirt.

I felt my face flush and my head started to throb. I even felt a burning in my eyes all of a sudden as my breathing sped up, and I started clearing my throat several times, though I knew there was nothing stuck in it. These could be symptoms of several different infections or the presence of a poisonous gas in the room, but at the moment, I knew it wasn't any of those things. It was an emotional response.

My alexithymia made it impossible to separate curiosity, fear, frustration, plus about a half-dozen others. I was feeling so many emotions, and I couldn't stop rubbing my hands on the knees of my jeans. I suppose it was pretty impossible to ignore.

"You all right, Logan?" Dr. Augustine asked. "Do you need a glass of water or a Mountain Dew? I've got several Mountain Dews around, I think."

I focused on the feeling of the denim on my palms, which helped get my breathing to slow down a little.

"I am not thirsty. I *am* curious if there are any photos from earlier, when she still had the hat on, where you see who she was traveling with."

Elena appeared to be able to see where my mind was headed, which is something I'm always impressed with.

"Logan, are you thinking she might have had her kid—or kids—with her?"

Dr. Augustine frowned and exhaled as she closed the image on her computer and logged out. "There's nothing else I can show you. MASC sent a rapid response team to the airport and there was a confrontation. I don't know many of the details, except that it was bad. More than a dozen of our soldiers didn't come back. It became a level-five Roanoke event."

Elena pursed her lips, either because she was confused or because her lips were dry. "What is that? Why do I know that name, Roanoke?"

"It's a famous piece of history," Dr. Augustine replied. "And a famous mystery. Huh, that almost sounded like a song lyric. Am I right?"

While Dr. Augustine grinned to herself about her accidental rhyme, I explained to Elena, "In 1587, one hundred and fifteen English settlers landed on Roanoke Island off the coast of North Carolina. The governor, John White, sailed back to England for more supplies and when he finally returned to the island in 1590, the entire colony was gone. Vanished. There was no sign of them at all, except for a single word, 'Croatoan,' carved into a wooden post. For more than four hundred years, the colony wasn't found and the carving was a mystery. Then, in 2020, an archeologist named Scott Dawson confirmed that the settlers simply moved to another island, called Croatoan Island. It turns out they joined with the indigenous tribe there and had generations of children together, so there really wasn't a mystery. It's just that the English colonial minds couldn't imagine them doing it, so they assumed the settlers had vanished."

Dr. Augustine nodded along. "If we could ever get you on a game show, Logan, you'd never have to work a day in your life. But yes, it's also the term we use at MASC when something big happens that can't be explained away, so it has to be erased instead. That's why there aren't more photos or video from the airport, you understand? But the idea that she would have a child, let alone multiple children, with her in a public place makes no sense."

Elena stood up straighter. "Why is that?"

"For the same reason that MASC has never allowed superheroes to have children before; it's a vulnerability. Logan, it's not that Colonel Gdula doesn't like you personally . . . well, actually that's not true. He can't stand you. But what he really can't stand is that a superhero might have to choose between doing their job and looking out for their kid. Or worse, a situation like Gil and Margie already faced where Necros tried to leverage you to make them switch sides."

I thought back a month to when my foster parents had almost made a deal with Necros to ensure my safety by erasing any memory of them. It was an extremely illogical decision by Gil and Margie, though I appreciated why they made it.

"So, if Necros did have children, she'd do whatever it took to keep them secret and out of reach," Elena reasoned. "Maybe even hiding her powers like my dad hid his from me and my mom?"

"It's possible, Lainie." Dr. Augustine leaned back, using a nickname for Elena that just sounded wrong. "But I think there's an even more extreme scenario that's just as likely. If Necros had a child—or children—I wouldn't be surprised if she sent them away to a boarding school or even to surrogate parents to keep them safe."

Elena frowned. "But Necros is, like, the most powerful person on the planet. How could her kids be safer anywhere than with her?"

Dr. Augustine shrugged. "With her powers, she might not ever be able to hold her own children. And considering her war against MASC, it's not like she could pick the kids up from school, bring 'em home for dinner and a bath, and then tuck them in before she heads back out to try and take over the world. It's possible the safest place for her kids would be away from her. In fact, if she really wanted them out of harm's way, her kids wouldn't even know she was their mother. It's easier to keep a secret if you never even know it. Am I right?"

As Dr. Augustine discussed the logic of it, I tried to decide if it made sense and realized it did. Again, I thought back to the deal Margie had proposed to Necros to keep me safe. If they had wiped my memory and sent me back to the orphanage, I would've been out of the equation and out of danger. Necros had called the idea "fascinating." At the time, I had thought she'd been surprised by Margie's novel solution. But what if it wasn't all that novel? What if it was a decision Necros had already made for her own children?

Elena and Dr. Augustine continued to discuss the idea back and forth. Elena was curious. Dr. Augustine was reluctant to share anything more. But frankly, I wasn't paying attention, because I had put everything I'd heard and seen together. The timeline of Necros being pregnant. The locations of the photos. The evidence showing that we were both at LAX on the day I became an orphan. The knowledge that MASC had covered up something huge the very day that I can't remember past. It all had to be connected.

I ran through the possibilities in my mind, as I often do, and tried to remain logical. I really did. But when I sifted through them, every permutation came down to four realistic options:

1. This was all a coincidence.
2. The timing was a coincidence, but MASC was the reason my memory doesn't go back further.
3. The timing was a coincidence, but something that MASC or Necros did made me an orphan and required my memories be erased.
4. The timing wasn't a coincidence. I was at the airport with my mother and my mother was Necros. That's why I was never claimed. Because my mother couldn't risk MASC learning who I really was.

I realize how unbelievable that last possibility sounds. But the more I thought about it, the more I couldn't ignore it, because it explained so much.

12:16 P.M.
FRIDAY, NOVEMBER 19

I have no idea how you'll react to what I just wrote about Necros possibly being our mother. It might totally confuse you or it might make you angry. It might be something you already had thought of, or it might be something you already know. Maybe you will just need a few moments alone to decide how you feel. As for me, I had more than a few moments alone to think it over, because I was pretty much left to my own devices for the next week.

Gil and Margie spent almost every waking hour bouncing from their secret identity jobs to MASC so they could ramp up Connie's training, which also meant she was pretty unavailable too.

"I'm sorry, Logan," Margie had told me just that morning when she stopped home for a change of clothes. "There's just so much going on at MASC. Whatever Necros is doing with the names you . . . well, the names she obtained, it's getting worse. You saw what she did to poor FemmeFlorance. I can only imagine what that abominable woman is putting all those missing people through. You understand, don't you?"

I did understand what she was saying about Necros being dangerous. However, hearing her talk about it felt worse than it used to for some reason.

Staying in touch with Elena was even harder now, since I wasn't allowed to visit her or MASC HQ without permission from Colonel Gdula, who was in no hurry to have me do either.

So, I spent a week alone, watching three hundred and eighteen new cat videos, including eleven from Princess Purrnella, all while trying not to think about whether I might be the secret offspring of the world's most dangerous supervillainess.

Also, to be clear, I know I wasn't technically alone when I was at school since I was in constant contact with other students. Even on the houseboat, I had Bohr. But during my years at the orphanage, I found the worst kind of lonely is when you feel lonely even when you're surrounded by other people. Then again, I knew I wasn't ready to talk to anyone, not even Elena, about my suspicions. So maybe it was good to have some time to myself.

During lunchtime on Friday, I was sitting on my own in a corner of the caf, adding to a very long list of options for trying to get myself into MASC to sneak another look at the top secret files. None of the ideas were any good—

93. Pose as a pizza delivery person bringing Colonel Gdula dinner.
94. Use magnets to cling to the bottom of one of the MASC vehicles.
95. Ask Gil to help me create an invisibility ray for a "science fair" and then use it to sneak in.

"Dude, you okay?"

That was Connie, who had sat down next to me without me even noticing.

"You look like you're trying to divide Earth's population by the number of elements on the periodic table."

"That's a nearly impossible calculation," I explained, "because even though the number of elements has been stable since it grew to one hundred eighteen in 2016, the population of the Earth changes every second and—"

Connie broke out laughing in the middle of my explanation, which I didn't enjoy very much. I'm used to being laughed at, but not by people who I like.

"Hey," Connie said, suddenly softer. "Sorry. My bad. I didn't mean to be a Gdula."

"A Gdula?" I asked, obviously recognizing the word, but not the expression.

"Yeah, that guy is such a butt, I've started replacing certain curse words with his name. It's low-key amazing. This morning, I told my homeroom teacher to take her tardy slip and stick it in her Gdula. She had no idea what I meant—but I did."

I thought about it for a few seconds and then felt my face drawing up into an uncontrollable smile. It felt like the first non-cat-video-related smile all week.

"That's very humorous," I admitted.

"Looks like you could use a laugh," she observed as she pulled out her lunch—a bag of Doritos and an unpeeled carrot. "I know I sure could. This training stuff is no joke."

"I assumed. You've barely been around. We missed you at D&D Club yesterday."

Connie looked down at her boots. "Yeah, I've been skipping out on a few classes too. I needed a break from everyone at Marina High treating me like a freak-o new kid."

I hadn't ever thought of Connie that way until she mentioned it.

"I may not be the best judge, but I haven't ever thought of you as a freak-o."

Connie cocked her head to the side and studied me like she thought I might be joking, or like she had noticed something in my teeth.

"You don't think having superpowers is strange, Logan?" Connie asked, lowering her voice.

"Your powers do pretty much what doctors do, just much more efficiently. I haven't met anyone who thinks doctors are strange, unless you count Doctor Strange, who I now realize may be a real person."

Connie shifted a little in her seat and gestured to her clothing and hair. "Okay, but I don't exactly fit in with the cool crowd either."

"That is a fact," I agreed. "But I can cite over two thousand psychological studies showing that at our age, our brains are pretty much hardwired to rebel and express individuality. From a developmental point of view, it's all the people who dress and act the same who are doing something that doesn't make sense. Besides, I have never gotten the impression that you care what other people think."

"I don't."

"This is a hypothesis, not a fact, but I believe being genuinely unconcerned with other people's opinions might be rarer than having superpowers. It's borderline unique."

Connie smiled at me with just one corner of her mouth.

"I think you're 'borderline unique' too, Logan. And even kinda cute . . . I mean, for a halfling wizard."

I felt the edges of my ears warm as Connie's crooked smile got wider. I suddenly had the urge to mutter the names of the constellations visible in the northern hemisphere, until she bumped into me with her shoulder and laughed.

"Speaking of which, did I miss anything big at D&D Club?"

Refocusing on her question, I informed Connie I could recount every dice roll we made.

"How about just the highlights, Logan. Lunch is only thirty-three minutes long."

It was a valid point, so I summed things up as concisely as I could. "Everyone in the party leveled up except for my character, Nogal. He died, but he'll be fine."

Chewed-carrot confetti came out of Connie's mouth. "What?! How is that possible?"

"They took me to a high-level cleric who brought me back from the dead."

Connie relaxed and leaned her elbows on the table, looking out the windows on the far side of the caf.

"Yeah, that's the great thing about D&D. There's always a chance someone might come back, no matter how long they're gone."

I had a feeling she wasn't talking about games anymore.

"Are we still talking about Dungeons and Dragons?"

Connie snapped out of her stare and turned to me.

"Actually, yeah. I just discovered a rad, underground gaming shop in Venice. It's like a ten-minute walk from here, totally off the radar. Legit gamer nerds only. They've got the best selection of dice in LA. We should totally go after school . . . unless you want to keep using those same cursed rocks that got you killed yesterday."

On a purely logical level, I knew that there was nothing wrong with my dice. They were well balanced and symmetrical.

But I didn't say that.

Spending the afternoon with Connie shopping for extraneous gaming supplies was so much better than anything I had planned.

"That sounds like a lot of fun. But don't you have training after school?"

Connie's grin soured dramatically as she rested her hand on her stomach.

"Actually, I may have to call in sick. Something I ate isn't sitting quite right."

This was concerning.

"According to the CDC in 2018, the most common foodborne illnesses are norovirus, campylobacter—"

"Logan. I'm not *really* sick, unless you count being sick of training."

I understood. Or at least, I was pretty sure I did.

"You're saying your stomach is fine. But your Gdula is killing you, metaphorically speaking?"

Connie laughed again, and this time I didn't mind. After all, I'd made a joke.

"Meet me after school and we'll walk there together. Got it?"

"Got it." I agreed as Connie got up and headed off toward class, only to turn one last time before she went.

"Dope. It's a date."

Then she was off and I was left sitting alone, wondering if "it's a date" was an expression, a joke . . . or a fact.

3:39 P.M.
FRIDAY, NOVEMBER 19

I was waiting for almost twenty minutes before Connie finally showed up, and I filled the time by perusing different sets of dice on my phone so I could know if the prices were fair at the store Connie had found.

"Sorry, dude," she apologized as she came out the door, stuffing her phone into a pocket and slinging her bag over one shoulder. "Mrs. Gupta caught me texting and she confiscated my phone. Was a whole thing. You still good to go?"

I assured her that I was. She led the way as we walked north toward Venice. For the first few blocks, I explained the relative merits of resin-based dice over stone, metal, and other materials. Then I moved on to an article I'd read on Dungeonsolvers.com about outcome probabilities when rolling a twelve-sided die versus two six-sided dice. By the time we got within a block of our destination, I realized I'd been talking for a solid ten minutes without Connie saying anything.

"I've been talking for a solid ten minutes. Do you have any thoughts on dice?"

"Dice?" Connie said vaguely, looking down the street for something as she slowed her pace. "Um . . . yeah. They're great. I think . . . I'm pretty sure that's where the place is."

Connie gestured to an alley between blocks about fifty yards away. The area was industrial, with very few shops on the street but a lot of garages and small, graffiti-covered warehouses around.

"That alley?" I asked, looking at the narrow passage up ahead. The sun was getting low and the entire alley was immersed in shadows.

Connie nodded and kept walking down the sidewalk. But as I followed, I noticed that just short of the alleyway, there was a matte black Dodge Challenger parked by the curb. It was one of those tough, muscle cars you see and hear roaring down streets pretty often in LA, but there were a few things about it that made it stand out.

First, its windows and windshield were all tinted,

which is a violation of California vehicle code 26708. And then, as I walked past the car, I noticed that it didn't have a license plate on the front or the back, which is another violation; vehicle code 5200.

It was enough to get me thinking about why:

1. The vehicle might be brand-new and have just been customized illegally after passing inspection.
2. The vehicle might be for use in a commercial, where they avoid showing license plates and sometimes show options that aren't street legal.
3. The owner of the vehicle didn't want anyone seeing inside or tracking the car.

It was that last option that was still top of mind when Connie called out to me from just inside the alley.

"Logan, you coming?"

I turned my attention back to Connie as she waved me on and gestured to something affixed to the cinder block wall halfway down the alley.

I picked up my pace as we started into the alleyway and I could see what she was pointing to. On the exterior wall of the warehouse on our left, there was a dusty sign above a few steps that descended to a door below. Written in a gritty, medieval font in lavender were the words "Gilmore's Game Grotto," and next to the railing stood a series of statues to add to the dungeon vibe. There was a full-sized Gandalf the Grey from J. R. R. Tolkien's *The Lord of the Rings*. Next was a mannequin in a surprisingly clean suit of armor with a sheathed sword and a billowing black cape. Finally, there was a werewolf figure that looked like it might have been rescued from a movie set.

"Kinda sick, right?" Connie asked as we approached the figures and the stairs down. But before I could respond, something drew my notice away. At the far end of the alley there was a gray panel van—the kind with no windows on the sides—and there was music booming from somewhere inside it. I didn't recognize the song, but it was that kind with ultradeep bass and a heavy beat. I didn't so much hear it as I felt it from half a block away.

But it wasn't just the music that got my attention. The van's windshield was heavily tinted and it had no front license plate, just like the Dodge we'd passed on the street. I knew that there was a chance that the two vehicles just happened to be violating the same two California vehicular codes, but I was growing increasingly skeptical of coincidences.

"Did you notice that car back there?" I asked Connie, interested to see if I was the only one who was now on high alert.

"Which car?" Connie replied, or at least I think she did. I saw her mouth move, but instead of hearing the words clearly, I was overwhelmed by a high-pitched ringing in my ears as a wave of dizziness crashed over me. Staggered, I stumbled sideways and leaned against the nearest wall. My mind raced, as it does. I knew there could be medical reasons for these symptoms. But in that moment, I didn't think I needed a doctor. I needed to get away.

"Run!" I yelled to Connie, although I couldn't actually hear my own voice as my legs gave way and I slid down the wall. Through the noise and wooziness, I knew Connie and I had to get out of there. But Connie didn't move away, making me doubt whether I was making any noise at all. Instead, she walked toward me.

My vision blurred at that point, but even as that happened, I remembered the watch on my wrist. Somehow, my fingers found the button on the side and pressed it three times in a row. The moment I did, the face of the watch started flashing red.

I don't know whether Connie thought it was a self-destruct device or was just confused, but she immediately took several steps away and started looking up and down the alley, frantic. I wasn't sure why at first, but then I saw the van's tires spin out on the pavement as it revved and roared toward us, sideswiping the statues in front of the game store as it fishtailed through the alley.

At the last possible second, I dove out of the way, or maybe I just fell in a generally beneficial direction. All I

Gilmore's
Game
Grotto

know is that the van sped by, its engine screaming, with that same unstoppable bass beat thrumming from inside. When it got to the street, the van skidded hard to the right, paused momentarily, and then raced away, followed by the suspicious Dodge only about twenty feet behind.

My heart felt like it was exploding out of my rib cage, but after another moment or two, the ringing in my ears started to fade, and with it, the dizziness left too.

I searched the alley for Connie, worried I'd see her body among the mangled mess that had been Gandalf and the werewolf, but I didn't see any sign of her, or any stray pieces of armor on the ground.

Suddenly, I was aware of the squeal of tires and roar of engines coming closer again. I was able to get to one knee and brace myself for another vehicular assault, but when a different dark van screeched to a halt at the end of the alley, I recognized it immediately.

A swarm of armed MASC commandos hopped out before the tire smoke had even cleared as two more military-grade Hummers pulled up at the far end of the alley, blocking off traffic at both ends. As the soldiers secured the area, Sergeant Bricker emerged from the van and headed directly to me.

"Where is the threat, Logan?"

Usually, I am very motivated to answer questions accurately. But at that point, I was not.

"I can't find Connie," I informed her in the strongest, most factual way I could. "We have to find her!"

"Trainee DeWitt?" Sergeant Bricker asked, her face stoic. "We're assigned to *your* protection. I need you to tell me whether you are in danger right now. Where is the superhuman threat?"

As you know, I am not a fan of being told what I need to do, especially when I'm certain there is something else that is more important.

"The threat is gone. Now order your team to look for—"

"Logan, I'm okay!"

Connie's voice called out from down the alley and when I searched for the source, I saw her poking her head up from the bottom of the short stairs down to the game shop. Making eye contact, she cautiously walked back up the stairs and crossed the alley to me.

"You're all right?" I asked, looking for evidence of injuries.

"Yeah. Are you?"

I nodded, although I wasn't sure it was a fact. The ringing in my ears had subsided, but there was still a faint echo of it in my head and I couldn't shake the feeling like something wasn't right, but I also couldn't identify exactly what was wrong either.

"Now that we've established that neither of you are

hurt," Sergeant Bricker interjected, "can someone explain to me why my team had to blow our cover in the middle of the afternoon?"

"There was a car with tinted windows and no license plates outside the alley," I explained, biting back something—agitation or frustration maybe—determined to share the important information as clearly as possible. "And there was a van with the same illegal windshield and no tags at the far end of the alley too. Also, the van was playing loud music. Then my ears started ringing, I got very dizzy and had a hard time breathing, so I activated the watch."

There was a pause. It was not a short one.

"That's it?" the sergeant asked. "You called us because you got an earache and a little bit light-headed?"

"No," I countered, feeling that same something uncomfortable rising up in me, barely below the surface. I knew I was telling her important facts and she just wasn't hearing them. "Something tried to get inside my head, and when I activated the watch, the van tried to run us down. It was an attack!"

Sergeant Bricker rested her hand on her heavy, tactical belt, but instead of asking for more details from me, she turned to Connie.

"What about you, trainee? Did you get a ringing in your ears?"

Connie looked at me for a moment and then shook her head.

"How about dizzy, short of breath? Or was that just Foster too?"

I saw Connie's eyes narrow at Sergeant Bricker. "Just because it didn't happen to me doesn't mean it didn't happen to Logan. So, you can stop being such a royal suck-hole about it."

Apparently, the MASC commandos were not used to people calling their team leader a "royal suck-hole" because they all encircled us to see what would happen next.

"Look who's sticking up for her boyfriend!" Sergeant Bricker's tone was unmistakably unkind as she smirked.

"That is not a fact. I'm not her boyfriend—" I began to clarify, but before I could finish, Connie got right up in the sergeant's face.

"You don't have to explain anything to this waste of space, Logan. She's got it all figured out. Don't you, Sarge?"

"Actually, I do," Sergeant Bricker replied, not backing down an inch. "I think there was an attack here. A *panic* attack. Logan, out on his first-ever date, with an older girl no less. She takes him to a dark alley, there's nerd puppy love in the air . . . and the kid blows a gasket. Maybe you told him he was cute or held his hand or—"

"Shut up!" I shouted, the words exploding out of me before I even knew I was going to say them as I stepped between Connie and the sergeant. "You need to shut up! I am telling you facts and you are not hearing them! You aren't listening!"

I vaguely felt Connie's hand on my elbow, but I pulled away. "You don't even know what facts are! You only know how to shoot your guns and hurt people and erase memories! That's all you do. It's all you have!"

My chest was heaving again, maybe even harder than a few minutes earlier, but the words finally ran out and suddenly I couldn't look at any of them—not Sergeant Bricker, not the commandos, and definitely not Connie. The ringing in my ears felt like it was getting louder again, punctuated by my heartbeat and it was all too much, so I turned away and crossed to face the cinder block wall of the alley, my back to everyone else.

"Huh! That was something. Guess you're not a full-on robot after all."

Sergeant Bricker's words elicited a few cruel chuckles from the others before she whistled down the alley. I wanted to say something back, but my jaw felt locked in place and I was so angry and frustrated, all I could do was grip my pant legs and try to focus on how the fabric felt on my fingers.

"I am deeming this a false alarm, which requires only a single piece of paperwork to reset the watch's panic button, versus a ten-page report on an *incident*. Everyone do a quick sweep and make sure there are no bystanders who require the Houdini buds. Then we will fall back to rally point beta," she ordered the soldiers with emotionless efficiency before turning to me and Connie one last time, "unless you want us to give you a ride. I'll let you two lovebirds share the back seat if you want."

Connie's tone turned even flatter.

"You're a garbage person."

If Sergeant Bricker reacted to Connie's insult, I didn't turn to see it. I just heard them load up their vehicles and drive away without us.

That was fine. I did not want a ride.

I did not want anything from MASC at the moment, except the one thing they wouldn't give me—the truth.

3:38 P.M.
THURSDAY, NOVEMBER 25

Thanksgiving may be a fun family holiday, but history shows it's also based on a lie. The pilgrims were actually *colonists* intent on taking the land away from the Native Americans—who were not in any way Indian—and while the two groups did share food and farming tips, the settlers didn't mention they were also sharing smallpox and other illnesses.

I point this out because my first-ever Thanksgiving week with a family was also a distinct mix of some information being shared freely and significantly more being left unsaid.

First off, after considering all options, I didn't tell Gil or Margie about my incident outside the game shop. It took almost twenty minutes for me to calm down enough to speak after Sergeant Bricker left, but when I finally did, Connie walked me to the bus stop and told me she didn't think I overreacted, which I appreciated. But she also pointed out that we didn't have any actual evidence of what happened, and that telling my foster parents would probably just mean having to go through the whole thing again with Colonel Gdula, who certainly wouldn't believe me, because he never does.

I did not want to do that. I didn't want to feel all out of control again anytime soon, especially in front of him. Connie suggested it might be a good idea to just to call Elena and tell her instead.

So, I did, and she freaked out a little. Still, she said I did the right thing and that Sergeant Bricker is a jerk. I told her I felt she was correct on both counts.

I should note that more than a month earlier, I had invited Elena and her parents to have Thanksgiving dinner with us when we moved out of the house on Kittyhawk Circle. I did it as a way of staying in touch and Elena accepted as a way of not having to choose which of her parents' houses to be at for the holiday. At the time, I did not know that I probably should've asked Gil's and Margie's opinions before I did it. Luckily, they agreed and, even though it took a while, MASC approved the request. So around midafternoon on Thanksgiving, Arturo, Vivica, and Elena became the very first guests we'd had on the boat.

I wish I could say it was a comfortable get-together, but it was not, and for four very different reasons:

1. Houseboats are not very spacious and our four-person table had six people around it.
2. Gil and Margie knew about Arturo's origin story, which meant Elena's mother was the only person at the table who was not aware that four of the six people at dinner had superpowers.
3. It turns out divorced couples don't often choose to spend holidays together under normal circumstances.
4. Margie had done the cooking.

"Be honest," Margie insisted as the two families sat, shoulder to shoulder, with full plates of what might technically have been food. "How is it?"

Everyone made eye contact around the table. I assume people were trying to decide who would speak and how honest they would be. I decided to go first.

"This meal is one of the best things you've ever cooked."

That was a fact. It wasn't good, but by virtue of being mostly edible it qualified as a success by Margie's standards. Margie smiled broadly, which apparently inspired others to join in.

"Margie this, um . . . I think you called it 'mashed turkey,' right?" Arturo gestured to a scoop of brownish paste on his plate. "I've never had anything with such a unique texture."

Margie beamed. "The key is pulverizing the bones so they have the same consistency as the potatoes."

"And the 'stuffed yams'—there's just so much stuffing in them."

That was Vivica, being equally polite.

"Yeah Mrs. Mo . . . I mean, Margie." Elena still sometimes almost called Margie by her substitute teacher name. "These are definitely the soupiest 'gravy beans' I've ever had."

Margie was almost glowing, which isn't one of her powers. Meanwhile, Arturo turned to Gil, who was sitting in front of an empty plate.

"Gil, man. I'm so sorry you have to miss out on this lovely meal."

"Yeah, I didn't realize I scheduled my physical for the day after Thanksgiving. Having to fast for twenty-four hours . . . that wasn't very *quick* thinking."

To be clear, Gil did *not* have a doctor's appointment. It was a pun-aided excuse for the fact that he does not and cannot eat. However, I guessed I wasn't the only one who was jealous of Gil's inability to eat at the moment.

"So, Gil and Margie," Vivica began, with the kind of high lilt on her voice I've heard before from people who are changing the subject. "Elena says you both have new jobs."

"We do . . . I'm running IT . . . for a TV company.

You know what they say about IT. *It* is a job."

No one laughed, but Bohr did bark once at Gil.

Vivica turned her attention to Margie. "And you're a trainer at that new gym down by Muscle Beach?"

"It's like being a teacher, but with more sweating," Margie explained enthusiastically. "There's so much I can teach them. Most of my clients, even the fit ones, can't come even close to bench-pressing a thousand pounds yet."

There was a moment of silence.

"The world record for unequipped, unaided bench press is seven hundred and seventy pounds and was set on March seventh of 2020," I pointed out. "So, if one of your clients were ever to lift a thousand pounds, that would make them the strongest human on the planet."

Margie blushed a little, her cheeks tinged in warm pinks as she smiled. "And that would make me the greatest personal trainer on the planet for helping them get there."

Now it was Arturo's turn to change the subject. "Logan, how's the new school?"

"So far, I have made one new friend, started playing Dungeons and Dragons, almost fallen off a cliff, and been reprimanded by a Spanish teacher for pointing out what the word *salsa* means in Korean."

"What does it mean in Korean?" Arturo wanted to know.

Elena stifled a laugh. "I'll tell you later, Dad—when we aren't eating."

Margie decided to change the subject as well.

"What about you all? How is life on Kittyhawk Circle?"

"Oh, it's pretty quiet, as you know," Vivica offered with a slow nod. "Although I think our Elena's athletic career might be about to take off."

Elena's head snapped toward her mother.

"I'm sure they don't want to hear you brag . . ."

"Elena, we're all friends. They'd be excited to know that you're being recruited by a new AAU basketball team. Her coach, Luther, has really taken her under his wing. She's practicing seven days a week, working on getting stronger and faster. Isn't that right, baby girl?"

"Sure is. Can someone pass the cranberry balls, please?"

Elena's expression was so clear even I could tell she didn't want to talk about her new "coach."

"So much to be grateful for," Vivica continued. "I mean, in addition to seeing friends and enjoying this truly . . . special meal."

Everyone agreed and people got back to eating however much they could ingest without endangering themselves.

Afterward, we cleared our dishes and Gil took over the cleanup. "Put your plates on the floor and we can let Bohr do the scrubbing. Then I'll take care of the rest."

Margie took Arturo and Vivica to the living area to sit and have coffee, but I saw Elena head outside to the front of the houseboat, so I followed and found her leaning up against the rail, looking out over the water as lights from the docks and boats danced across the ripples.

"That was awful."

"I know," I agreed, "but I don't think anyone will be sick from it."

"No, Logan. I mean, yes, that meal was disgusting. But sitting in there just felt so wrong. Being a hero should feel right! Right? Lying to my mom . . . that doesn't feel right. For the last few years, I couldn't tell her about what I could do and now I feel like I can't tell her about being a hero. I can't tell her about Connie. It's like I can't tell her anything."

"Why would you want to tell your mother about Connie's powers?" I asked, because that part of Elena's statement made no sense.

"Not Connie's powers, Logan." Elena sighed as she turned to face me, but seemed unable to look me in the eyes. "I can't tell her that . . . I think I like Connie."

"I like her too. She has many likable qualities, even if she doesn't show them to everyone." I told Elena this because it was a fact.

"No, I mean I think I might *like* her, which is not something I really do. I've crushed on people before; there was a guy at basketball camp one summer and we kissed once. Just once. And there was this girl I ran track with last year before she graduated, but I never did anything about it. She was a senior. Ugh! Do superheroes even date? Maybe I should ask Margie."

As you know, I am very interested in new information.

But at that moment, I was more concerned with how the information was affecting Elena.

"Does Connie know how you feel? Have you told her?"

"Oh my god no!" Elena finally looked up and directly at me with her mouth open. Either the emotions she was feeling required more oxygen than usual or she couldn't believe I would ask that question.

"I haven't told *anyone*, and neither can you, Logan. I mean, I don't even think I'd admitted it myself until I said it to you. After that whole lie-fest in there, sitting at that table keeping everything from my mom . . . I couldn't keep doing it."

She was right. I had counted more than a dozen times during the meal when people said things that were untrue or obscured facts. And as I thought about that, it made me realize that I had done the same thing several times over the previous weeks. In fact, I'd done it 136 times.

It also made me realize I was done lying too.

"Elena, I have something I have to tell you too. I may know who my real mother is."

Elena's face lit up. "Logan, that's—"

"It's Necros."

I don't know a good way to describe what Elena's face did at that point, but it definitely wasn't lighting up anymore.

6:21 P.M.
THURSDAY, NOVEMBER 25

I began by explaining the facts to Elena. On the day I became an orphan, Necros was spotted in the exact same place for the first time in nearly three years. Dr. A. confirmed that Necros's appearance was a large incident that required many people having their memories erased. I also noted that even with my eidetic memory, I could not recall anything that happened on that day or at any time before it. And lastly, I demonstrated that the timeline of my birth, and the birth of you, my younger sibling, lined up with the period when Necros was too busy becoming a mother to do any villainy.

Next, I moved on to observations that were more

subjective, like how Dr. Clarke's hair and my hair were similar and how Necros and I were both notably short. Also, I pointed out I was found at a gate where a plane had just left for Boston, and Dr. Clarke's last known address before joining Necros was in that city.

Elena started to reply, but then stopped. She actually did it three different times as she paced around the deck.

"Logan, this is a lot. But none of it *proves* anything."

"I realize that as well," I admitted, appreciating that Elena understood the difference between conjecture and proof. "That's why I need more information."

"From who?" Elena asked, her brows dropping so low, her eyes vanished into the shadows they made.

"That is the difficult part. I can only think of two sources. The first is MASC, but Colonel Gdula will not let me anywhere near their classified files."

"I'm not a fan of the guy, but you can't really blame him."

"I suppose not. Which leads me to the only other potential place to get more facts—Necros herself."

The whites of Elena's eyes suddenly were visible and wide, but before she could speak, the cabin door slid open.

"Pumpkin pie is on the table."

That was Gil, sticking his head outside. Apparently, Elena and I did not react the way he expected, which he attributed to our fear of Margie's cooking.

"Don't worry," he whispered. "It's store-bought. No need to run away and *dessert* the rest of us."

I don't think I would have laughed under any circumstances, but considering what we were just discussing, neither of us even smiled.

"Ouch. Tough crowd."

Gil ducked back inside and Elena turned to me immediately.

"Logan, I need you to promise me you won't do anything nutso and go looking for that . . . monster. You know what'll happen if she gets ahold of you, don't you?"

I did. Or at least, I thought I did.

"I think I do. But if I'm ever going to know what really happened that day, I need help."

"I swear I *will* help. I'll find a way. Just give me some time to figure out how. Okay?"

I thought about it and nodded, both because I believed she would do her best to help and also because it felt so good to finally have told someone else.

"In the meantime," Elena continued once she saw my nod, "let's get some pie, because I definitely didn't eat much dinner."

I agreed, and we headed back to the table for dessert, which was the right decision.

The pie was really good. The crust was flaky and the pumpkin was super creamy and sweet. Of course, it's possible that it was a very average pie that tasted special by comparison to the gravy beans and mashed turkey.

Elena and her parents left after dessert, and I helped Gil and Margie clean up. Bohr licked pie crumbs off the floor and I folded up our extra chairs, while Gil and Margie washed and dried the dishes. It felt very normal, or at least what I imagine normal feels like.

"That was really fun. Wasn't it?" Margie said aloud, looking back over her shoulder at me. "Our first Thanksgiving all together."

"The first of many!" Gil agreed, lifting a nearby wineglass despite his inability to drink it.

Margie turned off the faucet as silvery drops began filling the corner of her eyes. Gil crossed to her quickly. Not at super speed, just like he was concerned.

"Hey . . . I . . . I didn't mean to . . . are you okay?"

"Actually, I am," Margie assured Gil and then looked to me, her eyes still brimming with quicksilver. "I just realized that this is it. This is the reason I traveled halfway across the galaxy and ended up on this wonderful, silly little houseboat—to find my family."

Gil smiled and put his arm around Margie's broad shoulders, and she smiled back while extending her arm for me to join them. So, I did. We hugged, or at least, they hugged me and I let them. Then we finished the dishes, took Bohr for one final walk, and all went to bed.

But through it all, including several hours of not sleeping, I couldn't get the final three words she said out of my head.

Find my family.

I didn't need to go through a wormhole to do it. All my answers were right here on Earth. They just weren't there, on that houseboat.

I was going to have to go find them myself.

11:27 A.M.
FRIDAY, NOVEMBER 26

Do you enjoy leftovers? In 2013, the Grain Foods Foundation took a survey of two thousand American adults and found that six out of ten actually preferred holiday leftovers to the original meal.

However, it is statistically unlikely that any of those two thousand people had their turkey prepared by an alien superhero. So, on the day after Thanksgiving, when Margie and Gil suggested I meet them at Venice Beach during a lunch break from MASC, I enthusiastically agreed.

I knew for sure wherever we ate would taste better than anything in the refrigerator at home, plus I hoped they might invite me to come back with them to the underground HQ afterward.

However, while I was waiting for them on a bench by the bike path, watching a video of Princess Purrnella licking the outside of a fishbowl like she thought she could eat the fish through the glass, I saw Connie coming up the path at a high rate of speed, with an unmistakable look of annoyance on her face.

"Connie?" I called out. "Shouldn't you be training?"

Connie looked up at the sound of my voice and stopped in her tracks. "I don't care what I *should* be doing," she insisted. "In fact, I wish I never heard of MASC."

I immediately felt like she was saying all this too loudly, considering we were in public. However, for the first time in several days, I was thinking about something other than my own quandary, so I didn't say that. Instead, I tried to be supportive.

"I'm sure Colonel Gdula could arrange it if that's what you really want."

Connie leaned her back up against a light pole and stuffed her hands into her jeans' pockets, one of which had so many rips in it that I could still see her hands.

"It's like boot camp! Exercise sessions, combat lessons . . . I have to run a super-dork obstacle course on a daily basis so they can track my progress. I finally told them I wasn't doing it. Elena tried to chill me out and Dr. Augustine said if I didn't do it, it would affect my rating. I give exactly zero flips about my rating."

Connie didn't say "flips," but you get the point.

"What I *do* care about is the fact that MASC isn't doing anything to find my mother. I asked Colonel Sanders what the plan was, and he tried to tell me he didn't have enough superheroes and investigators. The only thing that guy has enough of is weak-sauce excuses."

I knew that she was referring to Colonel Gdula, and not Colonel Sanders, the man who founded Kentucky Fried Chicken in 1952. I also knew that MASC was experiencing a manpower shortage. But I realized Connie might not appreciate me sharing any of those facts.

"It's not like I need a bunch of heroes to help," Connie muttered, kicking at the sand under her boots. "I bet if *you* were on the case, we'd find her in less than twenty-four hours."

It was a very nice thing for Connie to say.

"That's a very nice thing for you to say, but I have no idea whether it's a fact."

"Why don't we find out?"

Connie was no longer looking down. Her eyes were locked on mine.

"My uncle works security for airlines. I bet he could get us a flight to New Orleans tonight. We could check out the apartment and look through her stuff. I can show you the places she used to work, hang out— Just one day, I bet that's all we'd need."

"Are you serious?" I asked. "Or are you joking? You may not know this about me yet, but I am not exceptionally skilled at telling the difference."

"Logan, I know, for a certainty, that you going to New Orleans with me is my best chance to see my mother again."

At that point, I knew she wasn't joking. So, there was only one thing I could say.

"Okay."

Connie's expression changed in an instant. Her eyes widened and her lower jaw went slack. I was almost certain it was the look of surprise.

"For real? I mean . . . you're just gonna come with me?"

"You did want me to say yes, didn't you?" I asked since I was now also confused.

"Yeah. I just didn't think you would."

Her response made sense, but only because there were details she wasn't aware of.

"There are details you aren't aware of," I explained. "Your mother disappeared because of information I shared while trying to save my life. That is a fact. So, since it's my fault your mom is missing, it only seems right that I should help you find her."

"Why . . . why are you telling me this?" she said haltingly. "You could've, I dunno, just said you always wanted to visit New Orleans or something."

"That would be true as well," I admitted. "I have never been to New Orleans and according to the website TravelAwaits.com, it's the birthplace of many fascinating things, including jazz music and dental floss. But I was in an orphanage for almost ten years, and then, once I moved in with Gil and Margie, they got kidnapped for a while. So, I definitely know what it's like to have parents who are missing. It's not fun. I also am aware of what it feels like to have no one you trust. That's even worse. It's probably why I like facts so much: they are significantly more reliable than people. But I'm trying to trust people more, and I want you to know you can trust me, Connie. So that's why I told you what I told you. However, I have also been told that I frequently overshare, so that might be another reason. In fact, I just realized I might be oversharing right now. Am I?"

"A bit," Connie replied before giving her head a little shake and regaining a bit of her swagger. "But I'm here for it. Okay, so I'll arrange the flights and text you the details this afternoon. I assume you can figure out what to do about Gil and Margie?"

I thought for a moment.

"Yes, I can."

With that, Connie gave me a nod and continued up the bike path, away from MASC.

Then I sat back down and waited for Gil and Margie, while thinking about the best way to help Connie. I knew it might be impossible to find her mother, but at that moment, it still felt more achievable than figuring out what to do about finding my *own* missing family.

9:13 P.M.
FRIDAY, NOVEMBER 26

When I walked through the doors of Terminal 2 at Los Angeles International Airport, Connie was already waiting for me at the near end of the ticketing counter, just like we had agreed after she texted me our travel arrangements. Connie walked over with a smirk on her face and a shoulder bag across her back.

"You showed up. I'm impressed."

I wasn't sure what was so impressive about me doing the thing I said I would do. But before I could inquire about it, something wiped the smirk off Connie's face as her eyes refocused over my shoulder.

"What the . . ."

Turning, I saw my foster parents coming through the door, Gil rolling a hard-sided suitcase behind him while Margie was tucking her credit card back into her purse and shaking her head.

"I still don't understand why taxi companies don't simply pay their employees more." Margie sighed in frustration. "It's ridiculous that the drivers rely on their passengers giving them a random amount of extra money at the end of each ride. And for what? Not crashing? It's bizarre!"

Gil shrugged and looked to Connie. "You'll have to forgive my lovely wife. She's been all over the galaxy, but the idea of tipping is still *alien* to her."

Margie's eyes narrowed, and I saw Gil's Adam's apple dip as he gulped nonexistent saliva.

"Why . . . don't we . . . get ourselves checked in," Gil suggested, changing the subject as he moved toward the counter.

"Connie, are you all set with your boarding pass?" Margie asked in a tone I've come to recognize as the one she uses when she's trying to seem casually cheerful.

"Uh . . . yeah."

As soon as Gil and Margie were out of earshot, Connie turned to me, her eyebrows elevated and her nostrils flared. Either she was upset or wanted me to check her nasal passages for obstructions.

"What are they doing here?"

"Accompanying us to New Orleans," I explained, although I felt it was obvious. "You asked me to 'figure out what to do about Gil and Margie.' I figured out that having them come with us made sense. They're very powerful, relatively smart, and they haven't let me have a sleepover yet, so I didn't think they'd want me traveling to a different time zone without them. This is what you wanted, right?"

"Yeah, but . . . but . . ." The words came out of Connie's mouth like each was a dead-end street. "I said I didn't need any more help. Just you and your brain."

"Right, because MASC couldn't spare any heroes. But Gil and Margie's assignment for the weekend was to make up for the training time you missed. So, when I said we wanted to find your mother, they thought it was a great idea."

"We told Colonel Gdula we were taking you for some fieldwork," Margie affirmed, arriving back with Gil from the baggage check. "He doesn't need to know how far afield we're going. After everything you've been through, Connie, of course we wanted to help. So, we bought tickets, put Bohr in a kennel, and here we are."

"With all of us working together," Gil added confidently, "we'll find any clue to your mother's disappearance, even the ones that aren't readily *a-parent*."

"Really, Gil?" Margie scolded him. "I'm sure Connie can do without the jokes."

"Sorry." Gil stuffed his hands into his back pockets. "Just trying to keep things light. But we really are here to help."

Connie looked at us, slowly coming to grips with how fortunate she was.

"So, Logan and I will be flying with two superheroes back to New Orleans?"

"Actually," announced a low, smooth voice from behind us, "there are four of us, if you count heroes in training."

Connie swiveled to see Stonefist standing by the terminal door. He was dressed in normal human clothes, jeans and a T-shirt tight over his huge chest and arms. He had a massive duffel bag over his shoulder. Peeking her head around the side of the baggage was Elena, smiling as she waved.

"Hey, Logan! Hi, Connie," Elena called out, scooting around Stonefist and crossing over to us. "Everything all set for the mission?"

Connie looked like she wanted to say something, because her mouth was open. But nothing was coming out.

"When I told Elena about your idea," I explained, "she wanted to help too."

Elena sidled up next to Connie but didn't look straight at her, instead keeping her eyes on her own feet. "I figured if there were more of us, we could cover more ground. And Luther thought it would be a good opportunity for me to learn some investigation techniques."

"Most trainees don't even get a taste of the field for months," Stonefist asserted, looking toward Elena. "No way I was gonna pass up the opportunity to get you some real experience, plus I love New Orleans."

"Did you know it's the birthplace of jazz and dental floss?" I asked him.

Connie finally found her voice as she turned to me.

"Logan, you shouldn't have done all this. It's . . . too much."

I did not think that was a fact.

"I think this is actually just the right amount, Connie. All of us were prisoners when I gave Necros the information that allowed her to take your mother. It's fitting that this is the group that should help you get her back."

I have no idea if Connie understood my point, because after a second of gritting her teeth, she turned and headed toward the security line alone. I was very confused.

"I'm very confused," I admitted to Elena. "Connie doesn't seem happy about this."

Elena shrugged and adjusted her backpack. "She might not be used to people doing right by her. But she'll get it. In the meantime, we just keep doing the right things for the right reasons. That's a Luther-ism, but I like it."

"Hey, you actually listened!" Luther chimed in as he

threw his arm around Elena's shoulder and led her toward the security line.

Gil, Margie, and I trailed along as I thought about the Luther-ism. Helping Connie find her mom was definitely the right thing to do. However, there was a small part of me that knew that finding Connie's mother might mean another encounter with Necros. I wasn't sure that was a good thing, not at all.

But there was no way I was going to let that stop me.

11:22 P.M.
FRIDAY, NOVEMBER 26

How do you feel about airports in general? I've read that some people enjoy them because of the anticipation of an upcoming adventure. But there are far more articles online about why airports are deeply unpleasant, including one 2017 article by Steve Blakeman on Inc.com that lists his top eleven reasons why airports are so irritating. Apparently a "top ten" wasn't enough.

All I know is that I am not a fan of airports at all. That is a fact. But while my experience leaving for New Orleans from LAX was less than ideal, it wasn't exactly for any of the reasons Mr. Blakeman listed.

First off, there was all the noise and lights and people

to navigate, none of which are my favorite. Then there was the security line, which presented its own challenges that weren't related to my sensory processing issues. Most of us made it right through, while Gil used his powers to beam past the guards at the exact moment a few tourists took flash photos with their camera. But Margie did not get along with the metal detectors since her entire body has a hidden layer of liquid metal beneath her skin. I was sure that our entire mission was over then and there, but after setting off the machines twice, I heard the faint echoes of her telepathic voice in my head as she "convinced" the TSA agent that their machine must be acting up. After that, she breezed through security.

Then there was the time waiting to board the plane, or as Gil said, "*bored*" the plane. I wasn't bored, to be clear. Once I was able to put on my noise-canceling headphones, which helped a little, I took time to look around the terminal. It was the first time I'd been there in a decade. There were little kids with their parents in the gate area, but none of the adults looked like they were about to leave their children or forget them. As I scanned the area and noticed all the security cameras and armed airport police, I couldn't imagine a child being left behind. There was no doubt in my mind that there was a secret to why I was at LAX that day and how I ended up an orphan. I just needed more information.

I assumed I'd be up all night once again, thinking

about it, but once I got on the plane with my special headphones on, I fell asleep hard. Maybe it was the rhythmic thrum of the engine, or maybe I was just exhausted. Either way, sleep came for me, and so did a dream.

In it, I found myself waking up in Margie and Gil's house on Kittyhawk Circle and smelling breakfast. But it wasn't the scent of a typical Margie breakfast. It actually smelled good. When I walked out of my room in the dream, Necros was in the kitchen, wearing an apron, whipping up eggs and waffles and bacon. Then she made a massive plate for me and held it out with an ungloved hand.

"For you, my child."

All I had to do was take it.

My eyes flew open, and I found myself in my airline seat, slumped on Margie's shoulder and drooling as the plane began its approach.

"You were out like a light."

That was Margie as she produced two tissues from her purse: one for the corner of my mouth, the other to pat dry her shoulder.

Gil leaned over. "Anytime you nap on a plane, you get a *descent* night's sleep. Right?"

From a row behind, I heard Connie and Elena sigh loudly and Stonefist quietly chuckle.

Once we landed, Stonefist gathered us around while we waited for the baggage.

"I doubt Necros is still active around here this long after Connie's mom disappeared," he reasoned, "but there's always a chance she's got operatives or maybe even other superhumans in the area. So why don't we check into our hotel, do a little sightseeing to blend in, and do some reconnaissance. Once we're sure we're not being followed, we can head for Connie's apartment. Agreed?"

We all nodded, but it looked to me like Connie's nod was a little less confident than the rest of ours. When I saw that Connie was off to the side, alone and checking her phone again, I approached her.

"If you don't like the plan, you can say something to Gil and Margie. Unlike Colonel Gdula, I have found they are capable of listening to ideas that aren't their own."

"You really are looking out for me, aren't you, Logan?"

I thought I'd been clear that I was.

"I think I've been clear that I am. But let me know if I have not."

Connie's half smile returned for the first time in a while, which I took as a good sign.

We all got into a shuttle bus that took us to our hotel in the French Quarter of New Orleans, but there wasn't much talking on the way. Maybe it was because no one wanted to say anything suspicious in front of the shuttle driver, but for me, it was because I found myself replaying my first encounter with Necros and analyzing every word of it.

Seismyxer had definitely wanted to kill me. That is a fact. But Necros had held him back more than once. And she had technically never threatened my life. Margie and Gil assumed she had, but as I combed through every exchange with her, I realized she threatened my foster parents and MASC, tossed Elena from a rocket saucer, and drained the life from FemmeFlorance, but never threatened me directly.

And as I reviewed our conversations, I realized she used the term "my child" with me.

Not just once. Twice.

Was she being formal . . . or was she being honest? I needed to know.

10:02 A.M.
SATURDAY, NOVEMBER 27

By midmorning, we had checked into our hotel, and I was feeling anxious, I think. Or maybe hungry. Actually, I know for sure I was hungry. But I'm pretty sure I felt anxious too.

We were pretending to be tourists, but since I had never been to New Orleans before (and neither had Elena), in a lot of ways, we kind of were tourists. We stood in line at Café du Monde for beignets, which are like little puffy pillow doughnuts covered in powdered sugar. They were maybe the most excellent thing I have ever eaten. There was a sign at the café that said theirs were the best in the world. The sign is a piece of advertising, so it is not necessarily a fact. I decided to ask Gil and Margie to get me beignets at several other cafés we passed in order to form my own opinion. I did not have a single bad beignet the entire day. I'm not sure such a thing even exists. I tried to get Elena to join my taste test, but she seemed more interested in talking with Connie than in trying beignets, which I thought was a bit shortsighted. Connie would be available to her when we got back to LA. Beignets would not.

By early afternoon, Stonefist circled us up. "We definitely aren't being followed."

Gil agreed. "So, enough sightseeing. Time to *see the site* of where your mom disappeared, Connie."

Margie held a map out to Connie. "What's the best way to get there on foot?"

"Well, um, we could . . ."

Connie considered her options, but since I'd studied maps on my phone on the way to the hotel, I interrupted.

"It's just over a mile away. We can walk along the riverfront on the Crescent Park Trail, then cut up on Clouet Street. Or we can follow North Peters Street to Chartres Street, which might be faster but less scenic, or—"

Logan! Margie said with her mind, as I heard her voice bouncing around inside my head. Then she spoke out loud to everyone. "I'm sure Connie knows the best way."

Connie looked on for a second and then shrugged. "My mom taught me to walk different routes and keep it random. So, whatever Logan's Google-Maps brain says is good with me."

We decided to take the trail along the river since that's what tourists would do. Connie and I led the way, while Gil and Margie walked behind us, holding hands like a couple strolling on vacation, and about fifty yards behind them, Stonefist was with Elena, teaching her how to follow people without being seen. Of course, since I knew that's what they were doing, I was able to spot them easily.

"Hey, Logan." Connie bumped her shoulder into mine lightly. "You know I wasn't making fun of you with the 'Google-Maps-brain' thing, right? I just felt kinda put on the spot and said something dumb. I actually think the way your mind works is pretty rad."

"I had been looking at Google Maps, so you were being factual. But can I ask you about something else you said?"

It apparently took Connie a moment to realize I was actually asking for her consent.

"Ask away."

"Why did your mother tell you to walk a different route every time you went home?"

"Not to get all dark or anything, but my dad died when I was really little and my mom has dealt with some shady people over the years. Folks who wanted to get their hands on her powers or make her do things she didn't want to do. She made sure I knew that the world isn't exactly a wonderland. Gotta watch your back. Can't let people take advantage of you, because they definitely will. But I don't have to tell you that, right?"

"That is a fact," I confirmed. "But now that you and Elena are going to be heroes, you'll be watching other people's backs, and MASC will watch yours."

Connie gave me what I think people call "side-eye."

"Do you trust MASC to have your back, Logan?"

It was a fair question. "I'm not confident in Colonel Gdula or Sergeant Bricker. But there are people in MASC who I trust, like Gil and Margie, Elena . . . and now you."

Connie shook her head. "Me? You literally met me, like, three weeks ago, dude."

I thought about it, and Connie had a point.

"You have a point. I will make sure I do not trust you as much as I trust Gil, Margie, and Elena yet. Of course, by doing that, I'm taking your advice, which means I must actually still trust you."

"Logan, you're not like anyone I've ever met before."

"That may be a fact," I admitted, even though I had a feeling it might be a compliment as well as an observation. "I haven't met anyone like me yet either."

Connie laughed, which was good, since it was kind of a joke, even if it was also solid logic. Then she took my hand in hers, and for some reason, I didn't feel an immediate reflex to pull back. I noticed our hands sorta matched each other. Like they looked all right together, but I wasn't sure why she had done it.

"Are you thinking that holding hands like Gil and Margie will help us blend in too?"

"Logan," Connie replied, looking down at our hands for a moment before looking off down the river. "Blending in is never gonna be a thing . . . not for kids like us. But it's fun to pretend for a little while."

After walking together past a few old, abandoned wharves and docks, Connie let go and directed the group away from the Mississippi River into a neighborhood full of music clubs and restaurants. After another five minutes of walking, the area got more residential. The streets were cracked and uneven, lined with two-story apartment buildings. A few had terraces framed with wrought iron and supports like you see in ads for New Orleans. But most of them didn't look all that different from the apartments in Los Angeles.

"It's there." Connie gestured to a faded tan building across the street.

"Did the police take any evidence from the apartment that we should know about?" Stonefist asked as we headed up a narrow staircase to a landing outside Connie's apartment.

"No. The cops weren't even convinced anything criminal had happened," Connie admitted in a tone that sounded like annoyance. "According to them, it was just as likely that my mother ran off for a few days. But I knew she wouldn't do that. Of course, they didn't believe me."

Connie looked down. It's possible she was looking for something on the ground, or maybe she didn't want any of us to see the look in her eyes.

"We believe you," Margie reassured Connie. "And we're here to find out what really happened. Okay?"

Elena went a step further, reaching out and taking Connie's hand. I saw her give it a squeeze. Since Connie didn't wince, I assumed it was just a regular-strength squeeze.

"Do you still have a key?" Gil asked.

Connie replied wordlessly, holding up a single key attached to a leather cord loop.

"Here's the plan," Stonefist said, even quieter. "Margie, you open the door. Then Gil does a super-quick sweep of the apartment and gives us the signal if it's cool to come in. Elena, you and I are on backup, making sure no one sneaks up on us."

Margie took a deep breath that sent a silver shimmer through her skin and then inserted the key. As soon as she turned the knob to open the door, Gil vanished, leaving a faint light trail behind him as he beamed into the apartment. Meanwhile, Stonefist let his hands and arms go full granite, ready for a fight if necessary.

Two seconds later, Gil reappeared on the other side of the door.

"Did someone borrow money from a bank? Because we are all *a loan* here."

Gil smiled sheepishly as almost everyone else exhaled and shook their heads. I thought it was one of his better puns.

One by one, we filed into Connie's apartment. It was small and clearly hadn't been cleaned in a while. The sun streamed in the windows, creating long shafts of light and dust, casting shadows that made the corners of the room feel even gloomier.

"I'm gonna open some windows," Connie announced. "It's stale in here."

As she went to the windows that overlooked the street and let the breeze in from outside, Margie, Gil, and Stonefist spread out looking for clues.

"Elena," Stonefist called out to her, "what's lesson number one?"

After a moment of thinking, Elena piped up, "Look for things that stand out because they shouldn't be where they are."

Stonefist gave Elena a fist bump that probably would've sent me flying.

With no other job to do, I crossed the room to join Connie at the windows and found her on her phone, as usual.

"Updating your uncle?" I asked, making an assumption.

"What?" Connie replied, her hands fidgety as she put her phone away. "Yeah, gotta stay in touch . . ."

I waited for her to finish her thought, but out the window, a bright reflection caught my eye. The sun was gleaming off what appeared to be a full suit of armor that was propped upright on a partially covered terrace of an apartment across the street.

This struck me as odd, because as far as I knew, armored knights were not part of New Orleans history. My mind started thinking of reasons why the suit would be there:

1. The owner might be a restorer of medieval armor who did their polishing work on the terrace because of solvent fumes.
2. The owner of the apartment had done an elaborate Halloween scene on their terrace and hadn't finished taking it down.
3. The owner had a job at a Renaissance faire and had left the armor outside to "air out" after a particularly sweaty joust.

But as I studied the armor and the black cape draped from its shoulders, I realized it looked familiar to me and after a few seconds, I figured out why; it was the exact same suit of armor that had been outside the game store in Venice.

I was about to tell Connie this fact when the armor moved.

And it wasn't like it tipped over in the breeze. One of the metallic gloved hands glided down and came to rest on the gleaming pommel of a sword sheathed at its hip. Then the helmet tilted to the side, like whoever was inside was looking back at me.

"When you talked about looking for things that stand

out," I asked Stonefist, "would a person in a suit of armor watching us from across the street count?"

Everyone stopped what they were doing and looked first at me, and then out to the terrace I'd indicated.

"Logan, I think you should move away from the window," Gil called out to me.

I did not feel any desire to disobey, although I did have questions. Still, I kept them to myself as I retreated into the far corner of the living room.

"Is that who I think it is?" Margie asked as she stepped forward toward the windows.

Stonefist joined her, standing shoulder to shoulder. "It sure looks like it: Shadow Paladin."

"But . . . I thought . . ." Gil stammered, joining the other heroes, "isn't he one of the missing heroes?"

At that point Shadow Paladin drew his sword, but instead of gleaming silver like the pommel, the blade was jet black and gave off no reflection at all. In fact, it seemed to drink in the sunlight.

"He definitely isn't missing anymore," Stonefist affirmed, his stony fists clenched. "And the way he's gripping that blade, I'm not so sure he's feeling all that heroic either."

"What's his deal, I mean powerswise?" Margie asked, glaring back at him through the window.

I scanned the database in my brain for the important

details. "He has a sword, which you can see. He uses it to teleport from shadow to shadow and he can also make bits of shadow come to life and fight for him."

"Is he the one who took my mom?" Connie demanded, stepping up toward the windows.

Margie responded in the mom-slash-teacher voice she uses to get my attention sometimes. "We'll find out, Connie. But until we know what he's up to, you kids have to stay back!"

Elena put her hand around Connie's shoulder and guided her back to the middle of the room.

"What are you thinking, Luther?" Gil asked, without taking his eyes off Shadow Paladin.

"We don't know for sure what he's doing here," Stonefist reasoned, "and he's still a part of MASC. So maybe Margie and I can go have a little chat while you hang back, Gil. But if he makes a move, you come in fast and heavy."

"Got it."

Stonefist looked over his shoulder just long enough to make eye contact with Elena. "This is not a training exercise, Elena. You stay here and protect your friends. We straight about that?"

Elena nodded. "We're straight."

Hearing that, Stonefist and Margie headed for the door, while we all held our positions. I am pretty sure I held my breath too.

“This is so messed up,” Connie muttered to herself.

Elena must’ve heard it too because she leaned into Connie and whispered, “It’s gonna be okay. I promise.”

Down in the street, Stonefist and Margie strode up to the sidewalk below Shadow Paladin and I heard her voice call to him. “We just want to talk.”

There was a pause as Stonefist and Margie both scanned the empty block to make sure no one was watching. Then they both flexed their knees and sprang off the ground with superhuman strength, landing on the terrace above.

In the apartment, we all waited to see if Shadow Paladin took an aggressive step forward, but he didn’t. Instead, he took a step back toward the shadowed part of the terrace.

“He’s going to teleport away!” Gil shouted from the apartment window before flashing toward the terrace. But he was already too late.

As soon as Shadow Paladin’s body touched the shadow behind him, the darkness swallowed him the same way his sword seemed to consume the sunlight, and he was gone.

A beat later, Gil, Margie, and Stonefist were on the empty terrace, searching for any sign of the enemy or an ambush.

But Shadow Paladin wasn’t on the terrace. That is a fact. Because at the exact same time, he stepped silently out of the shadows in Connie’s mother’s kitchen, right behind me.

3:11 P.M.
SATURDAY, NOVEMBER 27

I have gotten used to being the smallest, least coordinated kid in my class. I am starting to get used to having super-foster parents. I've even kind of gotten used to eating food made by an alien who may not have taste buds. But I don't think I will ever get used to being taken hostage by a supervillain.

I turned just as Shadow Paladin's gleaming form emerged from the darkness at the back of the apartment. He slung his black cape off his shoulder, and in one sweeping move, he wrapped it around me and dragged me back into the shadow.

"Elena!" I screamed just before I teleported for the first time.

That's another thing I do not think I will get used to anytime soon.

It felt much different than being whipped around at high speed by Gil. Instead, teleporting was like I stopped existing for a fraction of a second; kind of a blink where I didn't breathe, think, or feel anything.

When I popped back into existence, I was in the darkened hallway of Connie's apartment building, still wrapped in Shadow Paladin's cape.

Another blink and we were outside, in the shadowed doorway of a building across the street.

One more nonexistent moment and we were a hundred yards down the road, beneath an awning in front of a jazz club.

We weren't traveling all that far, always within view of our previous point. But with each teleportation, I felt like I lost something. Nothing physical. All my limbs were still attached, which I appreciated. But I felt weaker every time we emerged from the shadows until my legs gave out and my vision went blurry. Shadow Paladin put his arm under mine to prop me up, and I promptly barfed on him. It was mostly beignets. I throw up fairly often. That is a fact.

"What foulness is this?"

That was Shadow Paladin, speaking in a raspy British accent as my vomit dripped off his armor.

"Logan!"

My eyes regained focus as I squinted toward the sound of my name and saw Elena sprinting down the street in the distance, alone.

"'Tis troublesome, but we shan't tarry," Shadow Paladin hissed. "'The fool will stay, and then let the wise man fly.' I am sworn to return thee to my mistress intact."

I understood everything he said—he was telling me he planned to run and take me to his boss alive—but I had no idea why he felt the need to quote act two, scene four of *King Lear* to do it.

As if I weighed less than his sword, Shadow Paladin tossed me over his shoulder and sprinted toward the river. Elena put on a burst of speed, but each time she got within striking distance, he would dodge into the nearest shadow. Next thing I knew, we were several hundred feet ahead and I felt weaker and more muddleheaded.

Shadow Paladin finally stopped on a rickety dock, laying me down in the shadow of an enormous, abandoned steamboat, the kind with two tall exhaust chimneys in the center and a huge paddle wheel at its rear. "Lie still. Heed my commands, I swear no harm shall come to thee."

Before I could respond, a voice called out from across the dock.

"Save that noise, Ren Faire! Let him go . . . or else."

Elena was standing fifty feet away, breathing hard.

I tried to stand and run, but found that my legs still had

whatever version of jet lag you get from teleporting.

"I am charged with *his* safety, lass," Shadow Paladin replied, pulling his lightless blade from its sheath. "Thy welfare . . . is none of my concern!"

With that, he swung his sword through the shadows around us. At first, I thought it was just one of those cool sword-fighting flourishes. But then three pieces of the darkness seemed to be carved away from the steamboat's shade, and I watched them streak out toward Elena like dark, angular animals.

"What the . . .?"

That was Elena as she took one step back and prepared herself for the attack. The shadow shards were on Elena in a matter of seconds, slashing at her from multiple angles. But once she got a feeling for how the dark shapes moved, she counterattacked. I watched her fist pass harmlessly through the heart of one shadow as if it wasn't there. She followed up with a devastating kick that also hit nothingness. But when one shadowy attacker slashed back at her outstretched leg, the edge of the darkness left a thin cut across her calf.

Elena grunted with pain as Shadow Paladin nodded and then looked down to me.

"Dost thou see? My shadow shards are impervious to force. Though she may 'rage, rage against the dying of the light,' she shall fall."

Two things were becoming obvious to me:

1. Shadow Paladin likes to quote classical texts—especially Shakespeare and Dylan Thomas.
2. Villains who talk a lot often share things they shouldn't.

"They're impervious to force!" I shouted to Elena. "Use your light!"

Elena's pained expression turned into a grin I've seen before. On cue, her eyes flared and her hands burst to life, glowing with pure yellow light. Even from across the dock, I could hear a soft sizzling screech from the shadow shards and the faintest beeping from Elena's earring.

Elena's next punch found the center of one of the shadow shards; and this time, where her radiant fists made contact, the dark shape burned, amber sparks radiating from the middle, disintegrating the darkness until nothing remained.

Two more swings and the remaining shards evaporated too.

"Is that all you got, King Arthur?" Elena yelled out, straightening her shirt like the fight hadn't been much more than an inconvenience.

Shadow Paladin stood over me and held his lightless blade just inches above my head. "I am verily impressed. The question is . . . do my allies feel similarly?"

That's when two more people stepped out of the

abandoned steamboat, emerging from the shadows and onto the dock. First came a tall man with pale skin, spiked white hair, ice-blue eyes, and a body that looked more machine than human. He crackled with bluish energy and had frost at the edges where the metal on him ended. This had to be Cryoborg, another one of the "missing" heroes Colonel Gdula had mentioned. With him was a woman who I realized was also in MASC's files, but not as a hero—SubSonique. Her hair was in intricate braids, and she wore wraparound sunglasses. Her clothes were so cool, even someone like me who doesn't know what cool is could tell she looked more like someone who should be onstage at a concert than someone who was a supervillain.

"Cryoborg! SubSonique! Help me dispatch this young hellcat."

Neither responded to Shadow Paladin. Instead, Cryoborg brought his hands together, and his circuitry interfaced to turn his fists into a blue-glowing ray blaster. In a burst, freezing cold erupted from the muzzle, slamming into the ground in front Elena, freezing her feet and legs in place.

Frozen to the dock, Elena raised her right hand high above her head as if she was going to smash the ice. But before she could bring her fist down, SubSonique circled her to the left, beatboxing and stepping in time.

I wondered if this new supervillainess was challenging

Elena to some kind of dance-off like in the movies *Step Up 2: The Streets* or *Guardians of the Galaxy*. But instead, SubSonique's tune seemed to mesmerize Elena. I immediately recognized it as the same sort of music I'd heard coming from the van in the alley.

Some of the sounds SubSonique was making were so low, I couldn't hear them. I could only feel them.

And so could Elena. She began swaying to the sounds like she was in a trance, her feet locked in ice, her upper body moving to the rhythm.

I'd finally regained enough energy to stand as I worked through my options:

1. I could run and slide across the ice to Elena and try to snap her out of the trance.
2. I could run and tackle SubSonique off the edge of the dock into the water to try to break the spell over Elena.
3. I could run back and try to find help.
4. I could run onto the steamboat and force the villains to look for me, which might give Elena a chance to get free.

Unfortunately, all these plans had two big flaws. The first was they involved me running, which, as I've established, is not a thing I'm good at. The second was that while I was thinking, Cryoborg touched my shoulder with a hand, and it felt like all the moisture in the muggy, New

Orleans air around me froze instantaneously, turning my shirt and pants into an icy suit of armor.

"*Chill out*, kid."

Cryoborg's pun made me think of Gil, and the fact that the two of them might have even been friends when they worked together at MASC.

Elena was still stuck in ice and incapacitated by SubSonique's beatboxing. I was literally frozen inside my clothes, shivering either out of fear or hypothermia or possibly both. I remember thinking things couldn't be worse.

And then I heard the voice that told me I was wrong.

"Logan, you are harder to get ahold of than my old friend Houdini, the escape artist."

That was Dr. Francis X. Chrysler, who had just stepped off the steamboat, in his long, ever-present lab coat. Even though it had only been less than two months since I'd seen him, he looked much older and more frail than I remembered. And by his side, with a light smile, was Necros, looking just as powerful and perfect as ever.

"Houdini wasn't really an escape artist," I corrected Dr. Chrysler. "You told me that. Of course, at this point, I assume most of what you say is a lie."

But it wasn't Dr. Chrysler who replied to my accusation. It was Necros, her voice soft and familiar.

"There is no reason for lies anymore, my child."

I was already frozen in place, but hearing her voice made my brain freeze too. Again, she had called me "my child."

SubSonique stopped her beatboxing, and the dock fell silent except for the faintest beeping from Elena's earring. Shadow Paladin took a knee and paid homage to Necros like she was his queen.

My every instinct told me to run, even though I was frozen in place, while my curiosity told me to ask questions, even though it was clearly not the time.

But before I could do either, the dock rumbled and the ice holding me cracked and fell away. I spun around and saw that Elena's feet had also been freed.

Let . . . Logan . . . Go!

Margie's telepathy boomed through my head.

The supervillains must have heard it too, because they took a step away but seemed unsure why they did it. However, the uncertainty only lasted a moment. Their eyes refocused, and they all turned to the far side of the dock where Margie stood. Her entire body had turned pure silver and was vibrating with tension. At her shoulder was Gil, poised to strike as well. A few feet away, Stonefist cracked his rocky knuckles and gritted his teeth as Elena's eyes flashed gold and her hands lit up.

For what felt like a minute, no one spoke or moved. But then, SubSonique smiled.

"Finally! Let's dance."

3:27 P.M.
SATURDAY, NOVEMBER 27

SubSonique dropped a sound wave that boomed out with a single stomp, driving Gil, Margie, and Elena a few feet back as they all had to dig in their heels to do that cool, slide-back-and-stop superhero thing from the movies. Not me. When the wave got to me, I went flying and only stayed out of the water by grabbing on to a wooden post at the corner of the dock.

Scrambling to remain dry, I watched Cryoborg transform his cyberarmor into a freeze cannon on his shoulder and blast a column of ice toward Stonefist. Luther reared back and punched the washing-machine-sized ice blocks to the side with ease, while shouting, "I never thought you'd turn traitor, Cryoborg!"

"I didn't," Cryoborg answered back, firing another round of frozen artillery at Stonefist. "I just decided to choose *us* instead of them."

As chunks of ice exploded across the dock, I ducked behind a stack of rotting crates, searching for cover while trying to keep an eye on the fight.

Elena sprinted at Shadow Paladin, her hands glowing as bright as I'd ever seen as she parried his sword.

And then there was Necros, walking with purpose in my direction, her eyes on me and me alone. I felt the blood in my chest go cold, but not like when Cryoborg froze my clothes.

I had no idea if she was looking at me the way a supervillainess looks at a scrawny kid whose brain holds a thousand secrets, or the way a mother looks at the child she gave up. Thinking about either option just made my heart race at an unhealthy rate, so I tried to rub my hands on my pant legs and slow it down. All I knew for sure was that I couldn't bring myself to run away.

And I didn't have to.

Necros was about ten feet from me when I suddenly felt my skin pulling away from my bones. It was the familiar, if slightly painful sensation of Gil instantly transporting me up onto the roof of a low-slung brick building that overlooked the dock. Connie was there too.

"Logan? How did you . . . ?"

Before Connie could finish her thought, Gil got right up into my face without a stutter.

"No loopholes! No questions! Stay right here with Connie! We can't let Necros get to you. Do you understand?"

I nodded because I did understand.

That must have been enough for Gil because he beamed back off the roof and rejoined the fight, his light slamming into several shadow shards. Between him and Elena, the dock came alive with bright flares. Shadow Paladin was forced to retreat into the final few pockets of darkness nearby. A second later, he reappeared within the abandoned steamboat, calling to his comrades.

"Rally to me. We shall smite these foes together!"

Connie shook her head as she watched the action. I couldn't tell if it was because she was reacting to the fight below, or surprised that Shadow Paladin was using old English, even in the middle of a battle.

"No!"

That was Necros, speaking with superhuman volume. Even from the rooftop, I could hear her clearly. Apparently so could everyone else, because the combat paused. "I will not see another drop of superhuman blood spilled or another extraordinary life lost to this conflict."

"You are *all* on the same side," Dr. Chrysler added, stepping out from behind her, pushing his weak voice with whatever energy he could muster.

Elena wiped the inky soot left behind from punching shadows off her arms. "And what side is that, Necros? Because last time I checked, you threw me off a flying building like my life was worth less than a soda can."

Necros leveled her gaze at Elena. "I never meant to hurt you. It was only required to ensure my escape."

"If we're all on the same side, why are you coming after Logan again?" Margie demanded, stepping closer. Her posture made it clear she was ready to get back to fighting. "What kind of monster terrorizes a child?"

Necros calmly turned toward Margie. "What kind of parents would take reckless chances by bringing their child on a mission when they know he's being pursued by such a *monster*, to use your term? I've told you before, I have a goal that requires unwavering purpose. I am trying to liberate thousands of our kind from MASC's subjugation. That's why I need Logan. He's the key to all of us reclaiming that which was stolen by MASC. You cannot possibly overstate how important he is to me."

"And you cannot possibly understand how important he is to us," Margie assured her, glancing over to Gil, who nodded in agreement. "He's our son!"

"He wasn't always," Necros pointed out, turning her eyes toward the roof I was on. "And he may not be for long."

"Is that a threat?" Gil asked, his dark-matter-infused molecules starting to hum and radiate, suggesting he was ready for the fight to resume too.

"Merely an observation. Ask yourselves, who is more likely to try and separate you from Logan forever: me or MASC?"

Gil and Margie looked to each other again, but this time didn't speak, so Necros continued.

"This world will not change until all superhumans see each other as brothers and sisters. To prove I seek peace, not conflict, I will withdraw for now and leave your family intact. Shadow Paladin, Cryoborg, SubSonique, escort Dr. Chrysler back onto the boat. We are leaving."

Grudgingly, the rest of the supervillains took a step away, cautiously guiding Dr. Chrysler back across the gangplank without taking their eyes off the heroes.

I found myself wondering how they possibly intended to get away. I knew from a fourth-grade report I did on the Mississippi River that even steamboats built for river racing rarely traveled faster than fifteen miles per hour—at least according to John White's writings on InventionAndTech.com—and this steamboat looked like it hadn't had a tune-up in decades.

"You know we can't just let you go."

That was Stonefist, stepping forward toward Necros.

"I was not asking for permission," Necros answered,

her tone suddenly flatter. "I am choosing to leave . . . and to leave you all alive. Be grateful and step aside."

Necros turned in one smooth pivot back toward the steamboat. Everything that happened next seemed like it was in slow motion, even though I know it was not.

Stonefist took two hard steps toward Necros and as he did, his hands doubled in size, becoming even more encrusted in rock. He reached out with one of them and wrapped his fingers around Necros's gloved forearm, closing on it tight. But Necros's arm didn't move, not an inch.

"You dare lay a hand on me?"

"These hands are a solid ten inches of pure granite, lady. And in case you haven't heard, you can't get blood from a stone."

The actual expression he referenced was from an English priest and school headmaster named Vicesimus Knox who wrote, in 1788, "It is impossible to get blood out of a stone." But I never got a chance to correct Stonefist, because as he made his statement, Stonefist brought his other hand up to take hold of Necros's arm, grabbing her by the elbow, where her gloves ended.

I don't know if Stonefist assumed his rock form would insulate him or if he just thought he was strong enough to resist Necros's abilities, but the effect was immediate. As soon as his finger touched Necros's exposed skin, Stonefist's entire body went stiff. It looked different compared to when she'd drained FemmeFlorance. This time, instead of a gray sickness, Necros powers seemed to radiate down into Stonefist's body, cracking the stone and turning it to dust. His gigantic granite hands and forearms crumbled down to human size before Necros's erosive energy spread to his shoulders and chest. It was like his entire body was being turned to chalk.

"Luther, no!"

Elena's scream was unlike anything I'd ever heard.

Everyone else on the dock was too shocked to move, but Elena leapt forward, both of her hands flaring to life with energy on their own. At the same moment Necros's wicked power engulfed his torso, Elena reached out with both glowing hands to pull Stonefist away. For a millisecond, the two superpowers—dark and light—appeared to mingle and spark. Then, the air around the dock erupted in a flash of blinding brilliance.

I have no idea what happened next.

I couldn't see a thing . . . and I'm not sure I wanted to.

3:33 P.M.
SATURDAY, NOVEMBER 27

Flash blindness is something that overloads and burns the retinas inside a person's eyes. It can happen for all kinds of reasons. If it's from someone taking a selfie with a camera flash at night, the blindness goes away in a second or two. If it's caused by something like witnessing a nuclear explosion, it can be permanent.

After the blinding burst of light, my blindness wouldn't fade, so I could only listen to what was happening over at the dock—and it didn't sound good.

Necros was shouting at her hench-people, her voice more ragged than I'd ever heard it.

"This is impossible! SubSonique, help Shadow Paladin

up! Where is Dr. Chrysler?"

"He's unconscious," Cryoborg's voice rang out, "and you're hurt."

"Never mind that!" Necros raged. "I will recover. But my child . . ."

"Mistress," Shadow Paladin called out, "We have to flee! The girl's training beacon was activated during the melee. MASC is undoubtedly already on the way."

Then I felt a hand on my elbow and instinctively flinched.

"Are you okay? Can you get up?"

It was Connie's voice, somewhere in front of me.

"I can't see," I admitted.

A moment later, I felt Connie's fingers touch my eyelids and a coolness flowed from them.

"Logan, I can't . . . I'm sorry. I have to get down there!"

I heard Connie hesitate for another moment and then take off running.

Blinking away the blurriness, I could see now what was left of the dock: a disaster scene of blackened, ash-covered wood and concrete. There was movement at the edges, where Cryoborg and SubSonique were lifting up Dr. Chrysler. Shadow Paladin lurked near the shade of the steamboat; and Margie was slowly pulling herself back up out of the river, steam rising off her metallic skin. And there, at the center, barely up on one knee was Necros, her arms and chest scorched and smoking. A few feet from her, there were two forms lying on the ground nearby—Elena and Stonefist.

I refocused my eyes just in time to see Connie dropping from the roof to a dumpster and then to the ground, her black combat boots pounding with each step as she sprinted out onto the smoldering dock.

All at once, her approach caught the attention of Necros.

"Take her!" Necros ordered, her tone suddenly more certain as she rose to her feet. "Everyone back to the craft!"

"Wait!"

That was all Connie got out before Shadow Paladin wrapped her in his cape and pulled her into the nearest shadow, vanishing instantly. Necros retreated into the steamboat, staggering as she went with SubSonique guarding her back, followed by Cryoborg, who was carrying the limp form of Dr. Chrysler.

Even though Gil had told me to stay, I knew I couldn't just let them get away with Connie. I ran across the roof and peered over the edge, trying to judge whether I could take the same route down that Connie had.

I was about to throw my legs over the edge when Gil materialized behind me, grabbing the collar of my shirt and pulling me back from the edge.

I spun to face him, the words spilling out of me.

"We have to go! They've got Connie! They took her!"

That's when I noticed that Gil looked fuzzy, like he wasn't totally together. Only the hand he'd used to grip my shirt looked solid.

"You can't go down there, Logan," Gil grunted the words out like it was an effort. "We can't . . . we can't lose you too."

I knew he was right. I knew it was a fact. But it didn't make me feel any better. It felt terrible. My heart was like a jackhammer and my stomach lurched, so I leaned over the edge of the building in case I threw up. In the distance, beyond the old steamboat, I caught a glimpse of something in the river: a ripple rolling through the water as a black, metallic vessel pulled away for a dozen feet before disappearing under the churning, muddy current.

Whether it was a submarine or some supervillain escape pod, one thing was clear—Necros was gone, and so was Connie.

I felt Gil's hand on my back and when I turned my eyes back to him, I could see he looked more solid. For a moment, I felt something like relief, but then I heard Margie's voice calling out.

"Gil! Gil!"

Gil must have recognized that Necros was gone too, because he scooped me up and zoomed me down to the dock, where Margie crouched down next to a pair of fallen bodies on the ground. They were both so completely covered in a layer of chalky dust coating, it was difficult to tell which was which until I was only a few feet away.

"Please . . . please be alive!" Margie was whispering urgently under her breath as she wiped away the soot from Elena's face and neck and felt her motionless body for a pulse. Gil kneeled over Stonefist—or at least what had been Stonefist. Unlike Elena, there wasn't any part of him that was flesh anymore. He looked more like the victims of the volcanic eruption in the ancient Italian city of Pompeii.

Elena . . . wake up!

That was Margie's telepathic voice, so loud and emphatic in my head that I had to take a step back. Elena's eyes fluttered open and she took a sudden inhale, like a swimmer coming up for breath.

"What happened?"

"You're all right." Margie put both hands on Elena's shoulders, trying to keep her still, suddenly more mother than hero again. "Breathe, sweetie."

Elena took Margie's advice, sitting up slowly and resting her elbows on her knees while rubbing her fingers together, feeling the grit between them.

"Where did all this dust come from?" Elena asked aloud. Then the realization came to her all at once as her head whipped around and discovered Stonefist's chalky form lying only a few feet away.

"No . . . NO! Luther!"

Elena scrambled on her hands and knees to where he'd fallen. Her screaming turned to sobbing as Margie knelt next to her, laying a hand on Elena's back as she heaved and wept.

While I was trying to figure out what to do, Elena's crying stopped all at once and the dock went quiet again. Elena rose to her feet, her cheeks still streaked with tears; and a cold, almost white, light erupted from her eyes like the brightest headlights on the planet.

"Necros!" Elena shouted out, turning quickly toward the steamboat. "Face me, you coward!"

Before any of us could say anything, Elena slammed one of her hands into the boat's rear paddle. Giant planks of wood splintered and exploded on impact.

"Come out! You can't hide from me!"

With each sentence, Elena swung again, punching holes the size of trash can lids in the hull.

"Elena, they're gone!" Gil called out to no effect.

Margie stepped forward, reaching out to stop her, and Elena spun aggressively when she felt Margie make contact, like she thought she might be under attack.

I don't know if Margie communicated telepathically or just with her expression, but whatever it was, Elena's shoulders sank, her fists unclenched, and the blazing light disappeared from her eyes as she knelt next to Stonefist again.

I waited a moment and then did the same. I still had no idea what to say, so I figured whatever Elena did, I would do too. That way she'd know she wasn't alone.

After a few seconds, I felt Elena's hand take mine and I just held on.

It was all I could think to do.

11:09 A.M.
SUNDAY, NOVEMBER 28

What is the longest you've ever gone without saying a word? There are monks who take a vow of silence, but since you are younger than me, it's unlikely you would have had time for monastic training yet. Then again, there are a small number of people—less than 1 percent according to the website psycom.net—with a condition called selective mutism that prevents them from speaking except to certain people, in very secure surroundings. So, if you're among them, being silent for extended periods of time may not be unusual either.

Personally, I talk all the time so the idea of going a full day without speaking was totally foreign. But that's what I did after the MASC Rapid Response Team arrived at the dock, and I think I might have been grateful.

The team established a video uplink with the HQ in Los Angeles, and as soon as Gil and Margie mentioned the superhumans we'd just faced, Dr. Augustine insisted no one else speak.

"Answer by nodding yes or no. In the fight, did SubSonique use her sound waves to charm or confuse any of you?"

Elena was the only one who nodded.

Dr. Augustine let out a long sigh, "Okay. No talking until—"

"But what about Connie?" I interrupted, shocked that no one was asking about how she'd been abducted. "I saw how they got away. Who's going after her?"

Dr. Augustine made a shushing gesture toward me through the video screen. "The tactical team is on another secure line, putting a search plan in place, but we *cannot* discuss that right now. SubSonique can plant a frequency in a person's inner ear that allows her to listen to anything that person hears. I can neutralize it in my lab. But until then . . ." Dr. Augustine made a motion. It was either supposed to be someone pulling a zipper across their mouth or someone very roughly putting on lip balm. From everyone else's reaction, I assumed it was the first.

Soon after, the Rapid Response Team got to work,

making it look like the dock had been damaged by pyrotechnics from a superhero movie shoot. They even brought in cameramen and people in costumes to cover it up. Meanwhile, we were escorted into an all-black helicopter, though Elena refused to leave until she made sure the MASC team loaded Stonefist's body into a second chopper.

And so that began the silence. There was one helicopter flight to a government air base, one flight on an unmarked jet back to Los Angeles, and one van ride back to the HQ with zero talking. Once we arrived, Elena was treated by Dr. Augustine to remove the spy frequency from her inner ear, a process that took more than two hours. Gil, Margie, and I waited with her, but still, not one word was spoken until it was completed.

I had so much going through my mind, but at the same time, there was no one I could really talk to. I couldn't tell anyone at MASC about the possibility of Necros being my mother. If it was true, they might try and use me as bait to draw her out, or worse, a genetic guinea pig to learn about her powers. And even if it wasn't true, it would give Colonel Gdula another reason to claim I was a distraction and a security risk, not that he needed one. I thought about telling Gil and Margie, but they were interested in adopting me. That would probably change if it turned out I was the son of their enemy. And then there was Elena.

Elena was the only one who knew my suspicions, but

Necros had just killed her mentor . . . her friend. I didn't think Necros had meant to take Stonefist's life. He had been the one to touch her, but he was dead just the same. That is a fact.

So, being silent was hard. But it wasn't any harder than it would have been to speak at that point.

By the time Elena was cleared by Dr. Augustine, it was well after midnight. Arturo picked her up and brought her home, while Gil and Margie drove to the houseboat in silence, maybe because they were waiting for me to say something first. I usually do. But I didn't on that night. When we got back to the marina, I headed straight to my room and fell asleep instantly.

All I wanted was rest, but the dream came to me again.

In it, I was back in the house on Kittyhawk Circle. Necros was cooking a delicious-looking breakfast, looking more like a mother than a monster. This time, in the dream, I wasn't alone at the dining room table. Shadow Paladin was there, as were Cryoborg, SubSonique, and even Dr. Chrysler, who was quietly enjoying his tea and muffin. Necros sat down next to me and smiled, addressing the entire table.

"So, who are we going to kill today?"

I woke up to wet, sloppy dog kisses from Bohr and the light of the late-morning sun streaming through my bedroom window. I lay there with the puppy, not ready to get out of bed yet but also afraid to go back to sleep.

In 2012, Randolph T. Barker, a professor at Virginia Commonwealth University, proved that spending more time with dogs can lower the amount of cortisol a person has. Cortisol is a hormone produced when humans are stressed. But that morning, in bed with Bohr, I realized two things:

1. It was pretty funny that a professor named "Barker" did a study about the benefits of dog ownership.
2. I didn't really need scientific proof to know that snuggling a puppy was good for stress.

When I finally got myself out to the kitchen, Gil and Margie were there, waiting. Apparently, it was time for the silence to end.

"Hey . . . you're awake . . . I mean, obviously." Gil stammered and smiled. "Of course, when you're that tired, it's *snore-mal* to need your rest."

The awful pun sorta made me feel a little better.

Margie showed me a box of donuts sitting on the counter. "I went to Randy's while I was out getting Bohr from the kennel. I also stopped and got you this."

She held up a clothes hanger and on it was a suit. It was black.

"There's going to be a small service for Luther this afternoon."

"I didn't know that MASC did funerals," I admitted. "There was nothing for FemmeFlorance."

Margie nodded. "She had asked for no ceremony if she fell in the line of duty. Just a 'return to the earth,' she called it. You don't have to come today if you don't want to. Elena will be there, but it's up to you."

I had never worn a suit before. I had also never been to a funeral before. I would say that both have their purposes and that neither are very comfortable.

I put on the suit and Gil helped me tie the tie, but I found myself with questions that weren't about men's formal fashions.

"Will Stonefist's family be there?"

Gil paused in the middle of trying to get the knot just right.

"Probably not. Luther once told me that when he got his powers . . . well, he left his family to keep them safe . . . I don't think he'd seen them in a long time."

The idea of a superhuman protecting their family by separating from them felt like it kept coming up and couldn't be a coincidence.

"You look good, Logan," Gil announced when the tie was done. "The outfit *suits* you."

Gil stood and concentrated for a second. In a blink, his clothing turned into a black suit as well, with no tie tying required.

When we left my bedroom, Bohr barked at Gil, but Margie shushed him and smiled at both of us. I think it was a sad smile because her mouth curled up, but the corners of her eyes drooped.

"You both look so handsome."

We headed to a small cemetery on a cliff overlooking the ocean in Palos Verdes. I won't relay everything that was said at the graveside, because I don't think there was any new information you need to know. Also, there was something about it that felt private.

It was sad too. That was unmistakable, even to me.

After the service, while the adults were talking to each other, I found Elena standing by herself under a tree, looking out over the water. I didn't say anything, but eventually she did.

"He was so good to me. He taught me so much."

"I didn't know Stonefist as well as you did, but—"

"Luther," Elena interrupted. "His name was Luther. Not 'Stonefist.' You don't call Gil and Margie 'Ultra-Quantum' and 'Quicksilver Siren,' do you? Their hero names are just their job, not who they are."

Elena sounded angry, maybe at me, so I asked.

"Are you angry at me? I mean, because of something I did or who I might be?"

She exhaled and looked at me, with fresh tears in her eyes. "I'm angry at everything and just about everyone.

I'm angry that Luther's real family isn't here and won't even know this ever happened. I'm mad that MASC didn't find Connie, assuming they really even tried. I'm angry at myself for not stopping Luther before . . ." She trailed off, but I knew what she meant. "And I'm more than angry at Necros. I hate her, Logan. I know it might be hard for you to hear, but I do."

I didn't know what to say about that, so instead, I asked a question.

"Do you want me to go away from you?"

"No," Elena answered immediately, which was a relief. "I think being alone would be even worse. It's just, lately, I'd been talking to Connie a lot about stuff. And now . . . I know, it's stupid. But I really wish she was here."

"It isn't stupid to want a friend around when you're upset. I think it makes sense. Lately, I've felt fortunate that I've had a friend around when I've had those feelings. I'm speaking of you. You're the friend in this example."

Elena chuckled, shaking her head like she didn't actually want to laugh.

"I feel 'fortunate' to have you as a friend too, you big nerd."

Before I could point out that I wasn't at all "big" she put her arms around my shoulders and gave me a hug. You know I don't generally enjoy being touched, but this was an exception.

"I hate to interrupt a tender moment . . ." a loud, southern drawl called out. Elena let go of me and we saw Colonel Gdula standing with his arms folded across his barrel chest, staring at us. "But I need everyone from this unauthorized field trip back at the base for a full debrief now."

Elena released me from her hug and turned on him, her hands balled into fists.

Margie and Gil crossed to us, positioning themselves between Gdula and Elena, breaking the tension momentarily. "Colonel, please," Margie insisted. "We're here to honor our friend."

Colonel Gdula sniffed once. "You go right ahead and honor him. I'm more interested in avenging him. How about you, Arguello?"

With that, Colonel Gdula turned and stalked off toward his armored SUV, and after a beat, Elena followed.

3:03 P.M.
SUNDAY, NOVEMBER 28

When we got to MASC HQ, Colonel Gdula sat us down around a conference room table, lit a new cigar, and demanded a full account of what happened in New Orleans. All at once, everyone turned to me, so I did as requested, only leaving out details pertaining to my personal suspicions.

When I finished, the colonel looked around the table. "So, it's confirmed. Necros is not only behind these superhuman disappearances, but she's gotten heroes to defect to some sort of army she's building. That's why the boy here is still a target. This is a turd sandwich that just keeps getting bigger!"

"Colonel Gdula!" Margie admonished him in her teacher voice.

Dr. Augustine took a different tack, pointing out the positives. "It's not all bad. We now know who's helping her, which is important. And the big headline is that Lainie here survived contact with Necros's powers."

"*Indirectly*," Colonel Gdula said pointedly.

"Indirectly?" Elena asked, her face twisted in either disbelief or disgust. "You mean through Luther, who she *killed*! How can you act like that's just a minor detail?"

"He was a hero who gave his life doing what heroes do." Colonel Gdula's tone was flat. If Elena's outburst had affected him, he didn't show it. "You want to be angry? Feel free. But make sure you're pointing that anger in the right direction. You all walked right into a trap, and when that trap was sprung, who did Necros try to grab first before settling for trainee DeWitt?"

"Are you trying to blame this on Logan?" Margie stood, glaring at the colonel.

"I am stating a 'fact' as that boy likes to point out every time he opens up his mouth. Necros wants what Foster has in his head. And it's something you won't let me erase, even if it would make him and about eight billion other humans safer."

Margie had no reply, probably because that was, in fact, a fact.

"Here's what's going to happen," Colonel Gdula proclaimed. "I will debrief Arguello personally to see if there are any clues to how she countered Necros. Quicksilver Siren and Ultra-Quantum, get down to the comms center and run a Priority Alpha remote briefing with every available hero between the West Coast and the Gulf Coast. You will review the dossiers we have on SubSonique, plus Shadow Paladin and Cryoborg. Ensure every asset in the field is up to date on their powers, weaknesses, and aliases—and make it clear that they should be on high alert. Necros has stepped up her recruiting game. Understood?"

Margie still didn't look ready to speak civilly to the colonel, but Gil spoke up. "We will . . . bring everyone up to speed. And I don't mean that as a pun . . . because I'm fast."

Colonel Gdula moved on. "Dr. Augustine, Chrysler's encrypted files are the key to giving ourselves some kind of advantage. Pull *anyone* you need. Just get into those files!"

"What about Connie?" I asked, once again feeling like the only one who remembered her abduction.

"Our recovery team came up empty. But if we find Necros, we'll find DeWitt. Her best chance of surviving is us getting ahead of Necros. So, everyone get to work, and get me some results!"

The meeting broke up quickly. Colonel Gdula whisked Elena away. Gil and Margie explained they needed about an hour for their remote meeting, and I told them I'd wait.

It wasn't so much that I didn't want to go home. I just thought there might be an opportunity to learn more if I stayed.

"This is such a mess! I need to think. I *need* to think!"

That was Dr. Augustine, who waited until everyone else had left before putting one hand on each side of her head and massaging her scalp as if she was trying to squeeze something important out of her brain.

"I assume you aren't any closer to breaking into Dr. Chrysler's private files?"

"I've tried a thousand passwords and nothing! The fate of the free human race rests on me figuring this out. No pressure, am I right?"

"No, you are not right. There appears to be quite a bit of pressure on you," I reasoned, even though I suspected she wasn't really asking for a response. "Maybe I could help."

Dr. Augustine thought about my offer and then looked around to see if someone might be listening.

"The colonel did tell me I could pull *anyone* . . . Come on!"

The amount of trash, clutter, and chaos in Dr. Augustine's office had increased by double since the last time I'd seen it.

Still, Dr. Augustine appeared to have a passable grasp on where her most important documents were. She went to one pile of papers, moved aside a soda cup, and brought a folder to me as we sat down at her workstation. "The first ten pages are all the passwords I have tried so far."

I scanned the list. Some seemed to be variations on Dr. Chrysler's name or initials. Other digits were connected to his birth date, social security number, and MASC ID. But there was a whole section that appeared to center around a different, familiar theme.

"Are all these passwords about Houdini?"

"Dr. Chrysler was kind of obsessed with him. Houdini was the first important superhuman he studied. Isolating the mysterious radiation created by his powers is how Dr. Chrysler developed the chairs. And the way Houdini escaped his fame by faking his death became the model used for creating new secret identities."

Listening to Dr. Augustine, there was one word that caught my attention.

"You said *escaped* his fame. When I saw Dr. Chrysler in New Orleans, he mentioned his old friend, 'the escape artist.' I corrected him. I said Houdini never really escaped from any death-defying stunts, but what if that wasn't the escape Chrysler was talking about?"

Dr. Augustine shook her head. "I've typed in dozens of passwords with *Houdini* and even a few with the word *escape*. None worked. As soon as I hit the enter key, they were rejected."

I looked at her list of failed passwords, but for some

reason, I knew that the answer wasn't on the page. It was in something I had heard, so I kept replaying what she had said until it hit me.

"The enter key!" I said out loud. "I need to see Dr. Chrysler's workstation . . . or at least the one he used most often."

Dr. Augustine led me over to a small pile of computer parts. There was a dented monitor; a cracked keyboard; and a small, mostly crushed CPU all sitting in a pile.

"The recovery teams excavated the old HQ and brought this back, but it won't work. I mean, it had an entire Hollywood studio fall in on it. Besides, none of the information was actually stored on his CPU."

Those were probably all facts. But I didn't need the computer to work.

"I don't need it to work. I just need the keyboard."

I blew the dust off it and looked closely. The edge of the keyboard was broken and two of the number keys were missing. But the rest was intact.

"Have you ever played Wordle?" I asked Dr A.

"The word guessing game online? Yeah, for a little while. But, I don't understand—"

"Me too," I interrupted, even though I know I shouldn't. "So, according to analysis of the *Concise Oxford English Dictionary*, there are certain letters that are used far more often than others in English. For example, the letters *R*, *S*, *T*, *N*, and vowels like *A*, *I*, *O*, and *E* are used twenty to fifty times more often than letters like *Q* or *X*. That's why they're arranged on a keyboard where it's easy to reach them with your strongest fingers."

"I'm assuming this goes beyond a typing lesson."

"It's more of a lesson on erosion. On an older computer's keyboard, the most commonly used keys will be worn down a bit over time. The letters on the keys become smudged or faded, or even the plastic itself might be smoothed. So, if we find worn-down keys that aren't the ones used often in the English language, that might suggest . . ."

"Those are keys the user typed all the time, like for their password!" Dr. Augustine finished my thought, her voice rising and her bushy hair bouncing as her head nodded. "That's brilliant!"

Together, we examined each key.

"Tell me if I'm crazy," Dr. Augustine requested, before taking it back. "I mean, don't really tell me. I know you're very literal. But it looks like the *W*, the *K*, and the *Z* are pretty faded."

I held the keyboard even closer to my face. She was right.

"Now," she reasoned, "I just need to look at the password list to see which ones have a *W*, a *K*, and a *Z* . . ."

"No need. It's got to be 'Erik Weisz.'"

Dr. Augustine's head tilted to the side and her eyebrows scrunched down. "Is that a hunch?"

"That is a fact. Erik Weisz was Houdini's real name.

His actual identity. And it is the only potential password on your entire list that uses all three of those letters."

Dr. Augustine must have been convinced, because she immediately moved back to her workstation and began logging in to Dr. Chrysler's account.

"Wait! After you type in the password, don't hit enter."

Dr. Augustine's fingers froze over her keyboard. "Why not?"

I held the damaged keyboard out to her. "When Dr. Chrysler logged on to his secret server, he wasn't trying to *enter* anything. He was looking to *escape*, like Houdini."

I pointed to the esc key in the upper left corner of the keyboard. The *c* was almost totally worn off the key.

"What better way to make his log-in unhackable than using the one key that no one would ever use to 'enter' a password?"

Dr. Augustine hovered her hands for a second, like she was afraid to even touch the keys. Finally, she shook out her fingers and finished typing "ErikWeisz," at which point she extended her left pinkie and hit the escape key.

Nothing happened for what felt like a very long time, but it was probably only a second or two. Then the screen flashed.

We were in!

Dr. Chrysler's hidden files sprawled out in a long menu on the screen, well organized and clearly labeled. There were several folders with intriguing names, but there was only one that was named in all caps: "THE RECLAMATION."

"Logan, you did it!" Dr. Augustine practically shouted, which was strange because I obviously already knew we had been successful. "There is so much here. I don't even know where to start."

I knew where to start, or at least where I wanted her to start. That's when Dr. Augustine's voice snapped me back to reality.

"Actually, Logan." Dr. Augustine squinted at the screen and hesitated. "I can't open any of these with you just sitting there. No offense, but you seeing a supersecret computer screen is what got you in trouble in the first place. Am I right?"

She was right. I didn't like it, but she had a point. So, for the next fifteen, excruciating minutes, I sat across the desk from Dr. Augustine where I couldn't see the screen as she clicked, read, gasped, and took notes furiously. Then she picked up a phone.

"Colonel, you're going to want to get in here."

Less than a minute later, Colonel Gdula barged through the door of the lab, flanked by a security commando at each shoulder. Gil, Margie, and Elena were only a few steps behind.

"Tell me you have some good news, Dr. Augustine."

"I have several pieces of good news, and one that's not so good."

Dr. Augustine snatched up her notepad and began pacing as she reviewed her notes and spoke in what felt like one very long sentence without a breath.

"The first thing you should know is that Logan was able to get us into Dr. Chrysler's encrypted servers. I know you think his brain is a problem, but in this case, it really was a big help."

Dr. Augustine looked over to me and smiled, although when I peeked over at Colonel Gdula, his perma-scowl was still in place.

"The second is that we now have a lot of new information on Necros. I only skimmed, but there are hundreds of pages on her origins, her known associates, and an analysis of her powers. I took an extra look at that section and can confirm there's a specific kind of cosmic energy she cannot absorb, which could be her weakness."

I can't be sure, but I think Colonel Gdula actually looked impressed.

"This changes the game. With that information, we could take Necros down."

Dr. Augustine stopped her pacing and pursed her lips. Colonel Gdula noticed.

"You said there was bad news too?"

"The bad news is, her plans are already in motion. It's called the Reclamation and it could happen any day."

3:29 P.M.
SUNDAY, NOVEMBER 28

"According to several of the files I read," Dr. Augustine explained, "the Reclamation is Necros's plan to bring about the end of MASC while 'liberating' superhumankind. Those were Necros's terms for the mission. Phase one involves recruiting hundreds, possibly even thousands of superhumans, including some who are part of MASC."

"How far . . . I mean? How bad is it?" Gil wondered aloud and it appeared he wasn't alone as everyone's heads immediately turned back to Dr. Augustine.

"Considering the defections of Cryoborg and Shadow Paladin, as well as all the other missing superhumans, she's certainly well into the process. But the fact that Necros tried to reacquire Logan suggests she still has work to do before the next phase."

"Which is?" Colonel Gdula asked impatiently, grinding his cigar with his rear teeth.

"When she has enough support, she intends to organize the superhumans into cells in major cities on every continent. Then, they will all act at once to make a coordinated 'statement'—once again, Necros's words. This will bring about the end of MASC and a new dawn for Necros's followers."

"Our worst-case scenario." Colonel Gdula sat at Dr. Chrysler's computer and scrolled, grimacing with each line. "This 'statement' is clearly a global, coordinated offensive. They're going to try to take over the planet. The devastation will be unthinkable . . . and impossible to cover up. We must stop this Reclamation before it begins. It's humanity's only chance!"

"Speaking of only chances"—Dr. Augustine flushed, sneaking a look over toward Elena—"I still need to run tests, but Dr. Chrysler's notes may explain why you were able to survive Necros's powers, Elena."

Elena perked up at that, as did everyone else.

"Apparently, Necros is able to absorb and store every kind of energy found on Earth—electricity, nuclear, and even life force. That's what makes her so strong and basically immortal. But the one type of energy that her body's cells can't process is a certain extraplanetary radiation. It's called SGCR."

"You mean sub-galactic cosmic radiation?" Gil asked, then looked around the room. I wasn't sure why. "I figured I'd explain the acronym since most of you looked confused *initially*."

Dr. Augustine picked up where Gil left off, but without any puns. "It's deep-space radiation that never makes it through Earth's atmosphere, except when something literally falls out of the sky. That's why it's so rare. It's only found on crashed satellites, in certain meteorites, and right here in this room . . . inside you, Elena."

"I have SGCR in me?"

Elena looked at her hands like she wasn't sure they were hers anymore.

"You do. We've known that since we started studying your powers last month. But we had no idea it might be the key to stopping Necros," Dr. Augustine added. "You told us about how your father got his strength from that space object he towed out of the desert. Some of that energy passed down to you in his DNA, and now your body generates it. So, when Necros's powers interacted with yours and she couldn't absorb it, that caused the explosion."

No one in the room seemed to know what to say, except for Colonel Gdula. He was completely clear with his thoughts.

"Son of a biscuit! You're our secret weapon, Arguello. You're Necros-proof! This is it. This is how we win!"

The colonel took a long, satisfied inhale of his cigar and then let the smoke out with a grin.

"Colonel," Dr. Augustine offered, a small quaver in her voice, "it's too early to know if that's true. Like I said, I need to dig deeper. Elena is still human, and it's not like SGCR is the only energy in her body."

"What do you mean?"

Gil cut in then, not stammering a bit as he explained the science. "Imagine sunglasses with a protective coating. They reflect the harmful ultraviolet rays, but the rest of the light goes through. Elena only radiates SGCR when her powers are active. For instance, when she clashed with Necros. Since the energy couldn't be absorbed, it reflected out everywhere in the form of that explosion. But if Necros were to touch Elena when her powers weren't active . . . who knows?"

Dr. Augustine agreed.

"We need to run experiments. We need to—"

"What we need," Colonel Gdula interrupted, addressing everyone in the room, "is to end Necros once and for all, before this Reclamation ever happens. That means mobilizing all resources to sniff out her sleeper cells ASAP while getting our secret weapon up to full-hero level. Gil and Margie, you'll be running double training sessions for

Arguello, starting right now, because when we do find Necros . . ."

Colonel Gdula turned his attention and spoke directly to Elena: "You're gonna get your chance for some payback."

4:13 P.M.
SUNDAY, NOVEMBER 28

Do you have a favorite quote from a famous thinker or personality? According to a list compiled by Meredith Hart for Hubspot.com in June 2021, some of the top quotes of all time include Mother Teresa urging people to "Spread love everywhere you go," and Franklin D. Roosevelt telling folks "When you reach the end of your rope, tie a knot in it and hang on." While both seem like good advice, I do not have a true favorite. I've read and retained so many quotes that the idea of picking only one seems counterproductive. Instead, I believe there are quotes that fit specific moments.

So, when everyone around me in MASC HQ started

focusing on the problems they had to solve and stopped paying any attention to me, a famous quote often credited to Albert Einstein—but according to QuoteInvestigator.com, actually said by John Archibald Wheeler—crept into my thoughts.

"In the middle of difficulty lies opportunity."

Dr. Augustine was haggling with Gil and Margie over who would work with Elena first. Should she do a training session or have her SGCR potential measured? They settled on doing both at the same time, with Dr. A. bringing an armful of her equipment to the training room. Colonel Gdula was barking commands at scientists and soldiers, ordering them to send alerts across MASC's worldwide network. Sergeant Bricker took her team for a briefing on how to combat Shadow Paladin, Cryoborg, and SubSonique.

And then there was me, waiting for my foster parents to reclaim me, sitting quiet and alone in a chair near the entrance to the HQ, only a one-minute walk from Dr. Augustine's lab and her workstation. For the first time in weeks, no one was actively stopping me from getting answers.

But I couldn't just sit in Dr. A.'s chair and log in . . . or could I?

I felt a pressure rising within me, but then realized it was because I had to pee. Luckily, the restrooms were just down the hall past the lab, so I used the facilities and also used the trip to check out the situation.

Looking through the interior windows in the hall, I noticed that Dr. Augustine's lab was empty. Her workstation had gone into sleep mode, so I would need to reenter the password, but that was no problem. I was the one who'd cracked Dr. Chrysler's code in the first place.

This was the point where usually my mind starts considering all the permutations of how things could go, but for once, I just gave in to the curiosity that was building up inside me and acted before I could get in my own way. I ducked into the lab, sat down in the chair, and started typing. It took less than five seconds for me to get back into the secret server and find the menu I'd gotten a glimpse of only an hour before:

- THE RECLAMATION
- MASC Surveillance
- MASC Technology
- MASC Misinformation
- Necros Associates
- Necros Powers
- Necros History

There were dozens of documents and files under each of the headings, but it was the first and last labels that were most interesting to me.

If I wanted details on how Necros became a mother

and what happened to her children, the last folder might offer that information, and I felt sure it wouldn't just be a bunch of assumptions from MASC's research. There could be actual facts like birth dates, real names, and locations.

At the top of the directory was an entire folder about Necros's big plan for world domination. That was the section Colonel Gdula was probably focused on. If there was going to be any information that could reveal Necros's current headquarters—and also where Connie might be—it would be there.

Although my brain was ping-ponging between both options, my hand was frozen on the computer's mouse, unable to move.

"What are you doing?"

It was a good thing I had just used the restroom because the question caught me so unaware, I involuntarily shouted out "Pneumonoultramicroscopicsilicovolcanokoniosis!"

It's a lung disease and also the longest word in the English language. Fortunately, I was able to stop myself before I recited the next ten longest words in the list.

Collecting myself, I turned and saw Elena standing in the door to the lab, her eyes narrow and angry, her mouth wide open.

"Logan!" she shout-whispered, "please tell me you aren't in the encrypted, supersecret villain servers! It's, like, the only information in this place you don't already have in your brain."

"I could tell you that," I replied factually, "but that would be a lie and you know I am not good at lying. What are you doing back here?"

"Dr. A. forgot her compact skinnalator. I mean sinca-lator . . ."

"You mean her compact scintillator for analyzing exotic particles and galactic space radiation?" I asked.

Elena nodded, still clearly annoyed, although I wasn't sure if it was because I was on the computer or because I'd corrected her pronunciation.

"It's over there." I pointed to a device that was wedged between a Mountain Dew bottle and a half-eaten Fat-burger.

"Do you even realize how much trouble you could get into?" Elena shook her head, like she was trying to unsee me sitting at the workstation, as she crossed the room and picked up the forgotten technology.

"I do. But I'm already in trouble, Elena."

That was a fact I hadn't even admitted to myself yet until that moment. I felt all the thoughts I'd been keeping to myself forcing their way out of me.

"I know this is all my fault. It is. I'm the reason Connie lost her mom and the reason Connie's captured too. Luther died on that dock saving me, and for all I know, I wasn't even in danger. Maybe I was actually about to reunite with my mother. I have no idea what's right or wrong. I have no idea if I'm about to lose my foster parents and my best friend and everything else. The only thing I know is that this . . ." I gestured toward the computer monitor, my hands shaking in a way I knew I couldn't stop. "This may be my only chance to ever see what's in these files . . . to find out who I really am."

All the emotions I could barely name, let alone keep track of, came pouring out and I stood up, suddenly unable to touch the keyboard. I backed away into the corner of the lab and through the tears, saw Elena coming toward me with her hands reaching out to mine.

"Hey . . . it's okay. Breathe, buddy. It's okay."

Elena kept saying those words to me for what felt like several minutes, and even though I knew they weren't facts, they started to help. But just as the tears had started to dry, a speaker on the wall crackled to life and Dr, Augustine's voice blared out.

"Lainie . . . er . . . Trainee Arguello, please report back to Training Room C right away!"

Elena looked at the speaker for a moment and then back to me. I noticed for the first time that it looked like her dark brown eyes were brimming with tears too, but I watched as she blinked them back.

"I can't tell you what to do, Logan. I don't have any answers. I just know I have to do everything in my power to stop Necros. So, whatever *you* choose, do it fast, and please . . . PLEASE don't get caught."

Elena gave me one final glance before jogging back toward the training rooms. I watched her go, replaying her advice in my head as she passed all three windows facing the hall outside.

I was determined to think more and feel less as I dried my cheeks with the sleeve of my shirt. I'd learned that anyone walking by could spot me as soon as I sat back in the chair. That was a problem I had to solve before anything else.

However, as I scanned that exposed side of the room, looking for an angle that might allow me to hide while I worked, I noticed a button by the door that had the word *BLAST* printed on it.

I assumed it was a mechanism to insulate the lab in case one of Dr. A.'s experiments went wrong, but I also realized there was a small possibility that pressing that button could, instead, *create* some kind of blast. That would be counterproductive and possibly deadly for me. But I couldn't imagine why they'd want the ability to blow up the lab from the inside. So, I dropped down, crawled across the floor to the BLAST button, and hoped. Fortunately, my assumptions were right; and as soon as I pushed it, metal curtains descended from the ceiling, blocking the windows and door.

I immediately headed back to the workstation and knew I had to make the decision where to look first.

As much as I wanted to find out more about myself and you and possibly our parents, I *had* to see if there was anything that could help Connie.

For the next ten minutes, I was like a machine, opening every file in the Reclamation folder, scrolling through at high speed and letting my brain take snapshots along the way. The room was full of clicks and ticks: the mouse clicking every few seconds, while the clock on the wall ticked away. The phone rang in the lab several times, but I kept my attention on the screen. I wasn't even processing what I was seeing, knowing I could go back later and review it when I wasn't in the middle of committing several punishable offenses. There were planning documents, logs of conversations with Necros about progress, lists of potential locations for their synchronized "statement," and strategic briefs for what Dr. Chrysler expected MASC's response would be. It was hundreds of pages in total and I absorbed it all as quickly as I could, praying that somewhere within those files, there was something that would lead to Necros . . . and Connie.

Finally, I closed the folder and was about to get up, deactivate the blast curtains, and get out of the lab. There was no question I'd already been there too long. But then I felt myself drawn back into the seat by the label on the last folder on the screen.

- Necros History

Every logical part of my brain told me to go, but a small, hopeful voice inside my head insisted there was still time. After all, there had been no knocks on the door or sirens in the hall yet.

I started with a very promising document titled "Master Timeline." The only question at that point was how much I could learn before I ran out of time

The answer came less than a second later, when the door to the lab exploded off its hinges and skittered across the floor to stop at my feet.

At that point, I didn't need to wonder at all. My time had definitely run out.

4:27 P.M.
SUNDAY, NOVEMBER 28

Have you ever been sent to the principal's office? I certainly have, although I would like to be clear that in most of those cases, I had either corrected a teacher who taught inaccurate information or had upset a fellow student by sharing facts that somehow embarrassed him or her. I do not believe either of those situations represent occasions when I had done anything "wrong."

My current situation felt a bit like being sent to the principal's office, except the principal generally does not have a team of armed commandos leveling their weapons at you.

"Hands off the keyboard . . . now!"

Sergeant Bricker was the first through the door, barking orders at me. My mind raced with options:

1. Follow her directions since I knew those weapons could totally immobilize me, or worse.
2. Try to duck, hide, and sneak out of the room with a half-dozen commandos between me and the door.
3. Lie and claim that I was invited to help Dr. Augustine with her work.
4. Start speaking in another language and hope to stall while they look for an interpreter.

The last three options all had fatal flaws since I am not stealthy, not a good liar, and not fluent in any languages other than English. So, I raised my hands.

"What in the name of all things holy and moly are you doing in here, boy?"

The deep, southern drawl and commanding tone were unmistakable. Colonel Gdula stepped into the room. A few of the commandos by the door snapped to attention and saluted, but the rest kept their rifles trained directly on me.

"Sir," Sergeant Bricker spoke up. "We got an alert that the blast protection had been activated and no response when we tried to check in with Dr. Augustine. I ordered our tactical team to breach the door and found *him* logged in."

Colonel Gdula shifted his gaze from his officer to me. "Got anything to add?"

I did not.

"I do not."

The colonel nodded. His mouth spread into a lopsided grin as one corner held on to the ever-present cigar while the rest smiled.

"Then let's get you into a Houdini chair, pronto. Soldiers, secure the detainee and escort him to situation room Omega."

"Yes, sir!" Bricker replied. "I'll radio ahead to have a memory removal technician meet us."

One of the soldiers put me in handcuffs while the rest moved into formation around me, which they maintained as they walked me down the cold, echoey MASC hallways. It was a slow pace, though I couldn't be certain if it was because Colonel Gdula was being careful I didn't get away, or if he was intentionally drawing out the process.

"I knew this day would come. Everyone thinks you're so smart, but you can't even stop yourself from doing things when you know they're just plain dumb. Sneaking into there? Looking at those files? I'd be madder than a hound dog during flea season, except you've just done me the biggest favor possible. Now, I'll have no trouble explaining this to your foster folks. Speaking of which . . ."

At the sound of running footsteps in the distance, Colonel Gdula raised a single hand that halted our convoy as Gil, Margie, Elena, and Dr. A. came sprinting around a corner at the far end of the hallway.

"Colonel!" Margie shouted. "We were told there was a breach. Get Logan somewhere safe and we'll . . ."

Margie's voice trailed off as she got closer to us and saw that the commandos were not there to protect me. Gil must have noticed it at approximately the same time.

"Logan . . . why are you . . . are you in handcuffs? I don't . . ."

Colonel Gdula let Gil's stammering peter out before he answered.

"Quicksilver Siren and Ultra-Quantum, your *foster son* has violated nearly every one of MASC's critical security codes in the past half hour or so, and as such, we will erase his memories, effective immediately."

Margie took a step forward.

"Colonel, I don't know what happened, but—"

"No, you don't," Colonel Gdula interjected. "So let me illuminate you. Every time this child has come in contact with classified information, our mission has gotten more difficult. He knows this, and so do you. And yet, the second he wasn't being supervised, he let himself into Dr. Augustine's lab and accessed Dr. Chrysler's encrypted files. So now, in addition to the top secret information from our own databases he already had stored in that brain of his, he also has compromised the most important counterintelligence MASC has ever uncovered."

"To be fair, he was the one who uncovered it in the first place."

That was Dr. Augustine, speaking up on my behalf, which earned her an icy stare from Gdula.

"Is this true?" Margie asked, looking at me like she was hoping for a specific answer. I don't think I gave it to her, though.

"It is true. I snuck in, logged in, and was searching for information that might help us track down where Connie is, because I appear to be the only one interested in finding her. Then I was looking for details about the day I became an orphan, because I'm certain MASC had something to do with it; but once again, I am the only person who cares about that too."

You'll notice that none of what I said was a lie. But I didn't exactly tell the whole truth either.

Gil and Margie turned their attention to Colonel Gdula, who exhaled with a snort.

"He's proven time and again that he cannot be trusted with the information he has, and that as long as he's around, he'll keep accumulating more of that information, which will only make him more of a risk to MASC and the safety of the entire planet. For the good of our organization, our mission, and my own sanity, it's time to eliminate the risk and send the boy back."

"No."

That was Gil, responding with exactly one word and zero stutter.

The room went still, but I caught a few cues that the

tension level had escalated. I heard the safety switches on several of the soldiers' weapons flick off. The edges of Margie's fingernails shimmered silver. The end of Colonel Gdula's cigar glowed bright orange, but no smoke escaped his nose or mouth. And I started quietly reciting the state birds of all fifty United States.

"I wasn't asking for permission, Ultra-Quantum. That was an order." The words escaped with a curling mass of smoke from Colonel Gdula's mouth like a threat. But Gil stepped confidently through the cloud, his dark-matter-infused form repelling the smoke.

"My name is *Gil.* My wife's name is *Margie.* And we are done taking orders, Colonel. We will protect *our* son. His safety, his memories, and even his right to make a mistake without being threatened. We quit, as of right now. The only thing you get to decide is whether we walk out of here with Logan or we fight our way out."

Colonel Gdula's right eye twitched, possibly out of anger, possibly because of the smoke. A combination of the two seemed likely.

"I could have you court-martialed, son. Heck, I could put your entire family on the most-wanted villain list, right beside Necros. There would be so many heroes after you it would be like ComicCon on that houseboat of yours. Or why even wait? I could have these soldiers go guns hot, full-lethal right now."

The commandos raised their weapons.

"Just give the order, Colonel," Sergeant Bricker said. "It'll be a tune-up for the main event against Necros!"

Gil and Margie took up defensive positions in front of me as Colonel Gdula let the tension in the atmosphere build.

"The main event," Gdula grumbled, rolling the words in his mouth as he crossed his arms. "That's what's important. Not these two deserters. Sergeant Bricker, stand down. Uncuff the boy. I can't afford to sacrifice even one member of your team fighting a pair of quitters. These two aren't heroes . . . they're just *parents*." The word came out slathered in derisiveness so thick, even I couldn't miss it. "Let them go."

As insulting as he was trying to be, it seemed like a very good offer, and one that we shouldn't question. But I am not good at not questioning things. That is a fact.

"Why would you do that?"

The colonel looked down his nose at me as his men undid the handcuffs.

"Because unlike you all, I understand what's at stake. I don't have the time or energy to be constantly arguing with your *family*, and I certainly don't have time to keep babysitting a pint-sized, pain-in-the-butt security breach like you."

Colonel Gdula looked up and leveled his gaze at Gil

and Margie. "So, now that's your job. You're on your own. You protect him and keep him away from those criminals who want him so bad. But get it straight: he'll be under twenty-four-hour surveillance. And if I get even the slightest whiff that the information in Foster's head is about to fall into Necros's hands, I will do *whatever* it takes to make sure that doesn't happen, regardless of the collateral damage. Because there is nothing, and no one, on that houseboat of yours that is more important than protecting the rest of humanity from that demon woman's plans. Nod if you understand."

I nodded, because I did. Out of the corner of my eye, I saw Gil and Margie did as well.

Then the colonel turned to Elena. "What about you, Arguello? You may be the one person on this planet who can stop Necros from doing what she did to Stonefist and FemmeFlorance and countless others. You gonna make her pay for what she's done . . . or are you a quitter too?"

Elena's reaction to the colonel had been changing with each word he said. But a moment after his final question, her expression hardened and she looked to me.

"I'm sorry, Logan, but I have to go after Necros. I can't walk away from this. You understand, don't you?"

"I do." I admitted. Of course, I understood. I felt like I had to go after Necros too, but for different reasons.

Elena turned and headed into the nearest training

room. My foster parents put their hands on my shoulders and guided me in the opposite direction down the hall and out the doors.

Everyone had chosen their sides. Elena was staying, and Gil, Margie, and I were officially un-MASC-ed.

6:12 P.M.
FRIDAY, DECEMBER 3

You know by now I could tell you every single thing that happened after Gil and Margie resigned from MASC, but I won't bore you because each of the next five days was almost identical.

I'd wake up in time to say goodbye to Gil and Margie as they went to work at their now full-time jobs. Then I would go to school while a black van followed my bus from a block away. Next, I'd pretend to listen to teachers for several hours while mentally reviewing the files I'd seen in the secret server. Then I'd take the bus home, once again tailed by the van, and wait until Gil and Margie came home and told me about their distinctly non-super workdays. Finally, I would try to eat an inedible dinner and claim I was tired so I could go to my room and pore over more of Dr. Chrysler's data for clues as to where Necros might be holding Connie.

Of course, this description of my routine is an exaggeration and not a fact. Every day wasn't the exact same. I took time to think about other things, like when Princess Purrnella posted a new video where she learned how to ride on the back of a malamute named Pax while wearing a miniature cowboy hat. It was, in my opinion, one of her eight best videos of all time, providing several minutes of distraction.

But most of the rest of my days were deeply repetitive, so by the time the week ended and we decided to have pizza delivered, it felt like a big deal for several reasons:

1. The delivery guy was our first visitor to the houseboat since Thanksgiving.
2. It was my first meal in a while that wasn't prepared by Margie.
3. It gave me a chance to see just how serious MASC was being in terms of our lockdown.

When the delivery guy parked his beat-up hatchback by the dock, I watched as he retrieved the insulated pizza sleeve out of his passenger side seat. As he took the food out of the car, someone walked by on the sidewalk and bumped into him, causing him to drop our pizzas. The person stopped and appeared to apologize while helping to pick up the fallen food, but even from a distance, I could tell they were frisking the pizza guy.

It was MASC, following through on Colonel Gdula's promise.

Gil paid the driver and brought the food to the table where Margie and I were waiting.

"One large pepperoni, one small Hawaiian, both relatively hot, though they look like they were dropped."

Margie frowned. I nodded. We started eating in silence.

After a few minutes, Gil seemed to need to break that silence.

"You know, they say you get more pizza per slice in Italy because they make their pizza pies in a different shape. See, in America, pizzas are round, but in Italy *pie are squared.*"

Bohr whined from underneath the table. Margie changed the subject.

"So, Logan, any big plans for the weekend?"

"I only have two friends. One is currently spending every waking hour training in a place none of us is allowed to go and the other was kidnapped almost a week ago. Also, Colonel Gdula has us locked down, so, no, I have no plans."

Gil and Margie looked at each other in a way that suggested neither was comfortable with what I had said, but none of it was untrue. Elena had texted me early in the week to make sure I wasn't angry with her. I assured her that I was not. I understood her motivations. She stayed in touch, but she wasn't allowed to tell me much, other than the fact that she had been skipping school to work on her powers and that Connie was still missing.

I was thinking about that second detail when Margie tried to lighten the mood.

"We aren't really 'locked down,' Logan. MASC is just keeping an eye on us. We can go and do what we want. Like if you wanted to see a movie—"

"Mmmmmm, maybe no to the movies," Gil suggested with a slight stammer. "Last time still has me a bit *shaken*, if you know what I mean."

It was a reference to the time Seismyxer almost killed us in the middle of a theater.

"I'd say we could try biking on the boardwalk, but probably best to stay away from Venice Beach for a while."

Margie nodded but continued trying to make the best of it.

"What do *you* want to do, Logan? You choose."

I wasn't sure she wanted me to answer that question honestly, so I told her, "I'm not sure you want me to answer that question honestly."

Gil and Margie both immediately insisted they did without even checking with each other.

"I would like to locate Connie and rescue her as soon as possible."

Margie and Gil definitely checked with each other at this point. I was willing to wait for an answer, but I was tired of waiting for someone to do something about Connie's kidnapping.

"Logan . . ." Gil stammered. "I don't . . . we don't have any idea where she is."

"So, if we did?" I asked, following his logic. "Then you'd go rescue her?"

"Honestly?" Margie asked.

"I always prefer honesty."

"Our priority right now is you, Logan, and this family. If we were to do something reckless, like trying to evade MASC surveillance or acting *heroic*, we'd be facing enemies on every side."

Gil added a nod. "Can you imagine having to fight Necros and her squad while also being hunted down by MASC at the same time?"

Of course, I didn't have to imagine it.

"That's exactly the scenario we faced two months ago."

"And we were lucky to come out the other side, Logan," Margie pointed out. "If *anything* had gone differently . . . It was a one in a million chance that this family survived. And I won't risk it again."

That was disappointing news, but I couldn't pretend

it was surprising. However, what they said next did catch me unaware.

"Speaking of keeping us all together," Gil volunteered, even though we really weren't speaking of that. "Maybe this is a good time to talk about the upside of all this."

I must have looked confused because Margie spoke up.

"Since we aren't part of MASC anymore, we can move forward now with your adoption papers, like normal foster parents."

Margie let the announcement hang in the air. I left it there.

"What are you thinking, Logan?"

I wanted to answer truthfully while saying as little as possible.

"I'm thinking a lot of things, and I don't think I'm ready to share them right away."

Gil took a deep breath, even though he didn't technically need oxygen to survive.

"That's fair, Logan. We can give you a little space to think. After all, we want to be your mother and father, not your *smother* and father. Why don't you turn in and get some sleep? We can talk about it more in the morning."

I agreed and wished Gil and Margie a good night, even though I knew there was no way I would sleep anytime soon.

In my cramped cabin on the houseboat, I sat for hours,

my laptop open but no idea what I should be searching. The answers to my questions weren't on the internet. The clues about where Necros could be keeping Connie, the timeline of Necros's history, and every hint that might have been dropped were all somewhere in my head and I had to get them out before continuing that conversation with Gil and Margie in the morning.

And that's when it hit me.

"In the morning!"

I am certain I said the words out loud despite being alone. But hearing it started a chain reaction. Just before midnight, I texted Elena a short message with a set of very specific instructions.

"Logan," she messaged back, "I don't know why you want me to do this."

I gave her the only reply I could. "Because you are my best friend, and I can't do this alone."

8:41 A.M.
SATURDAY, DECEMBER 4

By the time Gil and Margie came out of their room in the morning, I had already dressed, eaten a piece of peanut butter and banana toast, and brushed my teeth.

"You're up early for a Saturday, Logan," Margie commented with a smile.

"Yeah, you could be in jail because you look like *arrested* guy."

I ignored the pun and said the thing I'd been waiting to say all night.

"I've decided what I want."

"In terms of adoption?" Margie inquired, her eyebrows rising so they almost disappeared behind her hair.

"No, in terms of this weekend. I would like to learn to ski."

"You mean, like on a mountain . . . with snow?" Gil sounded uncertain.

I nodded. "Yes, I was referring to the downhill, or alpine, version of the sport performed on slopes covered in snow."

"Logan . . . we don't . . . you need . . . skis to ski . . . and the nearest ski mountain is hours away. Not to be a bummer, but there's *snow* way we can go skiing today."

Gil was correct, as I knew he would be, so I responded. "All the equipment we need can be rented at the ski resort, except for the ski jackets, pants, and goggles, which means we will have to bring our own. I texted Elena and her family has all kinds of ski clothes they can loan us, but she suggested we get our own goggles. So, I propose we go buy the goggles today and then come home in time for Elena to drop off the clothing. Tomorrow morning, we can drive two hours and forty-two minutes to Bear Mountain. According to their website, the area is expecting fourteen inches of fresh powder from winter storm Beatrix tonight."

Margie's left eyebrow arched. She was either suspicious or intrigued.

"You've done all the research on this, haven't you?"

I replied truthfully. "You have no idea how much research I did last night. But I am very excited about this plan."

Apparently, that was all Gil and Margie needed to hear. Around midmorning, we drove together to Powder Hound's Ski-Topia in Santa Monica and purchased a pair of goggles for Margie and a pair for me. Gil made it clear that he'd just rearrange his molecules to look like he was outfitted for the slopes.

While we were out, we stopped at Fatburger for lunch and a grocery store to buy snacks for the drive up to the mountains. Other than the ever-present unmarked vehicle that was trailing behind us, it felt like we were an ordinary family.

In fact, it felt nice, or at least it would have, if I hadn't known what my real intentions were.

Around sunset, Margie served a dinner of Swedish meatballs, raspberry danish, and Swiss chard. She was excited to make a Scandinavian-style dinner in honor of our upcoming ski trip. It was, as usual, odd and disgusting, but seeing how happy it made her, I decided not to inform her that:

1. Swedish meatballs don't usually have Swedish fish in them.
2. Danish is more of a breakfast food than a dinner dish.
3. Switzerland, despite having three of the top twelve ski resorts in Europe according to PlanetWare.com, is not part of Scandinavia.

Instead, I ate as much as I could without putting myself in gastrointestinal peril and then retired to my room to watch a countdown of the top 100 cat videos of the year while I waited for Elena.

It was about an hour after nightfall when she arrived on her bike at the edge of the Marina with a huge duffel bag strapped across her shoulder. Peeking out from the window in my cabin, I saw MASC's surveillance operative approach her, but he must have recognized Elena because he dropped his cover and simply searched her duffel for a minute before letting her out onto the docks.

"Logan, Elena's here!"

That was Margie, calling from the main cabin a minute later. I found Elena in the middle of emptying her duffel onto the couch and showing Margie and Gil the ski clothes she had brought.

"This is so sweet!" Margie insisted, as she picked up a silver parka. "And these jackets are so stylish."

"That one is definitely you," Elena agreed.

Gil nodded along, but then turned back to Elena. "You're sure your folks don't mind you lending us all this?"

"We haven't all gone skiing since the divorce," Elena said, her voice getting a little crackly on the last word.

"I'm taking this one and the pink ski pants," Margie decided. "What about you, Logan?"

"I'm not sure. Is it okay if Elena brings the rest in to my room so I can try them on?"

Gil and Margie exchanged a look and then gave us a smile.

"Of course." Margie agreed, holding the silver parka to her chest. "I'm sure you two have plenty to catch up on."

"And just remember," Gil added as we headed to my room, "even if you can't find a puffy jacket that fits . . . don't let it get you *down*. You know, like goose down."

"Good one!" Elena said. She was lying. That is a fact.

Once we were behind a closed door, Elena dropped the duffel on my bed and also dropped the pretense of being there to help us prepare for a family ski vacation.

"Okay, I did exactly what you told me to. Now, can you please . . . *please* tell me why?"

"I'm almost certain I know where to find Necros and Connie."

Elena's eyes lit up. "Tell me everything!"

6:44 P.M.
SATURDAY, DECEMBER 4

You know by now that I am very literal, so Elena's asking me to tell her "everything" seemed, at first, like it could be more than she actually wanted. But it turned out she really did want to know every detail of what I learned and what I had planned.

"The big brains at MASC have been trying to figure out where Necros is, and they've got nothing," Elena explained. "Their plan is to send teams to all the biggest cities—since that's where her Reclamation scheme is supposed to go off—and scour the areas for any sign of Necros or her powers."

"That's why they can't find her. They're searching in too

many places and looking for something that they can't see."

"I'm officially confused," Elena muttered as she slumped down on my bed, right onto the pile of parkas.

"So was I, until I realized that when I read all of Dr. Chrysler's notes about his secret conversations with Necros, there was a pattern for *when* he made his entries. For the month during Seismyxer's attacks around Southern California, most of his communications were around eight a.m. But when I went back to look at their exchanges from the months before then, all their exchanges happen about three hours earlier, like around five a.m."

"So Necros is an early riser?" Elena asked.

"Possibly," I admitted, "but it seems more likely that she was in a different time zone—one that was three hours later than LA, at least until she established her lair under Cal Tech."

Elena nodded along. "Okay, I follow."

"Next, I realized that Necros's powers are easy to hide. They don't show up except when she's . . . you know, killing people. But her hench-people are not exactly under-the-radar types. So, I began searching for signs of *their* powers."

"You mean like super-low temperatures for Cryoborg?" Elena jumped in. "Or strange sounds for SubSonique?"

"Exactly. I was looking for reports that lined up with all three of them. It's called triangulation. I knew if I identified signs of Cryoborg, SubSonique, and Shadow Paladin, all in the same geographical area within the Eastern time zone, I could draw a triangle on a map and be fairly certain that Necros is, or at least has been, somewhere within that area."

"Did you find a triangle?" Elena asked, gesturing to my laptop.

"I did . . . in Boston."

Both of Elena's eyebrows shot up. "That's where the plane was going the day you were found at LAX, right?"

"Yes. It's also where Dr. Clarke was a professor when he met and joined Necros. But I was more interested in the current facts. Fact one: boat captains in Boston Harbor have been dealing with strange ice floes for several weeks. The harbor doesn't freeze often, and when it has in the past, it's been in January or February—not this early. It's getting blamed on climate change, but no experts have offered a meteorological explanation yet. Fact two: a month ago, a defense contractor in Weymouth, Massachusetts, sent several dozen employees to the hospital with dizziness, confusion, and a ringing in their ears. The hospital found no trace of infection or poison, but while their facility was basically empty, a prototype submarine disappeared."

"Not to talk like Gil, but that *sounds* like SubSonique," Elena replied.

"Yeah, it does," I confirmed. "And remember, Necros used a submarine to escape in New Orleans."

"So that's two," Elena observed.

"Indeed," I agreed again as I clicked to the next window on my computer. "Fact three: In late October, right before the harbor's ice issues, a ghost-hunting group was touring Fort Warren, an eighteenth-century fort built on Georges Island in Boston Harbor. Legend says it's haunted by the Lady in Black, the ghost of a Confederate officer's wife who died while trying to rescue her husband from the jail inside. There are no actual facts to support this account, which is why it is a legend. This ghost-hunting group had barely set up their gear when they all felt sick to their stomach and dizzy—"

Elena jumped in. "Like the workers at the submarine lab."

"They were evacuated from the island, but before they went, their remote high-speed cameras captured this."

I tapped the track pad on my laptop and a video window opened. In the grainy, compressed video, the camera showed a long hallway with stark shadows down the length of it. After a second, there was a glint of something bright in one of the shadows and then it was gone.

"I don't know what I saw." Elena's uncertainty made her voice crack a little.

"Neither did I the first time," I admitted, "but keep watching."

The video on the site then rewound and zoomed in, playing back in superpixelated slow motion. This time, it was clear. The glint was the polished, metallic edge of a knight's helmet, and right next to it was a female face. It was the face of Necros.

"Holy shnikes!" Elena shouted, although she definitely did not say "shnikes."

7:01 P.M.
SATURDAY, DECEMBER 4

"That has to be where she is!" Elena sputtered. "We have to . . . I mean . . . do we tell Colonel Gdula?"

"No!" I replied way too loudly and then wished I hadn't.

From the main cabin, Margie called out, "Everything okay in there?"

"We're fine! Logan just . . . didn't like my suggestion that he wear the purple parka."

It was not a perfect lie, but it was better than I would have done.

Once we were sure no one was listening, we continued the conversation in lower tones.

"Colonel Gdula doesn't care about rescuing Connie

and he certainly has no interest in helping me find out if Necros is my mother."

"You're still thinking that's a possibility? I mean, after everything she's done?"

"I do," I explained, "because the timeline I saw on the server confirms it's possible. More than possible. Almost twenty years ago, Dr. Clarke discovered that Necros could not absorb sub-galactic cosmic radiation, and they began searching for a source of it on Earth so they could neutralize her powers. You already know the story of what they found."

"Right, but why would Necros want that?" Elena asked. "Her powers are what've kept her alive so long."

"Because she wanted to have a child with her husband, Dr. Clarke. Their secret wedding was on the timeline too. I guess superpowered people falling in love with the scientists who are studying them is a thing. It happened with Gil and Margie as well."

Elena grimaced but I kept going.

"It all aligns. Almost fourteen years ago, Necros stopped using her powers and MASC lost track of her because the experiment worked. With doses of SGCR, she had no powers. She could get pregnant and carry a child."

"And you really think you're that child, Logan?"

I proceeded to give her all the information about the fact that Necros has never hurt or even threatened me directly and also the physical resemblance I bear to Necros and Dr. Clarke. I told her about Necros calling me "my child" now three different times.

"These all sound like coincidences."

That's when I told her the most important information I'd seen in the timeline.

"Eleven years ago, Dr. Clarke died while helping Necros give birth to their second child, and then Necros *sent both children away*; one overseas and one to the West Coast to keep them safe and separate, just like Dr. Augustine guessed. We also know that a year later, MASC encountered Necros for the first time in years, on the West Coast, in the exact place and at the exact time I became an orphan."

"So that means . . . ?"

Elena looked at me without blinking.

"It means she could be my mother, or at the very least, she is the only person outside of MASC who knows what really happened that day. If we tell Colonel Gdula where she is, he'll show up with an army and stop at nothing to take her out and make it all disappear. He doesn't care if people get hurt, and he definitely doesn't want answers."

"And you need answers?" Elena asked with a sigh, but it wasn't really a question. "Right, so what do you want to do?"

"I want us to go to Boston to rescue Connie . . . and find out the truth."

I have known Elena long enough to know her confused face at this point. I also know her worried face. She made both at the same time.

"How?"

"When we flew to New Orleans, we never used our return trip tickets, so there was a credit on Gil and Margie's account. I memorized their log-in and used it to book us tickets for tonight. Our flight leaves in about three hours."

Elena pointed to the door to the houseboat's main cabin.

"What about Gil and Margie? Our chances would be so much better with them coming along."

"I know," I admitted, "but they'd just stop us. I asked them to rescue Connie and they refused."

Elena's mouth dropped open. "Wait, you already asked them?"

"They said they wouldn't risk getting in trouble with MASC now that we're a *normal* family, whatever that means."

Elena buried her face in her hands and exhaled hard. "Yeah, whatever that means."

I sat on the bed next to her and just breathed alongside her. According to a *Psychology Today* article written by Whitney Goodman, that's one of the ten ways to help someone calm down.

"I know I'm asking a lot. But I also know you want to save Connie too."

Elena looked up, her eyes shiny, and she nodded almost imperceptibly. Then she looked down at the bed and the winter clothes surrounding her.

"So, that's the real reason you had me bring all the parkas. For Boston."

"Yes, but that wasn't the only reason."

Elena pursed her lips and scrunched her nose. She was either confused again or was smelling the leftover odors of Margie's Scandinavian feast.

"What was the other reason?"

"Before we can fly anywhere, I need to get off this houseboat."

8:08 P.M.
SATURDAY, DECEMBER 4

Are you someone who sweats when you're nervous or anxious around other people? It's not uncommon and it's nothing to be ashamed of. Excessive sweating, or hyperhidrosis, is experienced by up to 32 percent of people who suffer from social anxiety disorders according to Healthline.com. The article also said being anxious about sweating can actually make people experience hyperhidrosis even more often, which seems pretty unfair.

As far as I know, I do not have this condition. However, I am certain I was both anxious and sweating profusely when I left my room on the houseboat with Elena. I was in a duffel bag slung over her shoulder, bundled up and surrounded by a half-dozen ski jackets and pants. It was very hot, uncomfortable, and completely nerve-racking.

"I gotta head home," I heard Elena explain to Gil and Margie, though the sound was muffled through the layers of winter clothing and nylon luggage.

"Did Logan find a good fit?" Margie asked from not too far away.

Elena paused and then delivered the answer we'd rehearsed in my room. "Yeah, he got what he needed for sure. And then he quoted a study about the importance of proper rest as it relates to athletic performance and said he was going to bed right away. I guess he wants to be super ready for skiing tomorrow."

I knew this was the moment where things could all fall apart. At the same time, I felt something nudging the bottom of the duffel bag and heard a snuffling sound.

"Bohr, leave it!"

That was Gil. Thankfully, ever since Gil had stood up to Colonel Gdula, he'd gotten a bit more assertive with the dog as well. The Great Dane's nose stopped sniffing the bag right away.

"Sorry, Elena. He likes to smell everything," Gil explained, "even though he *nose* it's not okay."

The duffel bounced a little on her shoulder as Elena laughed. It felt to me like she might be trying too hard because that was not one of Gil's better jokes.

"Too funny!" Elena mused. "Anyway, have a great time on the slopes. See you . . . soon."

Gil and Margie said their goodbyes and I felt Elena head out the door, careful not to bonk the bag on the way off the boat. I appreciated it.

"Okay, now comes the hard part," Elena whispered as she walked up the dock, keeping what felt like a casual pace as the boards creaked under her feet with each step. Then I felt her reach the incline and the footfalls sounded more metallic. We were on the ramp up to the street.

"Trainee Arguello," a flat, military voice spoke out from a distance, "I'll need to check your bag again."

"Yeah, I know. No one wants to get in trouble with the colonel. It's still just ski clothes, minus the jackets they borrowed," Elena said, doing a good job of keeping any tension out of her tone. "Here, I'll just toss it to you so you can inspect it yourself."

We had planned for her to say that, so I wasn't worried that she'd actually throw me. But I also knew she had to convince the MASC operative that there wasn't anything important in the bag.

Elena slid the duffel down her arm and began swinging it around like it weighed nothing. That's a thing you can do when you're super strong. Of course, inside the bag it was like some cruel carnival ride, leaving me more than a little nauseated.

"That won't be necessary," the emotionless voice replied. "Just open it up and let me take a look."

Fighting off the extreme dizziness, I quickly lifted the

closest parka up and covered my head and shoulders with it just as I heard the zipper pull and felt a draft of night air pour into the bag.

Then there was the flare of a flashlight beam as I held my breath and willed myself not to move a muscle.

"Okay, you're good to go," the MASC soldier announced. "And be careful riding home. It's dangerous out there."

"Don't I know it," Elena responded earnestly. Then she zipped the bag back up, got on her bike, and we were on our way.

Even though I figured we were in the clear, just to be safe, Elena didn't let me out until she had pedaled almost all the way to the airport and locked her bike up outside a hotel on Century Boulevard.

"You look like you've been in a clothes dryer for an hour," Elena observed.

"Technically, you aren't that far off," I realized. "I mean, between the heat, the clothing items, and the spinning, the experiences are likely similar."

I let Elena try to fix my hair so it didn't look like a total mass of static electricity and then we went into the hotel and checked the duffel bag into their luggage storage, minus a parka for each of us. Next, we took the hotel shuttle into the airport, got off at our terminal, and loaded our boarding passes onto an app on my phone.

As we approached the airport security station, my

nerves were so on edge, I was quietly reciting the boiling point of all the alkali metals on the periodic table. One TSA agent got a bit suspicious, but Elena used my muttering to convince him we were both prodigies flying to Boston to apply for early admission to MIT's chemistry program.

He must have believed her because he let us through to the metal detectors. Elena and I removed our valuables, including my wallet full of all my saved-up allowance money, and put them on the conveyor belt through the X-ray machine. But when we got to the other side, we didn't reclaim all our belongings. Elena's trainee earrings and my watch with the panic button were both still in the tray.

"If we take them, MASC will know exactly how to find us as soon as they realize we're gone," I said aloud, although I was certain Elena was already aware of that fact.

"Right," Elena agreed, confirming my thought. "But if we leave them, that's it. No one's coming to save us if things don't go the way we hope."

We both paused to look at the items in the tray, and then each other.

"Guess we are officially on our own at this point," I said and turned away from the security checkpoint.

"No, we aren't," Elena corrected me, falling into step alongside. "We've got each other."

8:33 A.M.
SUNDAY, DECEMBER 5

It took me a while to fall asleep on the plane without my noise-canceling headphones, but another Necros dream came to me when I finally did. This time, she was teaching me how to make my bed, sweetly advising me on the finer points of tucking in the sheets and smoothing the blankets. But when I finished, she looked at me and her demeanor changed from motherly to menacing.

"You've made your bed. Now lie in it."

That is an expression that traces back to France in 1590, at least according to Phrases.org.uk. It means that a person lives with the decisions they've made.

My dreams were becoming less difficult to interpret.

When I jarred awake, we were landing in Boston, and

even as we walked down the Jetway, the cooler air made it clear the parkas weren't just a good escape plan. They were going to be necessary.

"So where do we go now?" Elena asked, blowing into her hands as we stood outside baggage claim.

"Georges Island," I replied. "It's the only place we have seen evidence of Necros. But between the ice in the harbor and the state closing it down a few months ago, there's no public transportation out there. I think our best shot is to go to the nearest mainland and attempt to rent a boat or hire a charter."

It took an hour in a cab, and we passed thirteen different Dunkin' Donuts on the way, including the one we stopped at for breakfast. Finally, by late morning, we were dropped off at the very tip of a town called Hull, on a rocky spit of land only about two hundred yards wide. The Atlantic Ocean roiled away on one side, and the calmer, dark green bay sat on the other.

I shivered against the wind that roared out of the north like it was coming straight from a freezer, sweeping across the ice floes that rose and fell as swells rolled in.

The parking lot was almost empty; only a few pickup trucks dotted the concrete. There was a ferry station, its gates locked and a tin "Ferry Service Suspended" sign hung from its chains. There were also a couple of small buildings that advertised boat rentals, but they were clearly closed too.

"That must be Georges Island!" Elena pointed west. "It's so close. I could swim there easy!"

I looked out and, indeed, there was an island, covered in low shrubs with hints of gray buildings barely visible. It was only a few hundred yards off the shore.

"That's not Georges."

The words were delivered with a dry, raspy grunt that came from the other side of an old white pickup with a logo for "Lobster Bob's Seafood" on the door. When we turned, there was an older guy with cool blue eyes, a thick gray-and-blond beard, and a navy-blue flannel shirt. He was unloading lobster traps from the back of the truck and speaking without looking at us.

"Georges is to the north—farther out."

"Are you sure? The one right over there looks like it has a fort on it," Elena pointed out.

"This is New England. Every island has a fort, a lighthouse, or some rich family's house on it. The one you're looking for is just to the left of that oversized pinwheel."

There was a massive wind turbine at the land's end, and beyond it there was what might be the shadow of another island, but the fog coming off the frozen seawater made it hard to see any detail. Instinctively, we followed the man as he carried his traps down to his boat—a thirty-two-foot craft with an open deck and the name *LindyLoo* across the back. There were already several dozen traps piled up as he arranged the final few, moving them around with a gaff, which is a long wooden pole with a hook on the end.

I had questions, so I started asking them.

"Are you Lobster Bob? Do you know if there's any way to get out to Georges Island? Have you noticed anything strange happening on the island recently? Have you seen any submarines? Have you seen any people dressed as knights?"

The man turned to Elena.

"Does he have an off switch?"

Elena gave him a shrug. "Not so much. But we really could use your help."

He grunted and continued readying the boat. "I'm the one who needs help. This ice and fog has just about put me out of business. It's been a month since I've been able to set my traps."

"It appears you're preparing to take your traps out now. Does that mean it's gotten safer?" I asked, adding it to my list of questions.

"Means I've gotten hungrier."

The lobsterman headed back up the dock toward his truck. Elena trailed after him, and I did my best to keep pace.

"Lobster Bob, can we please just ask you a question or two?"

"It's just Bob. Bob Mant, if you need to know. Ask what you want. I'm just not promising any answers."

"Fair enough," Elena agreed as Bob used both hands to

pull a heavy, oversized toolbox out of the pickup and heft it back toward the water.

"Have you noticed anything out of the ordinary recently?"

"You mean other than the damn humming?"

Elena looked at me and her eyes widened. "You mean like a strange vibration inside your ear?"

Bob put down the heavy toolbox with an echoing thump on the metal ramp down to the docks.

"No, I mean humming. The day it first got cold, there was a fog that rolled in and there was a humming sound that came and went. When the fog cleared, the whole blasted bay had chunks of ice choking the gut."

I didn't understand whose gut he was referring to.

"Whose gut?"

"The gut. That's what we call the water where the ocean and the bay meet. Every time it looks like the ice might break up, the fog rolls in again and there's more of that humming and more ice. That's why I'm trying to get out now, before it happens again."

Bob bent down to lift the toolbox, but Elena was quicker. She snatched it off the ground like it weighed nothing as we all headed toward the *LindyLoo.*

"Let me get this and you can tell us more about the humming."

Bob's expression changed ever so slightly. I am guessing he was impressed. "There's not much to tell."

"Can you describe the humming?" I pressed him for details. "Is it like a person humming or a cat purring or an electric toothbrush or a hummingbird's wings or—"

"That's what it sounds like," Bob interjected, his eyes suddenly up and scanning the water as he stepped onto his boat.

"A hummingbird's wings?"

"No, *that*. Listen."

Then I heard it: a distant humming from out in the fog that grew steadily higher pitched. This happens when a sound is approaching at high speed and is called the Doppler effect according to chapter 17 of *University Physics*, volume 1, which is one of the few books Gil owns. I don't know if Lobster Bob had read that book, but he understood the Doppler effect.

"It's getting closer. Never heard it do that before," Bob grumbled as he reached for his gaff and held it like a war club. "Why don't you kids get back on land."

Before we could respond, a burst of pale blue streaked out of the fog, slamming into the boat. Instantly, half the craft—including Bob—were covered in ice and frozen in place.

Elena and I had barely turned to look when Cryoborg exploded out of the mist, blazing straight at us on an ice-spewing Jet Ski.

"*Ice* see you!"

10:33 A.M.
SUNDAY, DECEMBER 5

You know how sometimes people talk about "freezing" in high-pressure situations? It's an expression, and it's also not a good thing. But it is still much better than literally being frozen when you're under attack from a supervillain who blasts liquid nitrogen. So, even though I am not exactly nimble, I did my best to force my body to move. My plan was to jump onto Bob's ice-encrusted boat and crouch down behind the traps. However, the finer points of my brain's plans were not understood by my feet; I caught a toe on the edge of the boat's railing and slid across the frosty deck face-first into a coil of rope.

It was not graceful, but at least when I came to a stop,

I was out of the line of fire.

I pulled myself up to peek over the side of the boat and saw that Cryoborg had created an ice ramp that he used to launch himself at Elena. Midair, his ice ski disassembled and became part of his legs, giving him extra armor as he threw a vicious flying roundhouse kick toward her head. Elena dodged at the last possible moment, but his metallic leg still got a piece of her shoulder, knocking her to one knee.

"Another two inches and you'd be out *cold*, junior hero."

"Ugh!" Elena spat, standing back up and getting into a fighting stance. "Your puns hurt more than the kick, Icebox."

"That's not my name!"

Cryoborg lashed out with a series of punches that Elena blocked, grunting with each impact. Every time Cryoborg attacked, I noticed the robotic elements on his arms hissing with liquid nitrogen and rearranging: a hammer for a blow, a shield for defense, or even a blade for a slash. His cold-powered cryogenic frame was transforming in real time to build whatever he needed.

"I'm tired of playing with you, girl." As Cryoborg spoke, his right arm formed into a cybernetic buzz saw with spinning ice blades.

Elena ducked his first two swipes and then, with her

back to the boat, caught his third, grabbing his forearm to hold the saw inches short of her face. Flecks of sharp frost flew off the blades, but Elena never flinched. Instead, her eyes flashed with bright yellow heat and the blade evaporated before it touched her skin.

"That's the difference between you and me," Elena retorted, as she pushed Cryoborg backward, step by step, until his back foot was up against a pylon. "I . . . don't . . . play!"

Elena punctuated her words with a shove, but at the same time, Cryoborg's hands transformed into clamps that created a pair of ice handcuffs around Elena's wrists.

"Overconfidence is a rookie mistake. But don't worry . . . it's the last one you'll ever make."

As he spoke, the rest of his cybernetic body began rearranging itself to form a cannon in the middle of his chest. Its muzzle was pointed at Elena, who was locked in place just inches away. From behind him, I saw liquid nitrogen tubes snake up his back to power a final pale-blue blast.

I knew I needed to help Elena, but the options that came flying into my head were somewhere between dumb and deadly:

1. I could distract him into turning and shooting at me instead.
2. I could tackle him, which would involve coordination and strength, two things I don't have a lot of.

3. I could shout several of the worst puns I'd heard from Gil and see if he responded with his own.

As I searched for a solution, I noticed Bob, frozen-still, with the gaff iced over in his hand.

I grabbed it and used it to pull myself to my feet. Then I twisted the gaff out of Bob's hand and swung the metal end toward Cryoborg's back. I knew it wouldn't even dent his cybernetic frame, but that wasn't what I was trying to do. The hook caught hold right at the base of where all the tubes connected and then I held on and fell backward, letting gravity do the rest.

All at once, a half-dozen tubes of liquid nitrogen pulled free and sent a cloud of frozen fog into the air.

"What the . . . ?" Cryoborg shouted as he turned. But he never finished the thought. Elena burst free, using her energy to melt the ice shackles.

Without a word, Elena went to work on Cryoborg's metallic exoskeleton. Her hands blazed as she literally dismantled him, tearing away components and tossing them into the bay. Every time one of his tubes tried to reattach itself, she welded it shut between her glowing fingers. Only when Cryoborg was totally stripped of everything except his bodysuit did Elena finally stop.

"Talking when you should have been finishing me off," Elena said with a smirk. "SUPER-rookie mistake!"

"Where's Connie?" I demanded, carefully getting

back to my feet. "Tell us where our friend is and we'll let you go."

"Your friend?" Cryoborg jeered through bloody lips. "I've got some bad news for you two dummies."

Elena lifted Cryoborg up by his neck, with a new intensity I hadn't seen from her before.

"If you hurt her . . ." With each word, her hand tightened around his throat. "Just tell us: Is she on that island?"

As his face turned as blue as one of his blasts, I saw Cryoborg register real fear as he nodded because he was unable to get a word out. Elena waited a second to decide if she believed him, and then her other hand came up with a straight punch to his chin that knocked him out instantly.

"He shouldn't have called us dummies," Elena explained as she found a coil of rope on the dock and started tying Cryoborg to a pylon. "But we still gotta figure a way out to that island. Oh shoot . . . Lobster Bob! I need to unfreeze him!"

"He said he would prefer you just call him 'Bob,'" I reminded her.

Elena hovered her glowing hands in a pattern around Bob's body, and the ice crystals melted away as the color returned to his skin. But it still took a fresh flannel from belowdecks and some jumping jacks to truly get Bob warmed up. Once he did, the old fisherman had so many questions, he sorta reminded me . . . of myself.

"What exactly happened to me? And what happened to my boat? And what happened to that guy tied up on the dock? Is he that guy from the movies? Why does he look so familiar?"

I was about to answer all of them when Elena stepped in and stopped me.

"If we tell you how you got frozen and how you got unfrozen and why there is an unconscious man in a frost-covered bodysuit on the dock, at some point, someone is going to show up and make you unremember what we told you. But if we don't tell you, then that's one less thing you have to worry about."

The expression on Bob's face suggested he didn't like the answer, or more accurately, the lack of answers.

"The one thing we can tell you is we really need a ride to Georges Island," she explained. "But if you can't do that, could you at least wait a half hour before calling the cops?"

Bob sized up Elena and then turned and did the same to me. "I'm pretty sure you two just saved me from being a permanent Bob-sicle. So, just tell me honestly . . . will I be putting you kids in danger if I help you get to that island?"

It was a fair question, so I decided to answer as factually as possible.

"We are in danger already. Nothing you do will put us in more of it. That is a fact. There are more people like him after us," I explained, looking over at Cryoborg, secured to the dock. "Our only chance of gaining an advantage is to take the fight to them."

Bob's eyes settled on me. "You a fighter?"

"No." I didn't feel I could answer any other way.

"But I am," Elena added, meeting Bob's gaze. "And I won't let them hurt him."

Bob shook his head slowly and then made his way to the wheel of the *LindyLoo.*

"Well then, make yourselves useful and untie the bowline. And put on your life vests. Last thing we need is someone falling overboard and drowning before you do something heroic."

Following Bob's directions, we were underway in a few minutes, heading out into the bay. There was still a fair amount of ice in the water, but whenever we were blocked, Elena went to the bow, there was a bright flash, and a steamy sizzle. With each, the path in front of the boat cleared.

"I dunno how she's doing it," Bob mumbled, "but if that girl ever needs a job, she's got it."

Just then, I felt a vibration in my pocket. A text from Margie.

"WHERE ARE YOU?!"

As you probably know, it's hard for me not to answer a question when I'm asked one, but I knew I couldn't. Even though I was sure Gil and Margie were worried, having just woken up to find a bunch of pillows under the covers in my bed.

Once again, I was flooded with too many emotions at once. Guilt, shame, even some regret. I couldn't identify them all, but none of them felt particularly positive. Most of all, I felt sure that I was doing what I had to do. I had to do it for Connie, and for me. So even though it did not feel good, I set my phone to "Do Not Disturb" and slid it back in my pocket.

"We're here!"

That was Captain Bob as he idled the *LindyLoo* toward an empty dock only a hundred feet away.

"Welcome to Georges Island, a possibly haunted, frozen hellscape-slash-historical site," Bob grumbled. "I won't be too far away, so if you kids get in trouble, call the number on my hat. You got it?"

His hat read "1-555-LOB-STAH." I think even someone *without* a photographic memory could remember that.

We stepped onto the dock and then the *LindyLoo* disappeared back into the fog, the chugging of its motor fading even after it was impossible to see the boat at all.

"Okay." Elena exhaled as she and I approached the fort's towering granite walls. "Before we go in, I need to know: If it's a choice between finding Connie and getting outta there or staying to get your answers, what are we doing?"

It was a question I'd been running through my mind for a while, so I told her what I'd settled on.

"You get Connie and go. Necros hasn't hurt me so far; and if she's my mother, she won't hurt us now."

"What if she isn't your mom?" Elena asked.

I had also thought of all the different ways this might go if Necros wasn't my mother, and all of them ended badly, not just for me but probably for the whole world.

"If she's not my mother, I don't think any of us will be going anywhere."

Elena listened and nodded.

"I hear that. But I need you to know something. Regardless of whether she's your mom or not, she's responsible for Luther's death, and I won't let her take another friend from me. You understand that?"

I returned her nod, because I did understand it. I just didn't know how I felt about it.

But there was no turning back.

11:39 A.M.
SUNDAY, DECEMBER 5

The fort's massive metal gates were frozen shut, a foreboding layer of salty ice encrusting the entire surface, but that wasn't an obstacle for Elena. Her hands flared to life, thawing open the doors as steam billowed up off the metal.

Together, we walked through the shadowy hall that led to the open area inside the fort's outer defenses. I don't know how Elena felt about this point of no return, but I know I must've been anxious or overwhelmed because I was quietly reciting the opening monologue from *Nicholas Nickleby.* It's an eight-and-a-half-hour play, and even though I knew I wouldn't get through it all, I just couldn't stop myself.

The interior of the fort stretched out ahead of us. Snow had drifted into massive piles in the corners of a pentagon-shaped courtyard and sunlight gleamed off the frosty, brown lawn.

"It's bigger than I expected," Elena admitted, scanning from left to right. "I guess we just keep our eyes open until—"

"Logan? Elena?"

Connie's voice called out to us, and when we turned, I spotted her standing behind a rusted, barred door set into the stone wall only a hundred feet away. Her face was just peeking out like you'd see in prison movies or occasionally at the zoo.

Elena moved like lightning, racing to the door while I ran to catch up.

"You two came. I can't believe it," Connie said, with no trace of her usual sarcasm.

"Of course we came," Elena insisted in a whisper. "Now keep it down and we'll get you out of here."

With one hand, Elena gripped the padlock on the door, twisting and pulling until the mechanism released with a clear pop. Then she tossed the lock aside, opened the door, and wrapped Connie up in a hug for a full three seconds before releasing her with a tinge of blush still on her cheeks.

"Sorry," Elena said quietly. "We were worried about you."

"Methinks thou should be worried about thyself, m'lady."

Shadow Paladin's raspy Shakespearean accent emerged from behind us, and by the time we turned to face him, he had fully appeared out of the dark hallway we had just come through.

"I am here to see Necros," I volunteered.

"See her, thou shall . . . after I dispatch this one." Shadow Paladin spoke as he leveled his lightless black sword at Elena.

"Good luck, Sir Sucks-a-lot. I beat you down once. If anyone's getting 'dispatched,' it's you."

Both of Elena's eyes and hands flashed with energy. She charged Shadow Paladin; but before she could get close, he melted away back into the shadows. Then he reappeared a hundred feet away in a breezeway at the base of the fort's walls.

"Such fervor! Come for me, shrew, and taste my inky blade."

Elena obliged, sprinting toward the breezeway so fast that she left a light trail behind her. But every time she was within striking distance, he'd vanish into the darkness cast by one of the columns, appearing dozens of feet ahead until he finally stopped in one of the open doorways that dotted the wall. With two flourishes of his sword, a pair of shadow shards sprang to life and bounded toward Elena. She chopped through the first one with a flash of her glowing right hand and then her eyes flared like spotlights as she headbutted the second.

"Curse thee, foul sorceress!"

Shadow Paladin appeared to be shocked by how quickly Elena dealt with his minions. He backpedaled into the open door behind him a moment before she reached him. Without hesitating, Elena dove through the door after him, but a half second later, Shadow Paladin reappeared in the shadows outside the doorway.

"Elena, it's a trap!"

I was already too late. Shadow Paladin used the tip of his blade to slam the door shut. As soon as it closed, a low hum came from beyond the door.

"In case you were wondering, that's what a sub-galactic cosmic radiation collector sounds like," a bored-sounding female voice said from somewhere behind Connie and me. When we spun around, SubSonique was leaning against a wall, checking the polish on her two-tone nails. "It's also a D. Thirty-six point seventy-one megahertz."

I don't have perfect pitch, but I did know she had the math right.

"Here's the deal," SubSonique continued, looking up at us for the first time. "Your neighbor pal isn't going anywhere, but you are. Now, I can drop a beat and make you zombie march down to see the boss in any time signature I choose, or you can walk on your own. Your call."

I knew she was right, but I was done being afraid. My best chance of helping Elena, at that point, was finding out the truth.

"Take me to Necros. I have some things I would like to discuss with her."

"I bet you do," SubSonique agreed and then turned to Connie with a smirk. "Why don't you come too? This should be fun. I'd hate for you to miss it."

Then she began walking toward a door at the far end of the courtyard. Connie and I followed silently while Shadow Paladin trailed behind.

Inside the fort's walls, it was clear some areas had been updated with electricity, heat, and simple furnishings. However, as we moved deeper into the fortress, we passed a hallway of gloomy Civil War–era cells. I tried to glimpse inside each to see if this might be where Necros was keeping the missing superhumans, but it was too dark to tell.

Finally, we rounded a corner to a pair of heavy, reinforced doors that looked like it would take a small army to move. SubSonique flicked a bit of lint off her shoulder, stamped her foot once, and then watched as the echo of the impact swung the doors open.

Within was a large chamber that was different from the rest of the fort. The granite walls were covered in art. The lighting was soft and warm. And the pristine, Persian carpets on the ground looked much older than the fort itself. At the far end of the hall, on a magnificent throne, sat Necros. Dr. Chrysler stood by her side like an attendant; and a dozen of her personal guards, all armed with plasma rifles, stood at attention behind her.

"At last." Her voice reverberated off the stone walls even though she spoke quietly. "I am so proud of you, my oldest child. I knew this day would come."

My brain went blank.

All of my suspicions. All of my theories. All of the clues and connections and facts had led to this. I struggled to find names for any of the things I was feeling, as the most complicated emotions of my life slammed into my alexithymia and left me utterly overwhelmed. Still, I somehow managed to speak.

"Then it's true? You are my mother?"

The room went silent as the echo of my words faded. Necros's head cocked a few degrees to one side, but she did not respond.

"Logan, what are you talking about?"

That was Connie, who turned to me and put her hand on my shoulder, with a look of confusion so obvious, even I couldn't mistake it for anything else.

"I'm sorry I didn't tell you, Connie. It was all just a theory. Not a fact. But now it's confirmed. I'm sure it's a shock that Necros is my birth mother, but it also means we are going to be okay. She won't hurt us."

I thought this would be good news, but Connie's expression went flat as she withdrew her hand from me.

"Logan, Necros isn't *your* mother. She's mine."

12:02 P.M.
SUNDAY, DECEMBER 5

You should know that I feel everything that other people feel. Many neurotypical people assume this is not the case, because I don't show how I feel the same way most other people do. But that is an assumption by them, not a fact. I get angry. I get frustrated. I get sad too. It's just that, usually, when an emotion hits me, I don't recognize it's happening right away. I need a little time to identify how I'm feeling and react. But in the moment when Connie admitted that Necros was her mother, there was no hesitation: I was flooded with all those feelings at once.

"That's not right. That can't be right! I'm the one . . . she's been looking for me . . . *your* mother is missing! Tell the truth. Tell the truth!"

The room spun and I felt like I was going to be sick, but I couldn't even get enough breath in to throw up. Or maybe I was breathing too much to vomit.

I dropped to one knee as Dr. Chrysler scurried over to me.

"Logan, breathe slowly. Slower."

"I can slow his breath down if you want, Doc." I heard SubSonique chime in from the edge of my vision with a cruel grin. "Wayyyy down."

"Mom, you can't let her . . ." Connie cried out before quieting herself.

"No one is going to hurt you, Logan," Dr. Chrysler insisted, drawing my attention back to him. "Count to five with each breath if you can. That's it."

I didn't want to listen to him, but as I forced myself to focus on inhaling and exhaling slower, my vision cleared over the course of the next few minutes. Up close, I saw that Dr. Chrysler looked much less frail than he had in New Orleans. "Good. Now, as calmly as you can, tell me . . . why on earth would you think Necros was your mother?"

Throughout my life, replying to questions with the most factual answer has always been my natural response. But this time, I couldn't do it, or, more to the point, I didn't want to. I had no desire to remind myself how I had made so many faulty assumptions. Still, as embarrassed and foolish as I felt, I also couldn't pass up the opportunity to know the truth.

"I thought . . . a lot of things that turned out to be wrong," I said as plainly as I could to Dr. Chrysler before looking to Necros. "But I do know you were in Los Angeles at the airport, almost ten years ago, and I was there too. That was the day I ended up an orphan."

Necros rose from her throne and moved slowly toward me, the train of her black and silver gown sweeping across the carpet and creating a low hush.

"I remember that day. It should have been a joyous occasion, but MASC made that impossible. You see, after the birth of Khan, or *Connie* as you know her, her father and I attempted to have another child. But the treatments that had made it possible began to fail."

"You ran out of sub-galactic cosmic radiation," I stated. "I read that in Dr. Chrysler's timeline."

"Indeed. And Wendell—Khan's father, my only true love—died while delivering the child. My powers returned in the middle of the birth, and he gave his life for our family. Khan was but a toddler, with no control over her abilities. Today, she might have been able to save her father. Alas, it was the darkest day of my long, long life."

I looked to Connie and saw tears welling in her eyes.

"For Khan's safety, I sent her to live with Wendell's

parents in California. Her brother barely survived the birth and required care only available half a world away. That left me alone in grief. It was a pain I had not known in all my centuries. But that day in Los Angeles was meant to be a step back into the light. I was there to receive Khan from her grandparents and take her back. But moments after she was with me, MASC's team of killers and superhuman traitors attacked. Lives were lost. I did what any mother would do to protect her child."

Necros was now only a dozen feet away. She held out a gloved hand toward Connie, who hesitated only a moment to look at me before joining her mother, careful to touch only the fabric.

I thought about what Necros had just said, careful to not make more assumptions.

"Does that mean you killed my parents?"

Necros turned back and studied me for a moment. I studied her right back, looking for indications that might tell me if what she said next was true or false.

"I have no idea."

She held my gaze, her eyes steady and unblinking. I saw no telltale sign of a lie, but I also may have believed her because I wanted to.

"Logan, I could help you find out what happened to your parents."

That was Dr. Chrysler, still standing close to me.

"What if we struck a bargain? You share the information that's still in your mind, and I will share the details of that day. That would be so much more effective and civil than the alternative."

"What is the alternative?" I asked, wanting to know the full list of options.

"The alternative," SubSonique piped up from the corner of the room, "is I turn up that ultra-high frequency I put in your ear a few weeks ago in the alley. Up to now, I've just been using it to listen in to your whiny 'who-is-my-mommy, where-is-my-Connie' drama. But if I pump up the volume, it'll rupture your eardrums until you tell us whatever we need to know. Want a taste?"

To prove the threat wasn't an idle one, I suddenly had a strange, high-pitched tone in my right ear that made me wince.

"That's enough, SubSonique!" Necros ordered with a new sharpness to her voice. The pain dissipated immediately. "I do not wish harm upon you. That is why I sent my only child to bring you to me. I could have dispatched any number of my lieutenants if I wished to use violence to obtain the knowledge in your mind. But Dr. Chrysler has helped me realize bloodshed is not the answer."

I felt a heat rising in me. I wasn't sure if I was angry about my own foolishness, feeling betrayed by Connie, or was struck by Necros's false claims. It may have been all three at once.

"How can you pretend that's true? I saw the plan for the Reclamation. How many people will die when your followers launch coordinated attacks around the world? How many lives will it take for you to make your 'statement'?"

I realized I was shouting again, which is not something I do often, but I couldn't hold it back. Strangely, Necros did not react in the way most people do when they're shouted at. In fact, she reacted more like I normally do, replying in a calm, matter-of-fact tone.

"You've made another incorrect assumption."

Necros turned and walked to a table off to the side, where there was a TV remote and a wireless keyboard. "Would you care to see what we have planned?"

With a click of the remote, a large flat-screen TV on the far wall flashed to life to reveal a document. It wasn't blueprints for some weapon or a battle plan. It was just words.

> Today, we, the superhuman citizens of the planet Earth, are revealing our presence to the world. For centuries, we have hidden our powers, hidden our identities, and hidden our potential, all out of fear of how the rest of humanity would react to our existence. Some struck unfair bargains with secret power brokers who called us heroes in name only but stripped us of our rights. Others fought against this oppression from the shadows, using our powers at the

risk of being imprisoned or destroyed. But the majority of us simply denied our true selves in a degrading attempt to fit in.

Those days have passed.

Today, we reclaim our rights. We will use our powers as we see fit. We will pursue the lives we desire. We will be the owners of our identity.

The signers of this declaration avow that we mean the world no harm. But we will defend ourselves if any person, group, or government seeks to impose their will upon us.

The era of superhuman denial and servitude ends today.

"This is our declaration of independence, though it's a good deal shorter than the one all those pompous men in wigs wrote two and a half centuries ago."

"It's a speech?" I asked and received a nod of confirmation from Necros. "I don't understand. Why do you need the database to make an announcement?"

"Because, Logan, it has to be something that MASC can't just cover up." Dr. Chrysler approached me, his voice thin and reedy. "And as long as they control hundreds of heroes, all convinced that Necros is the enemy and secrecy must be maintained, that's exactly what they'll do."

"Dr. Chrysler convinced me that information is more powerful than sheer might, and I've been swayed. You see how much we've accomplished with just a small portion of the knowledge you possess," Necros said, gesturing toward Shadow Paladin. "So-called heroes rally to our cause when we lay bare the truth of how they've been manipulated. MASC has no real power, only the illusion of control. With a list of every known superhuman on the planet, I can take that illusion away from them and give the power to those who deserve it."

"Imagine it, Logan," Dr. Chrysler implored me. "People like your foster parents, free to be whoever they want to be—protectors, explorers, or just parents—all without having to ask for permission."

It did sound good, but there was something being left out.

"What about the public pool paradox?" I asked Dr. Chrysler. "You're the one who told me about it: the idea that if humanity learns there are superheroes around, they'll expect them to fix all their problems and blame them if they don't."

"There will be no superheroes once MASC is gone," Necros declared, slowly returning to her throne with Connie trailing behind her, looking back over her shoulder at me every so often. "There will just be superhumans, with the same rights that every other free person on this planet enjoys and no obligations beyond that. When this declaration is made across the globe, it will fall upon the governments and people of the world to choose: respect those rights . . . or face the consequences. You have a choice to make as well, Logan. I'll give you some time to consider it."

Two guards broke ranks and approached where I was standing. They frisked me and removed my phone and wallet. Then they led me back into the hall. As I passed by SubSonique, she gave me a wink, but I do not think it was a friendly one.

"Keep your ears open, kid. I'm coming for you."

I was led back to the cells and escorted into the last one. The rusted iron door closed behind me with a dull, ringing impact, followed by the sound of a key turning in a lock. And then I was alone.

I know I should have been thinking about ways to escape and plans for rescuing Elena and ideas for calling for help. But I couldn't.

All I could think about was how wrong I had been, and not just about one or two things. I was wrong about everything.

6:14 P.M.
SUNDAY, DECEMBER 5

For six hours, I lay in one of the two cots in my cell and tried to distract myself. I reviewed every page I'd seen in Dr. Chrysler's encrypted files, hoping to find a weakness. There was nothing. I reexamined every map I'd seen of the fort online, but there was nothing new. I even rewatched thirty-three of my favorite online cat videos in my head, including one where Princess Purrnella gets a gift bow stuck to the top of her head. I didn't even crack a smile.

Within minutes, I was back to listing every fact I'd misinterpreted, each clue I missed, and all the times I should have shared what I knew with Gil and Margie.

I have been told I'm smart more than three thousand different times in my life—sometimes as a compliment, others as part of an intended insult—but at the moment, I was feeling so stupid, it was like none of those occasions counted anymore.

The only thing that interrupted me was when Shadow Paladin appeared without warning in my cell. In his arms was Elena, unconscious, with a pair of high-tech handcuffs on her wrists. He laid her on the cot nearest to the door.

"Thy compatriot is drained, but she shall recover with time. However, we have put measures in place to keep her from being a threat, rest assured."

He disappeared back into the shadows and once I was sure he was gone, I rushed to Elena. She was breathing and I saw no injuries, but her skin was cooler than usual.

I tried to wake her with a few gentle taps to her cheeks. That didn't work. I also checked her airway and raised her feet twelve inches above her heart, just like it suggested on a first aid poster I saw once in a hospital. I was considering attempting CPR when a hushed voice came through bars in the door.

"Why did you do it?"

That was Connie. She didn't sound as tough as she usually did.

"I've done a lot of inadvisable things recently," I admitted. "You'll have to be more specific."

"I made SubSonique tell me everything she heard when she was spying on you. She said that . . ." Connie's voice got harder. "Just tell me why you came after me."

"I thought you were my friend and that it was my fault you'd been kidnapped. I believed you would've done the same for me. Clearly, I was mistaken about that too."

I couldn't make out Connie's face in the shadows, but I heard air escape her mouth in a short burst, though I couldn't tell if it was a sigh or a muted laugh.

"When you got into Chrysler's server, SubSonique said you chose to look for me instead of finding out about your family. Is that true?"

Hearing her say it made my teeth ache. Then I realized how hard I was clenching my jaw.

"That is a fact."

Again, everything went silent except in my head, where there were too many voices reminding me of the mistakes I'd made. Then Connie's silhouette stepped into view on the other side of the bars, though her facial features were impossible to make out.

"Logan, are you okay?"

I didn't have an answer. I knew I wasn't hurt physically, but I also knew I was definitely not okay. Instead, I shifted the focus away from me.

"Elena is unconscious. I can't wake her up."

"Can you get her closer to the door?"

“I can,” I answered honestly. “I don’t know that I should.”

Connie rested both of her wrists on the rusted metal, her hands inside the cell. “I wouldn’t trust me either. But if someone was coming to hurt you, it would be SubSonique or one of Mom’s guards.”

Hearing Connie call Necros “Mom” made my stomach flip-flop. Either that or I was hungry. We hadn’t eaten since the Dunkin’ Donuts that morning.

“I don’t know, Connie . . . or Khan. I don’t even know what to call you now.”

“I’m used to people calling me Connie. Cryoborg’s the one who chose the fake last name *DeWitt* since my code name is Conduit. He’s like Gil that way—loves a good pun and loves a bad pun even more.”

“You have a supervillain name?”

Connie sighed and turned away from the door, leaning against the bars.

“You make it sound like I’m some Big Bad in a D&D campaign. I just wanted to be a part of my mom’s life, Logan. She is all the family I have ever known, and she needed me. I spent most of the last ten years at different boarding schools, always moving around, never seeing my mother for more than a couple of days at a time. She never asked me to do anything for her except heal up Dr. Chrysler a bit. She said she was keeping me away for my own protection. I begged her for years to let me help, so when she finally gave me a mission—getting close to you—it felt good to be asked. I felt important. But it got . . . complicated."

"Why?" I asked. "Your plan worked."

"How about when you saved my life on the bus? Or in the alley, when you were more worried about me than yourself? It sounds dumb, but you actually cared about me, and I started to like . . . I mean, I kinda started caring about you too. That was never part of any plan. So, when New Orleans went wrong, I thought it was over. But then you screwed everything up again."

I'd made so many mistakes, I wasn't sure which screwup she was referring to.

"Which screwup are you referring to?"

"You cracked Chrysler's password! Suddenly, SubSonique was telling Mom that MASC knew about the Reclamation. She also spilled the tea on Elena being an SGCR charging station. Suddenly, Mom and Chrysler wanted both of you. I was going to tell them to just let you both go, but before I could, you two gave MASC the slip and came here. All they had to do was sit back and wait."

As I listened, I couldn't dispute anything she was saying. We had made it way too easy for them.

Connie turned back around to face the bars, her eyes cast toward the floor. "I told you not to trust me too much, Logan."

"I figured you were telling me to be less gullible. I

didn't realize you were hinting that you were working for the most powerful supervillain on the planet."

Connie's eyes snapped up to me and narrowed.

"That's MASC propaganda! My mother is fighting for me and Elena and everyone like us, so we don't have to conceal who we really are. You know how that feels. I know you do. Logan, you're not like other people. You're honest, you're real, and you're not trying to be anyone but who you are, even though there's a world full of people trying to change you. The joke is, everyone should be more like you, not the other way around. Why should you have to get questions wrong on a test so no one knows you're special? Why should any of us have to hide what we can do?"

I thought about her questions. They were ones I had asked myself more than once.

"I'm not sure. But if it keeps the people I care about from getting hurt, I'll do it."

"I don't want anyone to get hurt either," Connie replied, reaching her hand through the bars. "So let me help. Okay?"

I'm not sure if I trusted Connie in that moment, or just wanted to trust her.

I do know that I took Elena's cuffed wrists and extended her hands toward the cell door until her fingertips touched Connie's.

In the low light, trickles of energy cascaded down Connie's hand into Elena for just a few seconds. Then Connie's arm dropped as she braced herself and let out an uncomfortable exhale.

Immediately, Elena's breathing quickened and her eyelids started to flutter. But before she regained consciousness, I heard Connie stand and push away from the door.

"I'm sorry, Logan. But think about what I said. Because if you helped my mother, maybe she could finally stop fighting and we all could stop pretending."

Connie's footsteps echoed off the granite as she retreated down the hall. I kept listening as they faded, until Elena's voice broke the quiet.

"What's going on?"

7:57 A.M.
MONDAY, DECEMBER 6

Are you a heavy sleeper or a light sleeper? According to a 2010 sleep study by Thien Thanh Dang-Vu, Scott M. McKinney, Orfeu M. Buxton, Jo M. Solet, and Jeffrey M. Ellenbogen, the answer to that question depends on the brain's thalamocortical rhythms. But after years living as an orphan, I can confirm that you can learn to sleep through almost anything if you have to: noisy roommates, arguing foster parents, even excessive farting.

But sleeping in a Civil War–era cell, assuming I was about to be tortured by supervillains, is different.

When Elena first regained consciousness, she was worried that Connie wasn't with us. After I explained to her that Connie was Necros's daughter and a spy, Elena was no longer worried. She was furious.

All she wanted was to tear the cell door down and go after Connie, but as soon as she tried to activate her powers to break us out, the handcuffs on her wrists started humming and Elena got super weak again. I reasoned that they must be miniature versions of the SGCR collector she'd been locked inside, but Elena refused to admit defeat. She tried to use her powers again one more time when guards brought us a bit of food and water. That time, she ended up nearly unconscious.

"I just need to rest a little. Then I'll get us out of here," Elena promised as she lay on the cot. Less than a minute later, it was clear she was asleep.

I lay down on the other cot and tried to sleep too, but every time there was a buzz in my ear or a shadow shifted on the wall, my heart raced and I recited Canadian census figures.

By the time the first rays of sunlight crept through the barred window, I was neither rested nor optimistic. So, when I heard heavy footsteps stop outside our door, I woke Elena, hoping she would be a bit steadier than the night before.

"I'm fine," she insisted as she started to stand, but then I caught her looking down at the cuffs and settling back onto the cot as the guard unlocked the door.

The soldier stepped inside, looming in the doorway with his helmet's visor down and his plasma rifle hanging by his side, inches from his hand.

"You're free to go."

My brain whirred, trying to comprehend the words:

1. I was sleep-deprived and had misheard his command.
2. I was still sleeping and this was a dream.
3. I was so anxious that my brain was replacing actual words with the words I wanted to hear.
4. Necros's newest superpower was pranking.

While I was sorting through these options, Elena managed to speak.

"What did you say?"

"You're free . . . to . . . go?" The guard said it like a question this time and began to shake his head until I heard another voice, but this one was inside my brain and it was Margie's.

Hold the door for them.

The guard's posture straightened and then he held the door.

Elena slowly rose to her feet. "Is this real?"

"If it isn't, I don't see how it could make our situation any worse."

Elena took the lead and stepped outside the cell, looking cautiously both ways. A beat later, she motioned for me. I inched out into the hall and then made a sudden, not-at-all-tough-sounding noise when Gil appeared in a flash right in front of me.

"Logan! Elena! You're okay!"

Gil awkwardly threw his arms around us. You're aware I am not usually comfortable with physical displays of affection, but it seemed appropriate and kinda felt good in the moment.

Hand over your keys and go lie down in the cell.

That was Margie's voice, which was soft and friendly in my mind, but must have been more persuasive in the guard's head. Necros's soldier handed Gil his keys and proceeded to lie down on Elena's cot.

Gil locked the cell and led us up the hall to where Margie was waiting in a shadowy alcove near the edge of the courtyard. The second I was within reach, she snatched me off the ground and gave me a hug that compressed several of my internal organs.

"I am soooooooooo mad at you, Logan!" Margie grumbled as she squeezed me even tighter. I felt something warm and wet on one of my cheeks and realized they were Margie's silver tears, rolling off her face and onto mine. That may sound a little gross, but I wasn't thinking about how unsanitary it was. I was too busy feeling ashamed for having made her cry.

After several seconds of pressure and tears, Margie released me.

"Do you have any idea how worried we've been?" Margie demanded before turning to Elena. "And your parents too. They called, asking if you were at our house. We covered for you."

"How did you find us?" I asked. "Did you reenlist with MASC and use their facial recognition software or hack into the TSA records of our flight?"

"We used the Find My Kid's Phone app," Gil volunteered, holding up his own smartphone that showed a map with a pulsing green dot on the island where we were. "It seemed *app*ropriate considering the situation."

The combination of Gil's pun and the normalcy of having my phone tracked by my foster parents made me almost forget how life-threatening the situation was.

"But how . . . or why . . . how and why did you find Necros?" Gil wondered. "You outsmarted all of MASC, for what?"

"I wasn't smart at all." That was a fact, but I knew I had to tell them more. "I was convinced that Necros was my birth mother and that I could rescue Connie and learn the truth. But the truth is, she's Connie's mother, not mine. Connie was never my friend. It was all just a trap."

"Logan, why didn't you just tell . . . ?" Margie started, her face questioning and her hands raised in what looked like frustration. But then her expression changed, the corners of her eyes and mouth drooping as she laid her hands on my shoulders. "Of course you didn't tell us. How could you?"

"Were you . . . I mean . . . Did you want Necros to be your birth mother?"

That was Gil, asking the question I realized I hadn't

had the courage to ask myself yet. But I owed them an answer.

"A part of me did. But I don't think it was ever about wanting her as a parent. Being her son would've meant I wasn't abandoned because I wasn't worth keeping. It would've meant I was special."

I was staring at my own feet as I said those words, but Margie dropped to a knee to look me in the eyes and refused to speak until I looked back at her.

"You are special, Logan. You are special to *us*, and it has nothing to do with your memories or who your birth parents might be. We love you, the person you are."

I felt one tear escape each eye, despite my best efforts. "I wish I'd told you before I messed everything up so badly," I explained, because I really did. "I'm sorry."

"It's okay. Well . . . it's *going* to be okay," Gil corrected himself, "assuming we can figure a way off this island. It's not like I can carry all of you."

"You don't have an escape plan?" Elena asked, her eyebrows disappearing behind her bangs.

"We had no idea we were going to find you inside Necros's lair. We just thought you'd run away. It was everything we could do to give MASC the slip and come after you," Margie explained, turning to Elena. "We're not part of MASC anymore, but you are. The tracker in your earring should alert them."

"I kinda took it off at the airport," Elena admitted,

brushing back her hair to reveal her ears with no jewelry on them.

"What about the emergency code on your phone? That should still work," Gil pointed out.

Elena frowned as she pulled a molten brick of glass and metal from her pocket. "It kinda got fried in this crazy cell I was in."

"So that's it, then," Margie said decidedly. "The three of us protecting Logan against Necros's entire army."

"Actually, just the two of you. I'm useless." Elena held up the heavy cuffs on her wrists. "These suck up SGCR. If I try to use my powers, I pass out."

"Then we better get them off you right away," Margie said, more like a mother noticing her child wearing muddy shoes than a superhero offering to remove high-tech power-stealing shackles. She pointed to an old iron cannon just past the hallway's exit into the courtyard. "There. Put your hands on either side of that."

Elena kneeled so the center of the cuffs lay across the back of the gun. Margie positioned herself alongside and raised one hand high as her entire body shimmered silver.

But before she could bring her fist down, something else metallic appeared behind Elena, materializing out of the long shadows cast by the morning sun.

Shadow Paladin.

His armored arms wrapped around Elena and as he dragged her back into the shadows, he shouted, "Intruders!"

8:27 A.M.
MONDAY, DECEMBER 6

People hate Monday mornings. That is a fact, which is confirmed by the twenty-five-million results you get in .56 seconds when you perform a Google search for "Monday morning memes." However, I would say that Gil, Margie, Elena, and I were officially having a worse Monday morning than most.

After vanishing, Elena reappeared in Shadow Paladin's grasp on the other side of the courtyard. Then Necros's guards started streaming out of doors to surround us. The sounds of boots on granite echoed in the halls behind us. And if that wasn't bad enough, SubSonique stepped out of a hallway a hundred yards away, surveyed the scene, and then shouted, "Ain't no dance party without me!"

With a flourish, she stomped her foot in a rhythm and each time she did, the ground cracked in a line coming straight toward us.

"This is not good."

That was Gil, abandoning the puns for understatement.

"Get Logan somewhere safer and then go help Elena," Margie ordered as her whole body went molten metallic and she crouched like an Olympic sprinter. "I'll take care of SubSonique."

Gil gave a nod and scooped me up as Margie ran at SubSonique. The ground between them was now jumping and fracturing in rhythm, but Margie bounded across the icy, broken lawn like it was a video game.

Suddenly, I lost sight of her as I went whipping up to the top of the fort wall courtesy of Gil.

"I need you to stay hidden until you see an opening and then get as far away from the fight as you can. Do you understand?"

I nodded because I did understand. Gil, Margie, and Elena were outnumbered and would be at even more of a disadvantage if they had to protect me too. But the idea of leaving them felt wrong. None of them would be there if it wasn't for me. As I thought about that fact, all the guilt and anger inside me came flooding back and I started listing off all the countries in the United Nations in order of population.

Gil noticed and put his hand on my shoulder. "I know

you're feeling a lot right now. But the best way to help us fight is for you to be safe. I need you to do the right thing, son."

Three things struck me about what Gil said:

1. It was the first time he had ever said anything fatherly to me without stuttering or making a dad joke.
2. It was the first time he called me "son."
3. He was right.

In a flash, Gil was down in the courtyard, delivering lightning-fast elbows and fists to commandos as he streaked back into the battle.

I was running too, staying as low as possible. The fort's southern wall had become overgrown with scrubby bushes over the centuries, so I was trying to hide among the frosty shrubs as I looked for a way back down to the docks. But before I got too far, I heard a voice bellowing from the courtyard.

"Why dost thou struggle so? 'Tis an exercise in futility!"

Peering over the edge of the wall, I saw Elena staggering away from Shadow Paladin, free of his grasp but still in the handcuffs. He drew his black blade and advanced, every few steps swiping it at the shadows nearby, unleashing shadow shards that pursued Elena. Each time one got near, Elena's hands flashed. It was enough to dissolve the shards, but with each burst of light, she faltered until she finally collapsed to the ground with Shadow Paladin towering over her.

"Yield, young maiden, or meet thy end."

And then there was a low booming from SubSonique. When I pivoted to look, across the courtyard, Margie was frozen ten feet away from the supervillainess, unable to move as the sound waves trapped her, forcing her to sway in place with the rhythm.

It looked hopeless. My only chance was to do what Gil had ordered: get as far away as possible and hope that there might be a boat, or at least a way to signal the mainland for help. But before I could even consider options, a pair of commandos emerged from the nearest stairway, weapons trained on me.

"Put your hands up!"

Reluctantly, I did what they demanded.

"Enough!"

Necros's voice echoed through the fortress and everything stopped. SubSonique's beats diminished to a low whisper. The plasma blasts ceased.

Necros stepped into the sunlight with Connie and Dr. Chrysler at her sides.

"Quicksilver Siren, Ultra-Quantum, one last time, I offer you a choice. The Reclamation is already in motion, but, like your former allies, you could make this revolution stronger. With Logan's help and your leadership, we could recruit hundreds more to join us and declare their independence. And with the rare radiation coursing through your DNA, Elena Arguello, you could give me the gift of being able to hold my children again. You all will have my gratitude . . . and your lives need not be wasted serving these mere mortals."

Necros held her chin high as her words echoed off the walls of the fort. But when I looked to Connie, the body language was very different. Her mouth was tight and her hands were stuffed into her pockets.

Dr. Chrysler took a step forward, looking so frail I wondered if a breeze might blow him over. "Margie and Gil, we know you're alone. SubSonique relayed everything you've said to Logan since you rescued him. You're here with no support. You've left MASC. Think of what your life with Logan could be with no restrictions."

"Listen to Dr. Chrysler," Necros added with finality. "This is your last chance to join us."

That's when Margie started to laugh. What started as a light chuckle grew to a full-fledged giggle. Neuroscientist Sophie Scott delivered an entire TED talk in 2015 about why people laugh at inappropriate times; but the more Margie laughed, the less convinced I was that she felt it was inappropriate.

"You think I am joking?" Necros asked, clipping her words.

"Not at all," Margie replied, quieting her giggles. "But all of you assuming Gil and I would forget about Sub-Sonique's spyware is pretty funny. And you know what's even more hilarious? The idea that only supervillains know how to set traps."

As the words left her mouth, the air filled with a distant thundering that grew by the second. From atop the wall, I looked out across the foggy harbor and watched as a half-dozen black, heavily armed helicopters exploded out of the mist. And when I looked back down to Margie, she was slipping something out of a hidden pouch on her belt.

My noise-canceling headphones.

"Enough talking!" Margie shouted, as she slid the headphones on and looked right at SubSonique. "You want to dance? Let's dance."

8:33 A.M.
MONDAY, DECEMBER 6

I wish I had my own pair of noise-canceling headphones for what happened next because it was so loud and chaotic, I felt myself physically twitching with each boom or blast.

With a single leap, Margie was up in SubSonique's face, her fists silver streaks. SubSonique dodged out of the way with fight techniques that looked more like break-dance moves. As she spun on her back, a wave of sound rippled out and nearly toppled Margie as the ground under her feet turned into a sinkhole.

Two battalions of MASC commandos came rappelling out of the sky, spraying force blasts at Necros's soldiers. I dove out of the way and managed to avoid the crossfire, but I ended up lying on my belly right at the edge of the wall overlooking the courtyard.

Directly below, Elena was still on her knees, exhausted and helpless with Shadow Paladin looming over her, his lightless sword poised to strike.

"'Parting is such sweet sorrow.'"

It was odd that Shadow Paladin was quoting act 2, scene 2 of *Romeo and Juliet*, arguably Shakespeare's most romantic play, while he was getting ready to kill Elena. But I didn't have time to point this out before the blade arced down toward Elena's head.

I almost looked away, but the instant before it made contact, Elena raised her hands so the sword hit the link between her handcuffs instead. There was a sudden spark that forced Shadow Paladin back a few feet; and by the time he regained his bearings, Elena was standing, her wrists finally freed.

"My turn."

Elena's hands raged with energy. She pulled the remaining pieces of the handcuffs off like they were made of wet toilet paper. Then she launched herself at Shadow Paladin, driving him back into the shadows, forcing him to reappear twenty feet away in another dark corner.

"Fight me!" Elena shouted as she sprinted after him, only to see him repeat his teleportation trick again and again, emerging momentarily to swing his sword and then dematerializing back into the blackness. As long as there were shadows, he'd be just about impossible to catch.

I considered options for eliminating the shadows:

1. A surprise solar eclipse.
2. Floodlights filling every corner of the courtyard.
3. A rainstorm, or at least clouds, to diffuse the sunlight.

They all sounded dumb and/or impossible at first, but then I realized the last one might have potential.

"Elena!" I yelled over the din of the battle. "Melt the snow!"

I wasn't sure if she fully understood my suggestion, but to her credit, she gave it a try, dodging Shadow Paladin's next sword thrust and planting both of her glowing hands into a snowbank at the base of the wall. An instant fog cloud formed all around her as the snow evaporated. It made it a little harder to see her, but the shadows grew less defined as the sunlight filtered through the vapor.

Elena got the strategy at that point. Instead of throwing punches at Shadow Paladin, she ran, jumped, dive rolled, and cartwheeled from snowbank to snowbank, plunging her fists into each. Within thirty seconds, the entire courtyard was enveloped in a low-hanging fog.

From on top of the wall, the details of what happened next were impossible to make out. But I was able to follow a pair of fist-sized light sources streaking through the mist. After a half-dozen metallic thuds, I heard the clatter of armor falling to the ground. When the fog lifted a little, Shadow Paladin was unconscious at Elena's feet, his lightless black sword shattered nearby.

Elena looked up to me and flashed a smile. I was about to try and return the grin when a rumbling from the far side of the fort grabbed my attention.

Margie had maneuvered behind SubSonique and was squeezing her arms to her sides. Having just been hugged by Margie, I knew this grip was unbreakable, at least for normal humans.

"Let me go!" SubSonique bellowed, and when she did, destructive sound waves filled the courtyard, shaking the foundations of the buildings. Necros's guards, MASC commandos, and even Dr. Chrysler and Connie had to fight to stay upright, but Necros didn't move an inch. She surveyed the battle intently, like she did not approve of what was transpiring.

"Can you do anything to muffle her?"

That was Gil, who had just materialized next to Margie.

Margie looked around until she spotted a heavy metal anchor that was as tall as I am.

"You need a little quiet time," Margie announced in her most stern, substitute teacher voice as she body-slammed SubSonique facedown into the frozen turf with the force of a dozen pro wrestlers. Before SubSonique could even think of getting up, Margie dragged the anchor over, leaving a deep groove in the earth, and laid it across SubSonique's back and neck, pinning her facedown with her lips pressed to the ground. Her sonic shrieks were muffled, but as they penetrated the ground, the earth vibrated and new sinkholes started appearing across the courtyard.

Margie leapt away to get clear of the crumbling earth underfoot, but as soon as she landed, something rocketed into her side, slamming her into a wall that cracked on impact. I called out to Margie, but she looked unconscious and there was a flattened hunk of metal lying next to her.

When I turned back in the direction the projectile had come from, there was Necros, holding a cannonball in her hand like it was nothing. Her expression had changed. Even I could tell she was angry.

"You fools! Now, you answer to me!"

According to baseballamerica.com, the fastest pitch ever thrown by a major league pitcher was on September 24, 2010, when Aroldis Chapman unleashed a fastball that was recorded as 105.8 miles per hour. But a baseball weighs just over five ounces. Considering what Necros did next with forty-pound cannonballs, I can only imagine what the Dodgers would pay to sign her to a contract.

Again and again, Necros reared back and flung the iron balls at MASC soldiers, forcing them to dive for cover as the walls shattered with each impact. On top of all that chaos, the ground was crumbling throughout the courtyard as SubSonique's screams were destabilizing the entire island.

I was in the midst of considering the merits of trying to hide or trying to help when the stone wall under me collapsed. Then I was free-falling toward the courtyard.

I hadn't even landed when a giant chunk of rock bashed into me and pain exploded up my arm as I felt the bone snap. I broke my arm once before—when I was nine during a failed attempt to learn how to skateboard—so I knew immediately what had happened. But before I could react, my legs crunched into the stony ground below and the agony doubled. And then I saw it. A small boulder falling right toward my head. I assume it hit me. I don't know for sure because last thing I remember is that everything went black.

8:41 A.M.
MONDAY, DECEMBER 6

The pain is what woke me, but not in the way I was expecting. My arm was throbbing and both legs were bent the wrong ways, plus the term "a splitting headache" was literal, considering the deep gash I had on my skull. Blood was oozing down my face, and I felt like I was leaving my body. But then suddenly, the pain started getting less and less. I wasn't immediately sure where it was going, but I didn't care. I was just so grateful.

I looked down and witnessed my legs unbending back to the way legs were supposed to look. My fingers started tingling, and I realized I could move my whole arm. When the pain in my head had diminished a little, I reached up to wipe away the blood, and the first thing I saw was Connie with her hand on my cheek.

"What . . . ?"

I only got one word out before she moved her hand over my mouth, which quieted me while still giving me the benefits of her powers.

"I didn't know it would be like this, Logan. I don't know what I thought it would be . . . but not this."

Connie's voice was hoarse and almost didn't sound like her. Maybe it was because healing me took effort or maybe it was all the rock dust from the collapsed wall. But from the way she was looking at me, I thought she probably was just upset and maybe even sorry.

"Khan! Come back to me this instant!"

Necros's voice boomed out through the fort, rising above the chaotic sounds of fighting and people in pain. Her voice sounded frustrated and impatient. It was a tone I'd come to recognize from Margie on occasion.

"Run, Logan," Connie urged as I felt my skin healing over with a sensation that simultaneously felt like an itch and a breeze. "Find Gil and Margie and Elena and get as far away as you can. Do you understand?"

I nodded because I did understand. I just wasn't sure why she was saying it, or if it was even possible.

"I wish you and I could've . . . I don't know. I just wish it was different. I'm sorry."

Connie took her hand away from my face, and then leaned down and touched her lips to mine. To be clear, my lips were totally covered with blood and bits of granite dust, so I assume it must have been deeply unpleasant. But it still counts as my first kiss. That is a fact.

I don't know if I technically kissed her back, though I think I kept my lips from going totally rigid. I was just so unprepared for it to be happening at all, but at the same time, I suddenly understood what she meant when she said things had gotten "complicated." It was a good word for it.

I was still rethinking every conversation we'd had again—from our first meeting to holding hands in New Orleans—when Connie stood and ran back toward Necros, picking her way around the sinkholes that were opening throughout the courtyard.

It was only after she was gone that I noticed a MASC commando, lying totally still, only a few feet away in the rocky rubble on the other side of where Connie had been. Moving closer, I recognized it was Sergeant Bricker, her broken and bloody hand outstretched in my direction, her skin withered, eyes gaunt and hollow like she had been sucked dry. The realization was immediate and sickening.

My injuries were gone and Sergeant Bricker was dead. Connie had been the conduit between us and taken a life to save mine.

"Logan!"

That was Gil, appearing next to me. He helped me to my feet, inspecting my face. "You're bleeding!"

But I wasn't. Not anymore.

"Not anymore. I'm fine. But Sergeant Bricker . . ."

I gestured to the body on the ground and Gil looked down. His expression hardened.

"Where's Mom? Is she okay?"

Instead of answering, Gil broke from looking at the body and snatched me up, whipping across the courtyard while dodging blasts and cannonballs. A second later, we found Margie leaned up against a pillar, out of Necros's firing line. She was still silver from head to toe, but her rib cage looked dented like a car after a crash.

"Your face." She wheezed the words out, trying to stand upright, but unable to do it. I tried to comfort her with facts as she slid back down.

"It looks worse than it is. Connie healed me. She also kissed me. They happened very close together but were not the same thing."

For a moment, Margie's silver expression changed from a muddled mixture of pain and worry to a clear look of surprise, with both eyebrows raised in the middle. I noted it and continued.

"She said we have to run, and while I still don't know if I trust her, I do believe her in this case. We need to find Elena and get somewhere safe."

Gil's head whipped around, scanning the fort. "I don't think she's looking to leave."

I swung around the pillar and saw where Gil was looking. Elena was on the other side of the courtyard. With a strength I didn't know she had, Elena picked up a fifteen-foot piece of a broken metal flagpole and brandished it like a club.

"Necros!"

Elena's voice rang out, and as it did, pure yellow light blazed from her eyes and the tips of her hair.

Necros sneered at Elena, and with a single powerful stride, she hurled a cannonball at a speed I could barely track. But Elena clearly could, because she swung the flagpole, knocking the cannonball away to the side. The pole snapped in the middle on impact, but Elena held on to the rest and pointed it at Necros.

"You're gonna pay for what you did to Luther. You're going to pay for everyone you've hurt."

"Foolish child," Necros replied, glowering down her perfect nose at Elena. "Stonefist died because he dared to touch me. And if it's vengeance you seek, you'll find the same fate."

I watched as the light radiating from Elena dimmed a bit for a moment, and I thought she might be reconsidering her plan. She wasn't.

"I don't need to touch you," Elena said calmly, before

her whole body erupted in the same yellow energy, "to kick your butt!"

The words were still echoing off the walls as Elena bolted forward, the flagpole in both hands. The ferocity of her attack must have surprised Necros a little, because she only barely dodged Elena's first swing. However, by the second time Elena tried, Necros had regained her footing and ducked under it smoothly.

Then Necros went on the offensive, lunging at Elena with her ungloved hands slashing through the air, trying to make contact. But Elena used the pole to keep her distance and counterstrike.

Elena caught Necros with a glancing blow to the shoulder, causing her to seethe as she shook off the pain. A few parries later, Elena sidestepped Necros's rush and delivered a punishing shot to her ribs that made her howl with anger. That rage pushed Necros to charge recklessly, and Elena reared back like a power hitter and connected with a swing that sent Necros flying into the fort's wall. The granite buckled on impact as the whole fort shook.

It didn't seem possible, but Elena was doing it. She was beating Necros.

Dr. Chrysler rounded up a squadron of Necros's guards and rallied to her side, forming a protective perimeter. They escorted Connie into their ranks, but she kept her distance from her mother. I was too far away to tell if she looked scared *of* her or worried *for* her. It may have been both.

"We have to retreat." Dr. Chrysler moved closer to Necros, pleading with her. "Think of the larger plan. The Reclamation. This battle—"

"This battle is *not* over and I do not retreat!" Necros declared as she pushed herself away from the impact crater in the wall. "I will not run ever again. This child knows nothing. She *is* nothing. I am death. I . . . am . . . Necros!"

8:47 A.M.
MONDAY, DECEMBER 6

The American poet and writer Maya Angelou famously said, "When people show you who they are, believe them." Ms. Kondrat had it printed on a poster at ESTO, so it always stuck with me, even more than most things stick with me. As someone who appreciates concrete facts, I feel it is solid advice. Like when we meet someday, this thing I'm writing will show I'm someone who has been thinking about you for a long time. And when Gil and Margie resigned from MASC, that showed me they really did want to be my parents more than anything else.

I say this because in that moment in the fort, Necros didn't just tell everyone she was death. She showed it.

Without hesitation, she grabbed two of her own guards by their necks, her delicate fingers finding the skin below their helmets and collecting their life force from them. In less than a second, both were gone. Their skin turned gray; their bodies limp as they collapsed to the ground.

"Mother, no!"

That was Connie, but it had no effect. Before any of the other guards had even turned, Necros laid her hands on two more, as her entire body radiated a dark energy. The last four guards realized what was going on, but too late. None was even able to fire a shot in defense before Necros had taken their life force for herself.

"What are you doing?" Dr. Chrysler begged, his already pale skin blanching. "I thought you understood this isn't the way. These are your men. They were here to protect you!"

Necros, despite being shorter than Dr. Chrysler, stood with a poise and power that made him appear tiny.

"What I understand is that these mere mortals are nothing. There are billions just like them littering this planet. I do not require protection, or your counsel. Only the power to see my will done."

Dr. Chrysler gasped, and that's when I saw Necros had taken his hand in hers. What little life force the elderly scientist had left was gone. His body fell, almost too light to even make a sound.

"Now," Necros asked, turning her attention back toward Elena, "where were we?"

Elena answered with an attack. She long-jumped over a sinkhole that was widening at the center of the courtyard, planted her foot on a massive rock, and launched herself into the air, the flagpole overhead like a barbarian's club.

But Necros didn't dodge. Instead, she raised both hands and caught the strike, only inches from her face. The muscles in her forearms and shoulders tensed and held, while Elena landed a half-dozen feet away, gripping the other end of the pole.

I could hear the metal groaning, but neither of the combatants was making a sound, silently locked in a tug-of-war.

That's when Necros leaned in, closing her eyes as she let the metal touch her chest. I watched the dark energy that had grown each time she stole a life, spreading down the flagpole. Necros was channeling her power, sending it toward Elena.

"Elena! Let go!" I called out. It was the only thing I could think to do.

But instead of letting go, Elena dug her feet into the unstable ground and unleashed her own energy. Her entire body erupted with brilliant light, and as it did, the radiation infused the metal, surging up the pole back at Necros.

As their two energies neared each other, the air hummed with static. It felt like all the oxygen was being sucked in toward the point where the dark and light intersected.

The humming swelled to a roar and people instinctively scrambled to get away. MASC soldiers and Necros's guards fled through doors or clambered into helicopters. Even Connie, who had been slowly backing away from her mother, retreated behind the nearest barrier.

But I couldn't will my feet to move, and I wasn't about to leave Elena.

The charge in the air spiked all at once, and then I felt something grip my collar and drag me back behind the pillar next to Margie on the ground.

It was Gil, standing over us.

"Stay down. It's gonna—"

That's all he got out before a shock wave of blinding light and concussive force blew him into particles and everything went white.

??? A.M.
MONDAY, DECEMBER 6

I have no real sense of how long I was unconscious. I think it was minutes, but if you told me it was hours, I couldn't disprove it. All I know was that after everything went white, I saw something that I've never seen before.

I saw the day I became an orphan.

It wasn't clear like the rest of my memories. But through a gauzy haze, I remembered standing in the middle of LAX, my point of view only two feet above the smooth, tiled floor. Our mother was sitting in a seat just a few feet away. She was holding a baby in her arms. She was holding you.

I couldn't see her face from my angle, but her hair was dark and curly, like mine, falling past her shoulders as she shook her head once and then again, the way a person does when they're trying to clear their mind or shoo a buzzing insect.

Then she stood, holding you in one arm while she strapped a diaper bag over her other, and she walked away without looking back.

But you did. With your tiny face poking up over her shoulder, you looked back at me, and our eyes met. You didn't cry, but you didn't look away either.

I felt the younger version of myself trying to call out to her. Trying to speak. Why was it so hard to make a noise?

Finally, the need built up until a noise erupted from me. A cry.

And then I was awake, lying on the chipped granite. The cry I heard was Margie, calling out.

"Gil?!"

I sat up and it took me a moment to understand what I was seeing.

Margie was limping around what was left of the fort, shouting into the air. The far end of the courtyard was blown apart like an ancient ruin or a bomb site. The area around me was crumbling, though I could see one thin piece of the pillar Margie and I had been behind was still intact. It was roughly in the shape of Margie's back, like she had held it up herself.

And in the middle of the courtyard—there was no

middle of the courtyard. Instead, there was a thirty-foot-deep crater that cut through several levels of the fortress hidden below. Approaching the edge, I saw that at the very bottom, seawater was starting to rise, and just above the waterline, there were two people, lying only ten feet from each other: Necros and Elena.

Neither was moving.

Low whooshes filled the air as several of MASC's choppers reappeared overhead, swooping in to evacuate anyone they could find. But there was another noise rising from below me too. The ground was vibrating underfoot as millions of gallons of the bay filled the belly of the subterranean hideout.

A flash of movement caught my eye, and from the far side of the crater, I saw someone sliding down. It was Connie, her black-on-black outfit turned gray with granite dust. She scrambled down the rocks toward the bottom, and when I looked back to Elena, I saw the cold water lapping at her ankles and she started to stir.

Elena's eyes fluttered open as Connie arrived by Necros's side, pulling up short, clearly afraid to touch her.

"Mother, wake up!" she pleaded, but Necros didn't move. Elena was still getting her bearings when she noticed Connie and Necros. At first, Elena's hands balled into fists, tensing for another fight. But after a moment of watching Connie crouched and crying over her mother, I could see Elena relax. She got to her knees and moved closer, extending a hand and gently touching Connie's shoulder.

"Connie . . . I'm sorry."

Without looking up, Connie laid her own hand on Elena's.

"No, you're not. But you will be."

Before Elena could react, Connie's other hand shot out and touched Necros's chest.

The effect was immediate. Pulses of life energy poured out of Elena, through Connie's arms, and down into Necros's heart. The first wave made both Elena and Connie gasp, sucking in as much of the cold ocean air as their lungs could hold. The second caused Elena's body to go rigid as her internal powers flared for a moment, but then fluttered like a candle about to go out. The third was so strong that Connie involuntarily let go with both hands as smoke rose from between her fingers.

Elena fell back to the dirt, motionless again. But a heartbeat later, Necros's eyes opened and found Connie, heaving deep breaths and on the verge of unconsciousness, her hands blackened and burned from the transfer.

"My child."

That was it. Those were the only words Necros spoke before producing a pair of black gloves from somewhere in her gown and picking up Connie in her arms. With her daughter held out in front of her, Necros looked up at me for only a moment. Then she picked her way across the crater to an opening into a lower level of the lair and vanished into the shadows.

"Logan!" Margie's voice called out to me from behind. She was down on one knee next to Gil. At least, it looked like it might be Gil. His molecules were struggling to re-form through whatever radioactive interference was still in the air. Neither of them was in any shape to help Elena.

It was up to me, which was not ideal.

Sliding on my butt, I descended into the crater, a cascade of dirt and rocks following me down. With water rushing in below, it felt like the island was being reclaimed by the sea, but I kept my focus on Elena.

When I got to her, I put both hands on her arm and felt her skin was still several degrees warmer than mine. As the water rose and the ground around me turned to mud, I did the only thing I could: loop my arms under Elena's armpits and start pulling her.

In movies, people can always lift another person up or at least drag them when they're unconscious. In real life, it's so much harder than that. I would hoist Elena two feet up the crater, but then the rocks would slide down a foot, the water would rise a foot, and I wasn't sure we'd moved at all. But that wasn't the worst of it.

With every second, the crater was getting wider as the sinkhole ate away at the ground from underneath. Huge chunks of the fort started sliding down into the pit. Across the way, waves had started slopping over the edge of what used to be the east side of the island.

I gave one final heave to pull Elena's feet away from the water and my arms gave out as I flopped back against the slope. Above and behind me, a wall was now teetering over the mouth of the crater. I knew that would be it. If we didn't drown, we'd be crushed. All I could do was wrap my arms around Elena as words flew out of my mouth. But they weren't random. They were every word of our first meeting, Elena's and mine, out in front of the house on Kittyhawk Circle. I was so cold, but holding on to Elena and reciting how our friendship started, at least felt a little warm.

That's when something blocked out the sun; the silhouette of a chopper, with someone on the skid, waving to us. I waved back and a second later, the figure rappelled down in one smooth, practiced maneuver, his combat boots planting into the crumbling surface next to us.

I looked up, past the boots, past the matching burgundy camouflage cargo pants and flak jacket, all the way up to Colonel Gdula's grinning face. He took the nub of his still-smoldering cigar out of his mouth, flicked it into the rising salt water, and looked me right in the eye.

"We are officially even."

I nodded.

"We are even. That is a fact."

8:58 A.M.
MONDAY, DECEMBER 6

Have you ever gone fishing? I have not and for several reasons:

1. I've never had anyone to take me on a fishing trip.
2. Until I was six, there was some concern I might have a fish allergy.
3. Giving me a sharp hook on the end of an invisible string is likely to result in a puncture wound.
4. I have too much empathy for the fish being yanked out of the water in such an upsetting way.

That said, being yanked out of the water and up into the air by a MASC helicopter was anything but upsetting.

As Elena and I dangled from a dual harness, I scanned the ground below and saw that a second helicopter had touched down by Margie and Gil, who had finally pulled his molecules back together. With her arm draped over his shoulders, they both limped over and pulled themselves inside, seconds before the ground underneath gave way.

I couldn't see what happened next because the safety line spun me away and then there were hands on me, which I do not enjoy. But they belonged to several MASC soldiers who lifted me and then Elena into the aircraft. Immediately, a field medic checked Elena for a pulse.

"She's breathing, but just barely."

Colonel Gdula ordered the pilot back to base. However, I knew that Necros was still down there.

"Necros is still down there, Colonel! Connie healed her. They're still on the island."

"No, they aren't. Look." Colonel Gdula's tone didn't seem quite as domineering as usual, so I did what he said and watched as what was left of the fort fell into the sinkhole. Massive slabs of granite tumbled into the water, and the dirt turned to sludge as the entire land mass was swallowed up by the bay. It was like the ocean erased any evidence of the island with each swell that washed over the rubble.

"It's gone. And so is anyone down there, including Necros. You did it, son. You and Elena and your folks . . . you did it. Sit tight. It's our turn to take care of you."

My mind was reeling. I was trying to comprehend several things that had just seemed impossible, or at least unlikely, but had all happened in a matter of minutes.

Necros was gone—buried or drowned or both. So was Connie, the first girl to ever like me, and the first girl to ever betray me. Dr. Chrysler died at the hands of the one person he was betting would keep him alive indefinitely. And maybe most shockingly, Colonel Gdula was being nice.

And then the memory of my mother walking away in the airport swept them all aside. But I didn't focus on her leaving. I concentrated on the vision of your face looking back at me over her shoulder. I studied the color of your eyes, the slope of your nose, and the freckles on your right cheek. I just wanted to take it all in, knowing for the first time with certainty that you are real.

I'm used to forming memories in an instant and knowing they'll stay with me forever. But having an old memory that was brand-new like that felt different.

I was snapped out of the memory when the sun glinted off the water and I turned to look, half expecting to catch the reflection of a submarine diving beneath the green water. But there was nothing. Still, I scanned the bay, searching for evidence that maybe it wasn't over, a shadow under the surface or the narrow wake of a periscope. However, the only thing I saw was a single lobster boat on the water, with a familiar, crusty fisherman at the wheel.

Lobster Bob gave us a wave and I waved back. It seemed like the polite thing to do, even if there was zero chance he would have any memory of me within the next hour.

11:22 A.M.
MONDAY, DECEMBER 6

I must have fallen asleep in the MASC helicopter, which isn't surprising considering I'd spent the previous two nights on a plane and in a Civil War–era cell. But what was surprising was that I dreamed of you, or at least a version of you.

It was similar to the dreams I'd had when I thought Necros was my mother, but this time I was back in the houseboat and it was like nothing bad had ever happened. Margie was microwaving a bowl of oatmeal for me, one of the only things she can't mess up, and Gil was fixing a leaking faucet. But then someone walked out of the bedroom and I just knew it was you. Even though you were almost as tall as me, your eyes were the same as I remembered from that day in the airport. You smiled and said, "Good morning."

Before I could reply, my eyes opened to Gil standing over me. He was smiling too.

"Good morning. Well . . . barely morning. I didn't want to *alarm* you . . . but I figured you'd want to see Elena."

I looked around and realized I was lying in a bed in a long, semi-permanent building, like a tent with walls, alongside a dozen other beds filled with recovering MASC commandos. Some were asleep. Others were having injuries tended to. The microwave beeping in my dream had been heart monitors. The leaky faucet was the IVs hung over the beds. I had so many questions.

"Where are we? How long have I been asleep? Where is Elena? Where is Margie? Why am I wearing a hospital gown? Where are my clothes? Who took them off me?"

Gil explained we were in a temporary base and field hospital MASC had set up at an abandoned airfield. My clothes had been pretty shredded from the explosions, rockslides, and other attacks. That explained the gown. Thankfully, Gil handed me a backpack of clothes he and Margie had brought for me from California.

"Colonel Gdula wanted me to keep you here until he could debrief you, but he's busy interrogating Cryoborg, who we picked up thanks to a tip from some guy named Bob. Get dressed quick, and we can go see Elena and Margie before he knows we're gone."

Once I put on jeans and a hoodie, Gil led me outside and I noticed the weather had changed. The air was a bit warmer and there were thick, low clouds hanging over the cluster of drab tents. We walked to a smaller tent across the way and inside, there were two hospital beds, side by side, both surrounded by a lot more equipment than I'd had.

On the left was Margie. She was sitting almost upright, with oxygen tubes in her nose and a thick, reinforced bandage around her ribs.

Elena was lying down flat on the bed on the right with Dr. Augustine standing by her bedside, scanning her entire body with a device. Dr. Augustine gave me a quick wave and went back to looking after Elena. "Lay still, Lainie. I'm almost done."

"Logan! You're okay!"

That was Margie, who held out her arms, beckoning me to come to her. When I got close enough, Margie pulled me into a hug. It wasn't a very tight hug, at least for Margie, and I definitely felt her wince a little.

"Are *you* okay?" I asked, because even though her skin was skin colored, her entire right side was bruised in a way I'd never seen: green and deep purple with tinges of silver running through it all.

"I'll be fine once they can get me a magnetic cast to pull the metal in my body back into place. But look at you! Gil gets blown apart, I'm laid up, and you come through with just a few scratches. You're a lot tougher than you look."

I thought about correcting Margie, but then I looked over to Elena, whose eyes were only barely open. I found my gaze drawn to the back of her hand, where there were now four distinct, angry burn marks, one for each of Connie's fingers.

"Does it look really bad?"

That was Elena, her voice thinner than usual.

"Yes," I answered honestly. I was done holding back the truth. "It looks like you tried to backhand a barbecue."

"It may heal up just fine," Dr. Augustine offered. "When your internal SGCR levels go back up to normal—well, normal for you—your cells should regenerate quicker again. Right now, your body is recovering from something that would've killed any other person on the planet. So . . . why don't I get you a Popsicle?"

Dr. Augustine left, ostensibly to find a frozen treat for Elena. I doubt that the treatment for almost having your life force sucked out is the same as for when you have a sore throat, but I didn't point that out.

"I heard you dragged me out of a crater."

That was Elena, who had raised one eyebrow higher

than the other. I wasn't sure if it was a sign she was impressed, or if she doubted what she'd heard. It didn't really matter which, because it was my fault she was in the crater in the first place.

"It was my fault you were in the crater. If you hadn't come with me—"

"Stop," Elena spoke up, reaching out to take my hand and waiting until I looked her in the eyes. "I wanted to save Connie and find Necros too, remember? I thought I could make her pay. *That's* what landed me here. I've been so angry for weeks and now, I just want . . ."

Elena's words seemed to dry up in her throat as tears rolled down both cheeks.

I didn't know what to say. But I guess Margie did, because she reached over from her bed and rested her hand gently on top of Elena's and mine.

"It's okay, Elena. Whatever you're feeling, it's all right."

Elena relaxed her head back down into her pillow as new tears chased the first ones down her face.

"I want my mom," she said, almost too softly to hear. "I want my mom . . . here. I want her to know who I really am. I need her."

Margie's fingers tightened around Elena's.

"Then we'll help you," Gil promised. "Whatever you need, we'll make it happen together, no matter what the regulations or Colonel Gdula says."

"Ahem."

Colonel Gdula had just arrived. There was no sign of his cigar, but his customary sneer was evident.

"Already planning your next insubordination?"

Gil and Margie exchanged a look like they weren't sure who should speak first. I was not willing to wait.

"Elena wants to see her parents—both of them."

Colonel Gdula leveled his gaze at me.

"They're three thousand miles away."

"You have supersonic, supersecret jets."

The colonel crossed his arms and widened his stance.

"They're outsiders. They don't even have security clearance."

"They're Elena's parents. Whatever is the highest level of clearance, parents should be one higher. If you can't trust them . . ." I broke eye contact with Colonel Gdula and looked back to Gil and Margie, who were watching with me with an expression that it took me a few seconds to recognize.

I'm pretty sure it was pride.

"There's no if," I corrected myself. "You can trust them. And you have to."

Colonel Gdula stepped in my direction, dipped his chin, and set his jaw.

"I don't take orders, son. I give them. So, you tell me . . . after being infiltrated *again* by one of Necros's moles and *again*, having to clean up the site of a major battle that destroyed a landmark, why do I *have to* trust anyone?"

I thought about his question. And I thought about myself.

"When I was in the orphanage, I didn't trust anyone. It made me feel like I was in control. But that was a feeling, not a fact. Because you can't really control what other people are going to do or feel—unless you have mind-control powers, which most people don't. I couldn't control Gil and Margie wanting me to be their foster son. Neither could you. They just did. And that's only two people. Even though Necros is gone, there are thousands of people with superpowers all over the world who are ready to come forward and be seen. I don't know when and neither do you. You can't control that. No one can. MASC started out as the Multinational Authority for Superhuman *Coordination*. Not control. It can't be about control anymore. You need to find a way to work *with* people with powers instead trying to be an authority over them."

"What are you suggesting? A name change? We go back to just 'coordinating' the heroes and everything's fine?"

"You could try 'collaborating' or 'cooperating,'" Gil volunteered. "There are plenty of words that start with that letter . . . as you can *see* . . . you know, like the letter *c*."

Margie must have said something to him telepathically because he closed his mouth.

"Do you have any idea what it would take to totally change the way MASC works?"

"Yes," I answered, because I did. "It would take trust. A lot of it. So why not start with Elena, the person who almost died doing the one thing MASC hasn't been able to do for a century? Why not trust her—and us?"

There was a long silence. After all the explosions and shouting and helicopters, I didn't mind it.

Colonel Gdula looked at each of us, one at a time. Then he took a breath like he was about to speak.

"I found Popsicles!"

That was Dr. Augustine, bursting in from outside with two different colored Popsicles in her hands.

"I didn't bring enough for everyone. What did I miss?"

I felt myself smile. And then I heard myself laugh. And then everyone in the room was laughing a little bit. Even Colonel Gdula. It wasn't as funny as a cat video, but it was close.

The colonel let out a sigh, opened a pocket on his flak jacket sleeve, and pulled out a thin plastic tube, just under a foot long. I worried that it was a weapon or something that would wipe all our memories at once. But when Colonel Gdula removed the end cap, he tipped the tube and revealed the most obnoxiously large cigar I'd ever seen.

"I swore I would light this up only when Necros was behind bars or in the ground. I was sure I'd be the one to make it happen. But it wasn't my way of doing things that got the job done. It was you."

He pointed to me with the cigar.

"I don't want your cigar, Colonel," I replied. "The Centers for Disease Control estimates five percent of high schoolers smoke cigars at least once a month. But I—"

"Sweet peaches and cream, son! I'm not offering you my blasted cigar. I'm saying *I'm* gonna smoke it, but only because you saw things my entire team of experts missed."

Then he pointed to Gil and Margie.

"And because you came back to us—even when we didn't want to listen—and used yourselves as bait to get Necros into the open."

And finally, he gestured to Elena.

"And because you turned out to be the strongest dang hero MASC has ever put in the field. I may not like it, but facts are facts. Isn't that what you're always saying?"

"Not exactly," I pointed out. "But it's close enough."

Colonel Gdula shook his head one more time. "Well then, fact is it's time to try doing things different, which is gonna be a humongous pain in my butt. Now if you'll excuse me, I've got to get the media team going on some sort of Hollywood-related cover story for why an entire island has gone missing. But first, I'm gonna go outside, light this victory cigar, and pretend I'm enjoying it."

Colonel Gdula turned on his heel, stepped outside, and a few seconds later, the faint odor of smoke drifted into the tent. And then I heard it: a few drops of rain spattering on the roof of the tent, getting steadier and steadier, and the unmistakable sound of Colonel Gdula cursing outside.

Then, all I heard was laughter again.

5:35 P.M.
SATURDAY, DECEMBER 11

Are you a video gamer? I am not, mostly because I have never owned a gaming console and my time on computers is usually spent searching for you or watching cats who can stand like people on their hind legs when they want treats. But I've seen enough video games to know that a lot have *save points*. If you're a gamer, you totally know what that is. If you aren't, it's a place in the game where, even if you screw up badly, you can go back to it and try again without having to start over.

When Elena and her parents came over to the houseboat for a "second Thanksgiving," that's what it was like—a chance to go back and do a bunch of things right.

This time, Arturo did the cooking. The turkey was in a green mole sauce that had everyone salivating, including Bohr. The stuffing was spicy with chorizo sausage; there was a pumpkin soup; and instead of the jellied cranberry sauce, he made his own cranberry and kumquat salsa. Elena was joking and smiling as she worked with her father in the kitchen, putting it all on serving plates.

Meanwhile, Vivica sat down with Gil, Margie, and me in the living area, all huddled around the coffee table.

"Y'all ready to get this done?" she asked us as she took out a small case from her purse, with an official-looking stamp and a booklet inside. "I notarize lots of real estate deals, but this is my first adoption. Then again, this has been a week of firsts, no doubt."

I probably should have mentioned that right away. I've decided to let Gil and Margie adopt me. The more accurate statement is that I've decided I *want* to be their son.

When we got back to California, the first thing we did was get Elena home and tell her folks everything that happened. Colonel Gdula and two of his security officers were there just to make sure Vivica didn't freak out too much. Elena and Arturo apologized for keeping their powers from her; and even though Vivica thought it was a joke at first, once Arturo picked up a couch with one hand, she knew it was for real.

Elena was crying. Vivica was crying. Arturo was rubbing

his eyes and apologizing for his tears, but I explained that in a 2008 study in the *Journal of Social and Clinical Psychology*, they found having another friendly individual present during cathartic crying was optimal for receiving positive social support. He had not read that study.

Elena was still weakened from her encounter with Necros, but despite the tears, she looked happier than I'd ever seen her, especially when Colonel Gdula granted her parents security clearance—not the highest level like I'd suggested—so they could be involved in her life.

We left them to have some family time. On the ride in the MASC van back to our houseboat, Colonel Gdula shared that I would be given clearance too. It was good news, but it led to a necessary question.

"Can I access the classified files from the day I became an orphan?"

"Officially? No," Colonel Gdula responded. "But if there's something in there that can help you find your folks, I'll see what I can do."

But I didn't need to find our parents.

"I don't need to find my parents, just my sibling," I explained. "I already have parents, and *they* found me."

"Wait," Gil asked, his eyes widening. "Does that mean you might want us to adopt you?"

"No." I replied. "It means I *definitely* want you to adopt me. I want to be your son, because I know you both love me. And I love you. That is a fact."

You remember the crying thing that happened with Elena's family? It happened again in the back of the van, with Margie's silvery tears pouring out and Gil making a crying face, though nothing came out since he doesn't have bodily fluids anymore. I'm pretty sure one of the security officers teared up inside their helmet too. Colonel Gdula sniffed twice.

When we got home, Gil and Margie invited Elena's family over to have a do-over Thanksgiving and witness us signing the papers. Vivica being a notary public was just a lucky bonus that saved us a trip to the post office and fifteen dollars.

"Arturo, come over here," Vivica called to Elena's dad. "You have to be the official witness."

Arturo wiped his hands as he joined us with Elena by his side. "If you like bossing me around so much, you should've stayed married to me."

Vivica raised one eyebrow. "Maybe if you'd told me what was up from the start, I would've. It's one thing when you find a good man, but finding a *super* man is something else."

Arturo's face flushed and I saw Elena mouth the words "Oh my God!" I couldn't tell if she was happy they were getting along or embarrassed. It could have been both.

Then Gil and Margie signed the paperwork, using the names Gil Grant and Margie Morrow.

That's the other thing I should have mentioned.

With Necros gone, we're moving back to Westchester and reclaiming our old identities. I'll be back in school with Elena, which is good news except for the possibility of dealing with the Hott Diarrhea Boys again. But after everything I've faced these past few months, I think I can handle a few bullies.

Finally, it was my turn to sign the adoption papers and I did it, taking my time to make my handwriting as smooth as possible. Then Vivica stamped the document, made a note in her notary log, and it became official.

I'm now Gil and Margie's son.

But I am also still your brother, and that will never change.

I made a whole bunch of bad assumptions about who I might be and who I should trust. But despite everything I did wrong, one thing went very right. I now am one hundred percent certain you exist. I've seen you. I know you're out there. And now that I might get a little cooperation from MASC, I know I'll find you someday.

I can't wait.

And even though there is no way to measure who is "The World's Best Big Brother," I promise that when I find you, I will do everything possible to be a *super* big brother to you.

That is a fact.

ACKNOWLEDGMENTS

I'm grateful for the opportunity to thank all the people who helped me pump out this sequel to my debut. Together, they were pretty much a publishing NASCAR pit crew; I have no idea how they fueled me up, fixed my flat tires, and got me back out into the race so quickly, all in what felt like a matter of moments.

The list begins with my agent, Rick Richter, who not only saw series potential in Logan Foster, but made it real when he got a two-book deal for an unknown, unheralded writer just a month before the world shut down. Thank you, Rick, and please know that as long as Logan keeps aging, so will the bottles of single malt I send each winter. Of course, I'm also beyond fortunate to be supported by the entire team at Aevitas Creative Management, and especially Caroline Marsiglia, whose love for Logan started this entire, amazing partnership.

Speaking of partners, I consider myself part of a dynamic duo largely thanks to my editor, David Linker, who may know Logan Foster even better than I do. At every phase of this one-year turnaround, you pushed me to make this book better, Dave. From structural swaps to emotional enhancements to the infamous "clash of the paddleboats," there was never a second when you weren't determined to make this sequel more nuanced and exciting than the original. Now, when I read these pages back, I believe we've done just that. Also, I'd be remiss to not shout out all the work Sherry Fisher did behind the scenes to help both me and David keep our eyes on the prize.

I'm grateful for the hard work, diligence and professionalism of the entire HarperCollins team, all of whom have made me feel like a legitimate "author" since the moment I signed my deal. They say you can't judge a book by its cover, but you *can* tell how talented your design team is from it, so thank you to Alison Klapthor and Corina Lupp, who ensured this book takes flight from the start. Turn the page and you'll find the outstanding, detailed work of production editor supreme Jessica Berg, copy editor Martha Schwartz, and proofreader Mary Ann Seagren, and editorial senior manager Sonja West throughout this novel. Thank you for making sure I dotted all my T's and crossed all my I's. (This is intended to trigger them all.) I'm also deeply indebted to the rest of those on "Team Logan," from Sean Cavanaugh and Vanessa Nuttry's production work in the midst of supply chain madness, Vaishali Nayak's marketing efforts on my debut and the sequel, and Taylan Salvati getting the word out as publicity manager.

Also, I must bow down to the great Petur Antonsson,

whose glorious artistic talents grace the cover and the interior illustrations in both Logan Foster books. You have a gift for adding drama, character, and energy to everything you draw, and I'm in awe of every sketch I see.

Speaking of people who contributed to the success of book one, there are several I didn't yet know when I wrote my acknowledgments a year ago, but I want to make sure they get their due. To my original publicity team of Jacquelynn Burke and Grace Fell, I thank you with the most ardent Chris-Trager-Parks-and-Recs GIFs available. Also, I must recognize the wonderful community of teachers, librarians, and reviewers who have helped my books get into young readers' hands. Some, like my oldest friend, Stephanie Shapiro, or my theater pal Tara Morrow, did it out of love. But I also acknowledge the army of folks in MGBookVillage.org, the #BookPosse and #BookAllies ARC sharing groups, plus voracious readers/sharers like Kate McCue-Day and the rest of her #LitReviewCrew, who spread the word because they just love middle grade books so much. I also want to thank indie bookstores like An Unlikely Story, Aesop's Fable, Wellesley Books, Park Street Books, The Silver Unicorn, The Book Jewel, Diesel, and Children's Book World, who all went out of their way to support me. Y'all rock!

Likewise, I've been blown away by the kinship and kindness I've gotten from other writers, from longtime friends like Antoine Wilson, Julie Abbot Clark, and the unstoppable Adriana Trigiani, to the entire group of #22Debuts who I didn't even really know to thank yet last time. Esme, Sonja, Erika, George, Naz, Erik, Karina, Refe, Rochelle, Jamar, Sylvia, Tom, and so many more . . . you are all stars, and I'm beyond lucky to share a little bit of sky with you all.

I recruited a truly amazing trio of early readers in Sue Gilad, Jennifer Lutzky, and Emmaline Kelly (who was one of my debut's earliest readers as a part of Mrs. Peters' 5th grade class several years ago), all of whom had been with me on Logan's journey from the start. I'm also deeply grateful for the honest and insightful sensitivity read I received from Sarah Pripas to help me focus Logan's traits in an authentic way.

Of course, I need to thank the original "Gil and Margie," my parents. You both gave me a love of the written word . . . and the written world. Thank you for opening that door for me and giving me everything I needed to step through.

To Hazel and Teddy, you're both too old for my books now, but reading to you two will always be my inspiration for writing stories for kids. Those bedtime rituals woke up the dreams in my head and made this all possible.

And lastly, to my wife, Sara. This book is dedicated to you and it's not nearly enough to express how much your love keeps me afloat. Thank you for showing up in every big moment and putting up with every little thing it takes for me to do what I do. I love you and can't imagine getting old with anyone else on this planet. That is a fact!